PRIDE *of* EDEN

PRIDE *of* EDEN

Taylor Brown

St. Martin's Press
New York

First published in the United States by St. Martin's Press, an imprint of St. Martin's Publishing Group

PRIDE OF EDEN. Copyright © 2020 by Taylor Brown. All rights reserved. Printed in the United States of America. For information, address St. Martin's Publishing Group, 120 Broadway, New York, NY 10271.

www.stmartins.com

Designed by Omar Chapa

Library of Congress Cataloging-in-Publication Data

Names: Brown, Taylor, 1982- author.
Title: Pride of Eden : a novel / Taylor Brown.
Description: First Edition. | New York : St. Martin's Press, 2020.
Identifiers: LCCN 2019037612 | ISBN 9781250203816 (hardcover) |
    ISBN 9781250203823 (ebook)
Subjects: LCSH: Smugglers—Fiction.
Classification: LCC PS3602.R722894 P75 2020 | DDC 813/.6—dc23
LC record available at https://lccn.loc.gov/2019037612

Our books may be purchased in bulk for promotional, educational, or business use. Please contact your local bookseller or the Macmillan Corporate and Premium Sales Department at 1-800-221-7945, extension 5442, or by email at MacmillanSpecialMarkets@macmillan.com.

First Edition: March 2020

10 9 8 7 6 5 4 3 2 1

For my mom

Until lions have their own histories, tales of the hunt shall always glorify the hunter.

—African proverb

Wherefore a lion out of the forest shall slay them, and a wolf of the evenings shall destroy them, a leopard shall watch over their cities: every one that goes out there shall be torn in pieces . . .

—Jeremiah 5:6

PRIDE *of* EDEN

PROLOGUE

The cattle of Sapelo Island live in a wild herd off the Georgia coast, marooned. The shell rings of ancient tribes stand among the trees of the island, and the area is storied for the doomed mission of San Miguel de Guadalupe, where enslaved Africans overthrew their Spanish masters—the first such revolt in North America. Since then, the island has been home to Catholic missions and antebellum plantations, to small communities of freed slaves and the grand estates of tycoons.

The feral cattle of Sapelo are descendants of the dairy cows of R. J. Reynolds, Jr., a tobacco baron whose mansion still stands on the island. No one is sure why he loosed them into the wild. Here they bred for generations, reverting to olden, feral ways. They are cryptic beasts, rarely seen, said to resemble the great aurochs, the fierce horned cattle of prehistory, which battled the cave lion and the saber-toothed cat and survived the ice-age extinctions. Today, these wild cattle roam the forests and savannahs of the island, leaving their heart-shaped prints before Geechee cottages or grass airstrips or the ruins of millionaires' greenhouses—great skeletons of iron, their ribs and trusses snarled with creeper vines. At low tide, they wade into the salt marsh, grazing on long shoots of cordgrass.

From time to time, single cows have been cut from the herd, killed, their carcasses ravaged as by tooth and claw. No one is sure what manner of predator could be at work. The island is located some five miles from land—only polar bears and Amur tigers are known to swim so far in pursuit of prey.

BOOK I

BOOK 1

CHAPTER 1

BLOOD HORN

The first squeal split the air like a fault line, a fracture in the world. It sang across the acacia trees, the veld of bunchgrass and thorny bushes. Malaya pushed the bridge of her sunglasses higher beneath her camouflage ball cap. Her gloves were fingerless, the knuckles padded to protect her fists.

Another squeal, heart-sharp against the white rising sun. Malaya's face didn't twist or scrunch. Only her nostrils moved, flaring like little wings. In front of her, the tracker, Big John, had his pistol out. It was an old revolver, patinaed like a grandfather's hand-me-down, overlarge in his small dark fist. He was bent to the red grass—*rooigras*—reading the way it had been canted, the passage of beasts and men. The spikelets rocked back and forth beneath his free hand, tickling his palm. Malaya watched.

"*Mkhumbi?*" she asked.

Big John nodded, frowning.

Rhino.

The moon was still visible, fat as a spotlamp, hovering low over the green canopies of the acacias. Such a moon drew men like worms from the earth, and they came with guns and knives and saws. Malaya's team had found a break in the fence just before sunrise, the dawn light puddled in bootprints that crossed the road. A hole had been cut in the wire, the snipped ends snarled outward where men—three of them, said Big John—had slithered into the reserve. The squad of rangers had stepped down from the Land Cruiser and entered the bush on foot, following Big John in his oversized green fatigues, a long blade of grass hanging from his teeth like an unlit cigarette.

Big John rose and waved them onward now, toward the squeals, spitting out the blade of grass. They stepped lightly through the sun-yellowed brush, into the shadow of a leadwood tree. Here was the tree that some called the great ancestor of all beasts and men. The shed limbs could burn nightlong, warding off creatures of the dark.

Malaya made nearly no sound, willing herself into something light-footed, predatory, a creature elided into the bush. On her right calf, she bore the tattooed scales of an eagle's claw, the triple talons inked over the bones of her foot. On her heel, the black scythe of the hallux. These were the weapons of the bald eagle, the symbol of her nation. On her left calf, she carried the spots of the Visayan leopard cat, native to the islands of her grandfather—a Philippine Scout who'd marched the death-road out of Bataan, when the fallen were beheaded by samurai sword. On the sole of that foot, the paw print of the leopard cat. Here were the bloodlines that rooted her, that sprang her coal-eyed and wild from the earth.

The six-man squad crouched in the tree's shadow, their shoulders dappled with morning light. Big John cocked his head toward a distant clearing half obscured in green bunches of shrub.

"There," he said. *"Makoti."*

A spiral of vultures, swinging black-winged over the trees.

Jaager, the unit commander, motioned for them to split into two elements, flushing the clearing in a pincer movement. Malaya would lead the second element, she and two other rangers. They rose and began circling the clearing. Malaya thumbed off the safety of her carbine. She hadn't been in combat since Baghdad, manning the .50-cal on a Humvee, watching her comrades spill wrecked and burning from the remains of their ambushed convoy. Her heart banged in her chest—*I-am, I-am, I-am*—and she denied its brag. She was cold, heartless. She was blood and bone, unsorry for herself.

The squeal split the air again, glancing off her sternum. The tattoo of a leopard's fanged face shielded her heart. She raised her left hand and motioned her team to advance. They stepped from the bushes, weapons locked in firing position, their feet moving neatly beneath fixed hips.

It was a bull rhino, gray and hulking like a battleship, fallen on its knees. This double-horned colossus of the veld, square-lipped and gentle as a wolfhound—someone had cut off part of its face. Two bloody stumps rose from the ruin of its head, like trees if trees could bleed, and the animal was still alive, beached in its own gore. Its great ribs swelled against the armor of its hide. Blood bubbled from its nostrils. Long rivulets streaked from its eyes, black as mascara where they cut the dust. This great beast of the field, it wept.

Jaager knelt alongside the animal, placing one hand on its shoulder as he inspected the wounds. The horns were made of keratin, the same as fingernails, but the poachers had cut deep into the quick, excavating the heavy base of the horn. He rose, his khaki shirt blotched dark against his back.

"Kettingsae." He shook his head. "Fecking chainsaws."

The horns would be sold to Vietnam or China, ground into a powder believed to cure fevers and strokes and impotence, or to Yemen, carved into the ornamental hilts of *jambiyas,* the curved daggers worn on the belts of men of status. A single horn could fetch half a million dollars on the black market—more per kilo than gold or cocaine—though the men on the ground would earn only a fraction of the profit.

Malaya squatted in the dust, staring at the butchery. Metallic flies jeweled the open wounds, swirling in glistening clouds. They alighted on her hands, her face, and Malaya didn't brush them away. She looked into the single dark eye before her, long-lashed in a wrinkled crater of flesh. She'd hunted deer

and turkey and squirrel in the Georgia pines of her youth. She'd
wrung the necks of chickens for her mother, felt the pop of spine
in her fist. She'd shot at men silhouetted on rooftops and balco-
nies and hunted ivory poachers through the bushveld. She was
not green. Still, she felt tears searing her eyes.

Big John returned from the edge of the clearing.

"Poachers gone," he said. "Two, three hours."

Malaya rose. She inched back the charging lever of her
rifle, the wink of a chambered round. The bolt snapped home.

"We better get after them."

Jaager, still squatting, shook his head.

"They're gone. We'll never catch them before they cross the
border."

"We can try. What the hell else would you suggest?"

Jaager stood and unslung the battered Nitro Express rifle
he wore across his back—a weapon chambered for elephant
and Cape buffalo. A relic of the ivory-hunting era, the heyday of
Hemingways and Roosevelts. He worked the bolt, chambering a
round, and looked at the suffering hulk.

"Die genade van lood," he said.

The mercy of lead.

Malaya was born under a full moon—so said her grandfather. In
the mythology of the Visayan Islands, the moon was Libulan,
son of Lidagat, sea-bride of the wind. He was made of copper,
melted into a planetary orb by the sky-god's thunderbolt. Malaya
was an *aswang*, said her grandfather—a nightly shape-shifter,
capable of becoming a bird, a wolf, a cat in the dark. That is what
they'd called him during his time in the Philippine Scouts, when
he'd hunted Japanese officers under the moon, piercing their liv-
ers and hearts. *Aswang*. These things, he said, they were in the
blood.

Members of his unit, the Philippine Scouts, were granted
full U.S. citizenship after the Second World War. He went on
to serve more than twenty years in the United States Army,
teaching guerrilla tactics at the Army Infantry School and

fathering one son who would carry on the military tradition, earning the tab of a U.S. Army Ranger. That's how Malaya came to be born beneath a full moon outside Fort Benning, Georgia—home of the 75th Ranger Regiment.

In high school, Beau Tolley, captain of the football team, asked Malaya if Filipinos had sideways pussies like other Asians—something he'd read in a magazine swiped from his older brother. This was on the quad, at lunch, amid the chuckling of boys with letterman jackets and glistening, acne-pocked faces. Linebackers and cornerbacks and wide receivers, their hormones fairly oozing from their skin. Malaya kept walking toward the lunchroom to collect her tray of square pizza and chocolate milk. Her cheeks blazed. She could feel their eyes as she passed, each imagining what was beneath her skirt.

Tolley, an all-state quarterback, drove a black Z71 pickup with a whip antenna, chrome exhausts, fancy mud tires treaded like alligator hides. He liked to play Tupac and Lynyrd Skynyrd with the windows down, his subwoofers pounding across the practice field, his seat cocked back while he fiddled with the dials. That afternoon, he found his tires stabbed flat in the school parking lot, four neat slits.

Horizontal.

After that, Malaya saw fear in the boys' eyes when they passed her in the hall, as if they were looking at a creature of some uncertain species.

She saw respect.

Malaya went into the army after graduation, like her father and grandfather before.

The moon was slightly ovate, like an eye just beginning to shut. It drew her from bed, from the dark of her platform tent set like a raft on the swell of grazing land. The bush was alive. The whoop of hyena, sounding the night, and the rifle-crack of broken tree limbs. She could feel heavy beasts shouldering through the dark. Elephants traveled at night, long herds of them rolling like boulders through the bush, leaving bent and broken trees in their wake, and there were black rivers of buffalo out there, huddled against preying eyes. The leopard hunted at night, the lion. Prides of golden cats, some of them man-eaters, ambushed kudu and eland, even giraffes, toppling them like four-legged towers of the wild. On dark nights, they hunted Mozambican refugees, tattered flights of them crossing the bushlands. Some said thousands had been killed. Lone bull rhinos stalked the fences, longing for moonlit crashes of females—cows—on the far side. Two thousand miles to the north, Kenyan rangers kept a northern white rhinoceros, last of his species, under round-the-clock guard.

Malaya was all of these creatures. She was none of them. She entered Jaager's tent without knocking. He was reading by lamplight when she came in, his hair cropped close to the skull, his chin shaved clean. He'd been a Recce Commando in the South African Defence Force, fighting in Angola, the Congo, and Iraq before taking command of the reserve's anti-poaching unit. The rangers called him Impisi White. The "White Wolf."

"You didn't knock," he said.

"Didn't I?"

He closed his book. *"Wat?"*

She sat on the edge of his bed, her hand next to his boot.

"The moon's out. We should be on patrol."

Jaager shook his head.

"Bravo Team is on tonight. If they detect anything, they will radio us."

"I can't stand around all night."

"You can sleep, like everyone else."

Her fingers had begun walking up his shin. They stood now on the bony dome of his knee.

"Sleep's for the dead."

"I told you, no more."

Her fingers kept on, crossing the lower head of his quadriceps, finding the trouser seam that climbed the inside of his leg.

"Ek wil jou naai," she whispered.

"No."

Her hand was high up the inside of his thigh now. She could feel him uncoiling to greet her. The leopard and eagle, they took their victims into the trees. She would clasp him in her thighs and wing him high into the black night of the mind, moon-eyed and awestruck, like something she'd killed. Her finger touched the tip of him.

His teeth glistened, wet and sharp, as if to bite.

"My wife," he said.

Malaya retracted her finger, curling her hand into a fist.

"*Jou vrou* didn't seem to bother you the first dozen times. In fact, you failed to mention her, didn't you?"

He slapped her hand away, hard.

"Get out."

Malaya rose and walked to the tent flap. She peered out. She could almost see them, the legion eyes of the night-veld. The beam of a flashlight and they would hover white-fired in the bush, some constellated in herds, the eyes of killers orbiting the weak like cruel moons. Her arms hung at her sides, her hands curled into fists.

"Malaya," said Jaager from the bed. "Don't have your feelings hurt."

Malaya said nothing, walking out.

The kudu hung upended in a wire snare, where it had starved. It was a bull, the great horns spiraled and twinned like the god-crown of some mythic beast. The throat of the animal was maned, the gray-brown coat drizzled with thin white stripes. It was a browser, an eater of shoots and leaves. Lions hunted it, and leopards and hyenas and black-faced dogs. Pursued, the great antelope would leap over gulches and shrubs, even small trees. The snares were waiting, strung invisibly through the bush.

One of the kudu's hind legs hung by a wire coil, straightened at an awkward angle, nearly vertical. The grass in a small radius was gone, eaten, the work of an outstretched neck. Only the scavengers had found the carcass. The eyes were gone, pecked out, and the antelope's tongue stuck moony from its mouth, coated in grit. Maggots sleeved the leg wound, where the wire had sliced through the meat, snaring bone.

Malaya felt a crackle of fire behind the wall of her sternum. It was hot, like panic. She thought of her trailer at Camp Liberty, in Baghdad, where three men in balaclavas had flexi-cuffed her to the bed. They wore rubber gloves and unmarked fatigues and they put a ball-gag in her mouth, red as an apple, so she couldn't scream. She was snared, trapped. The men were on her, ravenous as wolves, pawing at her uniform blouse, when the very bed juddered from the floor and the walls shook, raining dust, and a table lamp fell shattering on the floor. A mortar attack, raining onto the base. The men fled, leaving her strung to the metal bedframe, where she lay for two hours, gagged, fearing they would return.

Now she turned to Big John.

"Find them."

They found the bushmeat kitchen a mile to the east, a roofless nest in an island of scrub. The earth was carpeted with skins, riddled with bones. The offal appeared strangely arranged, as if cast by the hands of a *sangoma,* a healer. In one corner, a pyramid of skulls: eland and impala, kudu and Cape buffalo. The empty crania were still dark, unbleached by the sun, their black sockets looking in every direction—a many-headed watchman of the bush. Above them, irregular cuts of meat hung drying in the sun, strung in grisly pennants from tree to tree.

There was a crash in the brush and Jaager appeared, pushing a black man before him, his hands bound in plastic ties. The man was tall and lank, his mouth jumbled with crooked yellow teeth. He wore clothes better suited to some dusty city street: slacks, abused loafers, a collared shirt torn at the chest. Jaager sat him on the ground and squatted in front of him, calling Big John to help translate. The man admitted he was a poacher, a seller of bushmeat.

"Ask him if he poaches rhinoceros," said Jaager.

"No rhino," said the man, shaking his head. "No rhino."

"Ask him if he knows anyone who does."

The man dug his chin into his chest, shaking his head.

"Bullshit," said Malaya. "He knows."

"Tell him we will let him go if he gives us a lead on the rhino poachers," said Jaager.

"We'll do what?" said Malaya.

Still the man shook his head. He would not speak.

Jaager grunted and rose, brushing off the knees of his trousers. He ordered the rangers to confiscate the snares and salt, the bucket of gut hooks and skinning knives.

"What the hell are you doing?" asked Malaya. "He knows something."

Jaager stood with his knuckles on his hips, elbows out.

"What am I supposed to do? Beat it out of him?"

Malaya sniffed. She bent to pick up a coil of wire, then squatted in front of the poacher. She looked at Big John.

"Ask him how many animals he's killed with this."

The poacher's mouth clicked, his throat pulsed.

"He say his family is hungry," said Big John. "He say dinner walks in the bush."

She nodded, her bottom lip out.

"Ask him if he's ever imagined what it's like to be dinner himself. Strung to a tree, bleeding, wondering whether it will be the hyenas or lions to find you first."

The man's eyes were on her hands. She was shaping the wire, fashioning a simple snare like the poachers used. She held the noose just over his head, like the bent-wire halo from a church play. It was slightly too small. She clucked to herself, widening it.

"He say you will not do this," said Big John.

The rangers stood in a circle about them. They said nothing.

"Malaya," said Jaager. The word came small from his mouth, scarcely heard.

Malaya slipped the noose over the man's neck, tenderly, as if it were a necklace. She cocked her head to regard it, slowly tightening the cinch. "Tell him if he does not want the lions to kill him, enough pressure will cut his jugular. He can kill himself."

"Malaya," said Jaager again, in a whisper, like a lover might. But the man had already begun to talk.

She'd never reported the Camp Liberty incident, which took place during her second tour in Iraq. At the time, she'd been cleared for jump school after her return stateside. If she passed, she'd earn the silver jump wings of a paratrooper, pinned to the left chest of her uniform blouse. When the time came, she hoped to be selected as one of the first female candidates to attend Ranger School—a chance to earn the same tab once worn by her father.

She didn't know if that ambition was why she'd been targeted, but she knew that reporting the matter would compromise her chance of ever earning the tab. It was compromised anyway, a week later, when a chief warrant officer made a crack about her ass in the hallway of the mess. There was a knowing glint in his eyes—or she thought there was. She shifted in an instant, attacking him with knees and elbows, edged hands and inked shins. He was reduced to a sack of bones huddled quivering against the wall, leaking from the nose and mouth.

"You want to tap it now?" she asked.

She was dropped from the list of candidates. She told herself it didn't matter. Even if she earned her wings, she couldn't serve in a direct combat role. Only men could be trigger-pullers.

Jaager stood at the entrance of her tent.

"Malaya."

She was lying propped up on the bed, her bare feet crossed, her ballcap sitting beside her thigh. Hemingway's *The Old Man and the Sea* lay open in her lap, the old Cuban fisherman dreaming of the pride of lions he saw on an African beach.

"*Wat?*" She imitated his accent.

He stepped into the tent. He was still in uniform, wearing the mid-thigh shorts he always wore in the bush, which showed the thick bulbs of muscle over his knees.

"The other night," he said.

"*Uit*," she said. Out.

He stepped closer. "You don't want me to leave."

"That's irrelevant," she said. "I told you to."

He stepped to the edge of her bed.

"You don't give the orders here. You seem to have some trouble understanding that."

"You came to teach me a lesson, that it? Show me who's in charge?"

His nostrils flared. His eyes were the palest blue, chipped from ice.

"I want you."

"You have a wife."

"At home, in Durban, I am a pet dressed up in bright colors for parties, barbecues. Out here, with you, I am myself."

"You mean you are Impisi White."

He said nothing. His assent.

This man, she had tested him. He was strong enough, sharp enough to cut her, to pierce the angry leopard inked over her heart, and she knew only one thing to do. She looked him up, down. She narrowed her eyes.

"The White Wolf?" She shook her head. "No, I see only a dog."

He stiffened, as if ordered to attention. His right eye twitched.

"Please," he said.

"And you beg like one."

"I could kill you," he said.

"It might be harder than you think."

She slid the small pistol from where it lay hidden beneath her ball cap, tapping one finger on the receiver. His face was drum-tight, bloodless. His teeth showed. His eyes roved her. They stopped on the sole of her foot, the one bearing the print of the leopard cat.

"You know, the *luiperd* is bigger than the *hiëna*. It has five weapons instead of one. Teeth and claws. But when the hyena comes? The leopard, it always runs."

Malaya leaned forward.

"That's a good story, Jaager. Have you heard the one about the African white wolf? With a bullet in its brain? It dies like any other dog."

He smiled, a wide white blade of teeth, and walked out.

She dreamed that night of the elephants that first brought her to Africa. They were war orphans, survivors of bloody Mozambique. They had seen their parents killed, their siblings, whole herds of their kind murdered by truck-mounted machine gun, by helicopter gunship. Their tusks had occupied endless rows of warehouses in Maputo, white forests of ivory that financed the wars of men. The survivors bore the scars of shrapnel blasts, like flocks of tiny dark birds against their skin. Their great ears were riddled like country road signs, their brains laced with dark snares of trauma, waiting to be tripped.

The elephant never forgets.

They overturned safari trucks in the reserves, the iron beasts that once killed their families, and they fled the giant flies that chopped the sky, that stung their rumps and put them to sleep. Gangs of poachers haunted the land, armed with automatic rifles and night-vision goggles, chainsaws to remove tusks and horns. The elephant would go extinct, the rhino. Scientists gave them a decade each. Veterans were needed who could train rangers and patrol reserves. Who could, if need be, pull triggers.

She'd come.

In her dream, Malaya was high on the back of a war-elephant. It was woolly, with great snarls of tusk crossed like swords. She was riding in the howdah, the armored carriage that rocked upon this boulder of muscle, and the moon was hot copper above her, as if newly formed. Her right foot was an eagle's claw, her left a leopard's paw. In her hands, a rifle. It bore a cyclopic green eye that could see at night, a drum of steel-jacketed lightning. The barrel was an extension of her, like the arm of a god. There was an elephant before her, another behind. They were traveling in convoy, clasped trunk to tail, and she realized what would happen before it did. *Ambush*. Like Baghdad, there was an explosion first. A blast of the reddest hell, sprung from the core of the world, and the elephants screamed and lurched through the bush, their ears winged and flaming, their pain trumpeted through the night.

Then she saw them, a gang of poachers come surging through the red-grass, dark-skinned and light, each slavering with desire. She turned the green eye of the gun upon them, keen as a leopard's, her finger flexed on the trigger. She was mindless instinct, the dream of herself. But these were not men, she realized. They were a cackle of spotted hyena, bright-toothed in the dark, and they were laughing at her.

She couldn't shoot.

They washed over her, a white flood of teeth.

The cairn was just where the bushmeat poacher said it would be. A small pile of stones set at the edge of the tar road that ran alongside the eastern boundary of the reserve. Here, a narrow gulch twisted down through the dry red earth and carved right under the fence. There was an opening just big enough for a small man to slither through. Big John squatted before it, picking a lint-sized piece of cloth from a snag of fence wire. He rolled it between his fingers, sniffed, then studied the tracks.

"They come two, three hours ago. They are already in the park."

"How many?"

"Five, maybe six."

"Fuck," said Malaya.

Jaager cradled his rifle in the crook of one arm, frowning.

"They will use the same flaw to escape. A perfect bottleneck. We remain here and ambush their escape."

"They won't be leaving without horn."

"They may already have it."

"And they might not. We haven't heard a shot. Let me take a tracking element after them."

"It will be dark soon," said Jaager. "I cannot split the team."

"We can't let another one go down."

"There's nothing we can do."

"The fuck there isn't."

"Malaya. Malaya!"

She didn't look back. She was already disappearing into the bush.

The moon hung low over the edge of the world, curved and sharp. Malaya's breathing was almost back to normal. She'd had to outrun them for the first mile, into the red fire of the west, until it was too dark to track her. Night fell quickly here, something about the angle of the sun. Jaager would have caught her and bound her hands, telling her it was for her own safety.

The trail she walked was pale in the dark, like moonstone. The sea of grass was purple, furrowed by the passage of beasts, strewn with thorny shrubs. The night was alive, choral. The cicada roared, a mania of tiny engines, and over them the sustained churr of nightjars, sight-hunting against the moon. She stopped beneath a leadwood tree and sucked on the straw of her hydration bladder. A troop of baboons, like dog-snouted old men, watched her from the high branches. They were silent, the color of ghosts.

She adjusted the sling of her carbine and kept on, moving west through the veld. She knew she was being pursued. There was the White Wolf and his pack of rangers, tracking her through the bush, and the shades of lions and leopards that hunted at the night. Still she didn't stop. She stole through the long blades of grass, barely a shiver in her wake. She bled from shadow to shadow. She was trained, armed. She was a crossbred shadowwalker, born to this.

She came upon a mound of rhino dung, laid to mark the territory of a bull. It was fresh; the beetles had yet to find it. She must be on the right track. The acacia grew denser, a long train of trees strung low over the horizon. They marked the river, she knew, and she quickened her pace.

The soil was basalt, a layer of prehistoric lava risen from deep fissures in the earth. She thought of the bull rhino's squeal of three days ago, the hell that flashed the world of men. The ground descended beneath her, softened, and she was beneath the cool night-shadows of the trees. The dark snake of river appeared, coursing through the land. Its banks were pale under the moon, almost white.

She found him there, the one she sought. He came bouncing through the tall grass on the far side of the river, heavy as a dreadnought, and turned broadside on the beach, as if just for her. He looked like the ugly brother of a unicorn, the brunt of laughs. An oxpecker stood on his shoulder like a tiny guardian. Seeing him, her heart roared.

The rhino bent his head to drink, and that's when she saw them. They were coming through the grass behind him, their heads floating disembodied over the chest-high blades. Poachers. A skulk of them. An unkindness. Her heart was stammering, beating at her breast. Her fingers were numb. She brought them under the barrel of her gun.

"Stand down."

It was the White Wolf, slunk up behind her.

"You are not cleared to engage."

The poachers crept from the grass over the river. They were carrying dusty AK-47s at hip-level, approaching the bull. Malaya was neither leopard nor eagle nor wolf. She was only herself. If even one of the poachers fell, the rest might run.

"Don't," said Jaager. "They must be first to engage."

She thumbed off the safety of her carbine. She could not hear the squeals again, the pain of the world unseamed.

"Stand down," said Jaager. "That is an order."

The men that knelt on the beach to aim, they were hungry. They had children to feed. They had come miles through the bush, braving lions and leopards and rangers with guns. They had their reasons. Their hungers and equations. They were men.

They were in no danger of going extinct.

"I will kill you," said Jaager.

The men raised their weapons to the bull, this horned relic of prehistory drinking from the river, and Malaya laid her crosshairs over the nearest man's temple. The shot was less than one hundred yards. By the time Jaager fired, her bullet would already be sent, passing through the poacher's brain like a judgment.

"Please," said Jaager. *"Ek is lief vir jou."*

I love you.

The rhino raised his head, as if he'd heard the words.

Malaya pulled the trigger.

CHAPTER 2

LION COUNTRY

Lope knelt before the fire engine, rag in hand, polishing the silver platters of the wheels. An old song rose in his throat. Muddy Waters or Howlin' Wolf, begging his baby not to go, not to be her dog. Lope let the words hum against his lips, unvoiced. There was heat in the blues, he knew, as if the singer's heart were held over the blue hiss of a gas flame.

Lope started to part his lips, to sing to the sleeping engine, when a whistle rose in accompaniment, like the train songs of old. A turbocharged diesel came whining up the drive, a black Ford dually with smokestacks risen over the cab like a pair of chrome horns. The truck skidded to a halt before the firehouse bays, rocking on its wheels, as if summoned here.

Little Anse Caulfield jumped down from the cab, his back-cut cowboy heels clacking in the gravel. He was a square-jawed bantam, built like a postage stamp, bowlegged like the old jockey he was. He wore a bush hat, the brim pinned on one side, and the small round eyeglasses of a small-town clerk, his nose smashed broad and flat against his cheeks, as if by God's thumbs. His eyes were iron-gray. In one hand he held a double rifle, like for shooting elephant. He stood before the open bay, squinting at Lope.

"You ain't seen a lion, have you?"

Lope stood from the wheel. He snapped the rag at the end of one long, dark arm.

"Lord," he said. "Not again."

Her name was Henrietta. She was a golden lioness, born on the grasslands of Africa, sired by a black-maned king of the savannah. She was still a cub when poachers decimated her pride, killing the lions for their teeth and claws and bones. The cubs were rounded up and sold on the black market. She became the pet of an Emirati sheikh, who later sold her to a Miami cocaine lord who enjoyed walking her on a leash amid the topiary beasts of his estate, ribbons of smoke curling from his Cuban cigar.

After a team of DEA agents raided the place, she found herself under the care of Anse Caulfield. His high-fence compound on the Georgia coast was a sanctuary for big cats and exotics of various breeds. It was located an hour south of Savannah, where the dark scrawl of the Satilla River passed beneath the old coastal highway—known as the Ocean Highway in the days before the interstate was built. On this two-lane blacktop, laden with tar-snakes, tourists had hurtled south for the beaches of Florida while semis loaded with citrus and pulpwood howled north. Sometimes they'd collided. There had been incredible wrecks, fiery and debris-strewn, like the work of airstrikes.

Now traffic was scarce. Log trucks and dusty sedans rattled past the compound, which was set back under the mossy oaks and pines. Behind the corrugated steel fence, there lived a whole ambush of tigers, many inbred or arthritic, saved from roadside zoos or private menageries or backyard pens. Some surrendered, some seized, some found wandering highways or neighborhood streets. There lived a duo of former circus tigers, a rescued ocelot, and a three-toed sloth once fenced in a family's backyard jungle gym. A range of smaller big cats—servals and caracals popular in the exotic pet trade. An elephant that once performed circus handstands, a troop of monkeys, and a lioness.

Anse called the place Little Eden.

No one knew why he kept the property, exactly. His history was vague, rife with rumor and myth. Some people said he'd been with an elite unit in Vietnam—a *snake-eater*, operating far behind enemy lines. Others said a soldier of fortune in Africa. Some claimed he was a famous jockey who'd fallen one too many times on his head. But Henrietta was his favorite— everyone knew that. He'd built a chain-link enclosure for her, sized like a batting cage for Paul Bunyan, and people said his big dually truck cruised the night roads, rounding up strays to feed her. Others said it was Henrietta herself who stalked the country dark, loosed nightly to feed. Why she would return in the morning, no one knew.

"You reported it yet?" asked Lope.

"What you think I'm doing now?"

Lope got on the radio. The schools would be locked down, the word put out. The county cruisers would begin prowling the backroads along the river, looking for tracks. The firefighters would take their own personal trucks. When he emerged from the radio room, the firemen had paired off into two-man search teams. Anse stood bouncing on his bootheels, grinding his teeth. The odd man out.

"I'll ride with you," said Lope.

They aimed up the old coastal highway at speed. Lope had one long arm extended, his hand braced against the dashboard.

"This fast, ain't you afraid you could hit her crossing the road?"

Anse was hunched over the wheel, his chin pushed out like a hood ornament.

"Serve her right, running out on me again."

Lope eyed the elephant gun rattling on the rack behind their heads.

"Where's your tranquilizer gun?"

Anse sucked his lips into his mouth, then popped them out.

"Forgot it."

They passed the old zombie neighborhoods built just before the market crashed. *Satilla Shores, Camden Bluffs, King's Retreat.* Whole housing developments killed mid-construction, abandoned when the housing bubble burst. Their wrought-iron gates stood twisted with vines, their guard shacks dusty and overgrown, vacant but for snakes and possums and the odd hitchhiker needing shelter for the night. Their empty streets snaked through the pines, curling into cul-de-sacs, skating along bare river frontage.

They turned in to one called Plantation Pointe, the sign weedy and discolored. The community was neatly paved, with greening curbs and sidewalks, periodic fire hydrants standing before overgrown lots. There were four or five houses built, pre-recession dreams that petered out. They were empty, their windows shining dumbly in the morning sun, their pipes dry, their circuits dead. Squatters had been found in some of them, vagrant families with their old vans or station wagons parked in the garages, the flotsam of Dumpsters and thrift stores strapped to the vehicles' roofs. The vagrants cooked only at night, in fireplaces of brick or stone, like people of another age. They kept the curtains drawn.

The dually rolled through the neighborhood, the tires crackling around empty cul-de-sacs. The windows were up. Lope had his ballcap turned backward to press his face closer to the glass, scanning for a flash of golden fur in the trees.

"How'd she get loose?"

Anse frowned. "Same's last time."

"And how was that, exactly? I never got it straight."

Anse chewed on his bottom lip.

"Look," he said, pointing over the wheel. "A kill."

They stood in the overgrown yard. It was a whitetail doe, or used to be. It had been torn inside out, the guts strung through the grass. The rib cage was visible, clutching an eaten heart.

"Lord," said Lope. "You been starving that thing or something?"

Anse spat beneath his bush hat and looked up. A white clot bubbled in the grass.

"She's born for this. What do you expect?"

Lope looked out at the tree line. Fragments of the Satilla River shone through the trunks and vines and moss. The lioness must have stalked the doe from the woods, bursting forth to catch her across this man-made veld.

Anse had the elephant gun cradled against his chest, still staring at the mess in the yard.

"Used to be lions all across this country, hunting three-toed horses and ground sloths, woolly mammoths."

"You mean saber-toothed tigers?"

"They ain't tigers. They're saber cats. Smilodons. Then you had the American lion, too—*Panthera leo atrox*—four foot tall at the shoulder. Them cats owned the night. 'Course they disappeared at the same time as the rest of the megafauna, ten thousand years ago."

Lope shivered.

"Thank the Lord," he said.

Anse's upper lip curled in sneer.

"They would of ate your Lord off his cross and shat him out in the woods."

Lope stiffened. He thought of the hymns sung in the small whitewashed church of his youth, where his father, a deacon, had often preached on Sundays, his face bright with sweat. Songs of chariots and lion dens and flying away home.

He looked at Anse.

"Not Daniel they didn't. 'God hath sent his angel and shut the lions' mouths.'"

Anse smiled at the killed deer.

"*Hath* he now?"

Lope could remember his first structure fire more clearly than his first kiss, than his first fumblings for buttons and zippers in the dark of movie theaters and backseats. The stable fire peeled back the darkness of the world, so bright it seared him.

He was ten at the time. He'd already developed a fascination with fire. Under his bed, he kept a cardboard box filled with cigarette lighters he'd collected. He had a vintage Zippo, a butane jet lighter that hissed like a miniature blowtorch, even a stormproof trench lighter made from an antique bullet casing. He would sit cross-legged on his bed and thumb the wheel of a Zippo or Bic, relishing the secret fire in the house. Sometimes, after school, he would erect small temples of kindling and tinder in the backyard, then set them alight, watching rapt at the transformation—the twist and glow of their dying architecture, the chemical brightness.

The day of the fire, he followed a black pillar of smoke home from school, weaving down the shoulder of the road on his BMX bike as the fire engines roared past. His heart raced faster and faster as he realized what was burning.

The stables where his father worked.

The man had grown up on one of the sea islands, riding bareback on marsh ponies while other children were still hopping around on hobbyhorses. A hard man among his family, but strangely tender with animals. He spoke to horses in Gullah—a tongue Lope never heard him use among men. His loose-jointed body seemed built for horseback, his seat and shoulders bobbing in time to their trots. With his long limbs, he could trick-ride with gusto, swinging low from the saddle like an Apache or standing high atop their spines, his arms spread like wings. He worked as the barn manager and groom for a local equine community.

Lope straddled his bicycle before the blaze, his face licked with firelight. Antlers of flame roared from every window, like the blazing crown of a demon, and the smoke looked thick enough to climb. An evil hiss pervaded the scene, pierced now and again by the scream of a frightened animal. Only later did Lope learn that his father had been inside trying to save the last of the horses when the roof beams collapsed.

Ten years old, Lope could not help but feel there was some connection, that his secret fascination had sparked this awful happening. His secret desires or jealousies. So many times, he'd wrapped his arms around himself and wished for the gentle touch and cooing voice his father gave only to his horses—never his son. So many times, Lope had huddled over his yard-built temples and pyres, watching them burn.

Back at Anse's truck, Lope called his wife. He told her to stay inside with the baby until she heard from him.

"Larell Pope," she said, using his full name. "I got a cut-and-color at ten. One of my best clients. I'm not canceling on her because some *zoo animal* is on the loose. I already have a girl coming to watch Lavonne."

Lope turned toward the truck, gripping the side mirror.

"Please," he said.

"That new dryer ain't going to pay itself off, Larell."

"It'll get paid."

Lope could sense Anse waiting behind him, his bootheel grinding into the pavement.

"Just cancel it," he said, hanging up.

When he turned around, the old man was sliding a giant, double-barreled pistol into a holster slung under one arm. The gun looked like something the captain of a pirate ship would carry, with twin rabbit-ear hammers and double triggers.

"The hell is that thing?"

"Howdah pistol," said Anse.

"Howdah?"

"An elephant carriage. Back in the colonial days, hunters carried these pistols on shikars—tiger hunts—in case a pissed-off tiger tried to climb the elephant they were riding."

Lope swallowed.

"Hell," he said.

The old man took the double rifle from the backseat and held it out.

"Can you shoot?"

Lope looked at the old safari gun. The twin barrels were huge, the stock scarred from years in hard country. He sniffed.

"I can shoot," he said.

"Four-fifty Nitro Express." Anse handed him the rifle. "Designed for dangerous game. That cartridge brought down Hun fighters like pheasants in World War One."

"How is it for lion?"

Anse shrugged. "Great. If you don't miss."

Lope followed him through high, weed-ridden yards—tall as savannah grass in some places. The old man knelt here or there, examining the ground.

"See any prints?"

"Pugmarks," said Anse, rising. "We call them pugmarks."

Lope trailed him, cradling the double rifle against his chest, stepping high-kneed through the weeds and creepers. Like always, he felt clumsy without a man-made surface beneath him, asphalt or concrete or milled wooden floors. Like his father, he was all hinges and sockets, a long-boned creature that seemed to have a few too many joints. His head rode high atop his shoulders, his arms long and ropy. People assumed he was good at basketball. Anse was small and square beneath him, neckless, his skin leathered a cancerous brown. They seemed of two different species almost, a race of over-tall princes and cowboy-toed dwarves.

"People say you were a jockey once," said Lope.

Anse didn't turn around.

"That's right."

"Thoroughbreds or quarter horses?"

Anse looked over his shoulder.

"You know horses?"

"Grown up on a horse's back. Daddy was a groom."

"Quarter horses, mainly. Back in the days they ran on Winstrol and cocaine. They weren't but claiming races, mostly. Out in Texas, Oklahoma. I did race in the All American Futurity once."

"At Ruidoso Downs?"

Anse nodded. "That's right. A horse called Thunder Boy."

"You win?"

"I thought about it," said Anse. "But I didn't want to get shot."

Lope followed him into the trees. The cathedral pines shunted the sun. It fell over them in irregular scrawls, hunting for earth. Lope thought of Henrietta slinking from blaze to blaze, invisible in the light. Even now she could be stalking them, a cat the color of afternoon sunlight.

For years, he'd dreamed he started the fire that killed his father. A lit book of matches on the dry bales of hay. A jet lighter touched to a ragged bed of straw. The yellow stalks curling and blackening before him, swirling aloft like burning flies. In the dream he stood watching the fury he'd loosed. The flames seemed alive, an orgy of snapping, singing tongues. They licked their way up king posts and raced across roof beams, turning the barn into a roaring maw of fire. They leapt from the barn, flickering across the fields to set the surrounding trees alight. They would spread and spread, consuming the whole world if they could.

Young Lope would wake guilty each time, slimy with sweat, bedsheets coiled around him like a straitjacket. His blood thundering. To calm himself, he would imagine wielding a fire ax or hydrant wrench or attack hose—weapons against fire. He would become part of the thin red line that kept the flames of the world at bay.

Now came the drone of an outboard motor. An old skiff rounded the bend of river, the pilot unaware of what exotic creature could be lurking along the shore. Lope watched the boat round out of sight, the sound dying. When he looked down again, Anse was bent on one knee, his hand pressed to the earth. His shoulders were quaking. Lope approached him. He thought to reach out, to touch the old man, but he wasn't sure he should.

"You okay, Mr. Anse?"

Anse rose and turned to face him. He was short as a child,

his eyes bright with tears. Beneath him, the paw print where his hand had rested.

"I can't believe she done me like this."

"We'll find her, sir."

"Her of all of them," said Anse. "You seen the enclosure I built her?"

"I seen it."

Anse shook his head.

"'Bout the size of Swaziland. She eats like a queen."

Lope shifted his weight.

"Some people . . .'course they're only kidding. Some people say you feed her strays."

Anse straightened. He sniffed, wiping his nose with the back of his hand.

"She eats like a queen," he said.

They nooned under a big laurel oak set alongside the river, the shade heavy as lead. Anse said they could relax. Henrietta would be bedded down this time of day, avoiding the heat the same as them.

Lope wicked the sweat from the back of his neck.

"We ain't avoiding it too well," he said.

Anse picked his nose with his thumb, examining what he'd found.

"You ought to try Africa, you think this is hot."

"What were you doing there?"

Anse flicked the booger away.

"I was in Rhodesia."

"I heard that."

"It's Zimbabwe now."

"Yeah, I heard that, too."

Anse seemed a long way off, his gray eyes steered distant.

"They shot 'em just for fun."

"Shot who?"

Anse sucked his teeth.

"Lions, rhinos. Baboons. I seen them drop a mortar once into a herd of elephant." He shook his head. "You know they call a herd of elephant a *memory*. That's the fucking word."

"Who was doing all this?" asked Lope.

Anse looked at him for the first time in the conversation, his round little glasses fogged by the heat.

"Us."

Lope hadn't been on a horse in years. Now he preferred the saddle of his Suzuki sport bike, a 1300cc Hayabusa—*falcon*, in Japanese—which could reach 193 mph if you had the nerve. His knees stuck out like wings when he rode it, like the legs of a frog about to spring, and his helmet rumbled high up in the wind. But when he was paged for a multi-alarm fire, he would twist the throttle and the world would turn to flame, a green blaze of pine beneath the white torrent of sky. He would feel the elation of pyromania in his blood, like a man sparking demons from thin air and flint. He would pass through them, a fire-walker, kin to the heat.

"Lope," said a voice. *"Larell."*

A hand touched his shoulder. Lope came hard awake, grabbing the wrist of that hand. Sweat stung his eyes. He blinked it away, looking up.

Anse stood over him, looking at Lope's hand where it gripped him. Lope let go.

"You fallen asleep," said the old man. "It's time to get moving."

Lope stood. He was slick with sweat, birthed from dream.

"Right."

He followed Anse, wading through a maze of saw palmetto. The sun was streaming slantwise through the trees now, a canted forest of light. They broke onto the riverbank and the breeze was cool and pure, crusting the sweat against his skin. He could almost forget the beast skulking through the woods at his back, crackling like golden fire.

"Look," said Anse, pointing to the mud at river's edge. "She drank here."

Prints stove the bank, clear as a mold.

Anse shook his head. "River water. At home, she drinks only the filtered stuff."

"I'm sure it won't hurt her none."

"Hurt her?" said Anse. "She was born to drink it. I'm worried she won't want to come home."

"That's what we got these for, I reckon," said Lope, tapping his rifle.

Anse glared. "You ain't pulling that trigger 'less I tell you to."

"Four hundred pounds of angry cat coming at me, I'll pull it whenever I damn well want."

Anse growled and turned, leading them farther through the woods. It was nearing dusk when they broke from the trees onto the overgrown lawns of a second zombie neighborhood. White street signs, empty cul-de-sacs. A single model home stared blindly across the expanse of waist-high weeds. Great earthmovers had roamed this ground, fellers and crawlers and mulchers that chewed man's vision from the forest. Then the pavers and rollers, laying down ribbons of asphalt. The river swept past the empty lots, unsaluted by evening whiskey or barking dogs or the *squeak-squeak* of trampoline springs.

Lope looked out over the tall grass, thinking of the lion.

"Must look like home," he said.

"Come on," said Anse, wading into it.

"She could be laid up in here."

"She *could be* right behind you."

Despite himself, Lope glanced over his shoulder. Then he waded into the high grass behind Anse, the pair of them heading for the model house in the distance. It was a lowcountry design, a porched behemoth raised on brick pilings with dormer windows and storm shutters—the kind of house from which men had once looked out across cane fields or rice paddies, a storm rolling heavy and purple over scattered knots of slaves or field hands.

Lope followed Anse up the porch steps. The old jockey draped his pistol from a porch post and squatted down, peering across the overgrown lots.

"What now?" asked Lope.

Anse spat on the planks, rubbed his chin with the back of his hand.

"Sun's dropping. We bait her and wait."

"What are we gonna bait her with?"

Anse rubbed his hands together, a papery rasp.

"You got a knife?"

Anse ran the flame of his cigarette lighter along the blade, again and again, sanitizing the edge. He squinted, thinking.

"*Man-Eaters of Eden*," he said. "That's the book. A study of man-eating lions in South Africa. Turns out, lions are most likely to attack humans under a waning moon, like we have tonight, especially if the animal is sick or wounded." He blew on the blade, briefly, then drew the edge across the heart line of his palm. "Some say they eat hundreds of refugees a year. Sometimes whole prides turn man-eater, have to be killed."

Lope swallowed.

"Did hers?"

Anse made a fist to force the blood from his hand, dripping it onto the front steps.

"Hard to know."

"You think she'd attack you?"

"I don't believe she would."

"So I'm the one that's bait?"

Anse shrugged, holding out the knife to Lope.

"You're perfect."

Lope looked at the blade, still edged in the old man's blood. He reached out and took the knife, his dark fist closing around the handle.

"Why is that, exactly?"

Anse grinned, watching him wipe the blade on the cuff of his turnout pants.

"Because she likes anything with fight."

It was nearly midnight when she came. Lope had been lying for hours on the porch planks, the double rifle stuck between a pair of white balusters. He'd been trying to stay awake, his lids fluttering, his eyes rolling back in his head. The womb of sleep seemed safe, so safe, no matter that he was in lion country.

When he first saw her, he was not sure if he was dreaming. He could see only her furred back sifting through the weeds, the muscular slink of her shoulders. She was moving like a lover might, her ribs clicking through the grass, her tail poised.

"Anse," whispered Lope. *"Anse!"*

The old jockey lay on the other side of the porch. Lope realized he was snoring. He looked back and Henrietta was much closer now, as if she'd bounded toward him when he wasn't looking. She stepped from a patch of weeds, and he watched the spheres of her eyes float through the night, incandescent. She crossed the paved road and he could almost hear the pad of her feet beneath the old man's snores, the thump of her blood.

She entered the yard on the near side of the road. She seemed to be moving in tempo to the old man's breaths, moving only when he inhaled. As if she were drawn by his very lungs, the beat of his heart. By whatever dreams were alive in his skull. She moved like a flame in the grass, flickering in and out of sight. A creature of pure instinct, mindless and true. Seeing her, Lope knew how firebugs longed to release flames from darkness, to stand glazed before their creations like worshippers, and how his own hand twitched on the throttle, itching to pour fuel into the hot heart of his sport bike. To make the world burn. He knew how the old man must long to uncage this killer, to let her rove his property in the night.

He turned and saw that Anse had risen on the other side

of the porch. He was hardly taller than a child, and he moved in a sort of trance, bandy-legged and slow, his eyes open and unseeing as he passed before the dusty windows, making for the front steps. His bush hat was pushed back, haloing his head.

"Anse!"

The old man did not seem to hear him. His face shone with sweat and he'd left the pistol hanging from the post behind him. He turned a right face at the stairs, as if on a parade ground, and started down them, his cowboy heels banging on the wooden steps. The driveway was long and white-paved, and the old man stood motionless at its head. Slowly he opened his arms.

"Henri," he said. "Baby."

She emerged onto the driveway some ten yards in front of him, her forepaws so close they touched, her tail flicking flies from her back. Lope saw no recognition in her eyes, colored a desert gold.

"Come home," said Anse. "Come to Papa."

Lope was breathing hard now. He had her under the barrel of the rifle.

"Anse, get back on the steps."

The old man ignored him, standing there with arms spread wide, as if he would embrace her when she came.

"Anse!"

Lope watched the lioness flatten herself low to the pavement, her haunches swelling, her body compressing into a fistlike knot before she exploded up the drive, leaping for the old man, her paws stretched out for him—for blood or embrace—and Lope felt the rifle slam back against his shoulder, the night illuminated for an instant in the stark daguerreotype of man and beast clenched upright in each other's arms, the man's head buried in the wreckage of the lion's chest, the two of them toppling into the returning darkness.

Lope found them at the foot of the stairs, still clutched, the old man sobbing into the blown ruin of the animal's heart. She was dead, her claws hooked inch-deep into the meat of his shoulder blades, her bone-colored nails curved like a second set of ribs. Anse looked up, his face painted with strange red designs, his eyes round with faith.

"She won't let me go," he sang. "She won't let me go."

CHAPTER 3

LITTLE EDEN

Tyler had heard them whispering in bars and on beaches, even on the campus quadrangles of Cornell, where she'd studied zoology. She was nearly six feet tall, with long-muscled limbs and angular hip bones. She'd rowed crew as an undergraduate, those long dawns of pain on the steaming water. Her back could still spread winglike with power from a backless dress.

Whoa, they whispered. *Damn.*

It was her size that made them whisper, she knew, and the muscles that shaped her arms. Her square unpolished nails and wide, hard shoulders. She was all angle and tendon, tanned leathery from the sun. She'd never worn makeup or sunscreen in all her years of subtropical living, and her smile lines were many. Her long hair was the color of wheat, the same as her face. Only her breasts were white.

Tyler watched her reflection in the mirror across the room, a pool of light mounted in a battered vanity. The wooden frame was nicked and scarred, the bulbs mostly blown, the little shelf lined with nail clippers and cologne bottles and talcum powder. In the glass she saw herself riding the small man beneath her at a canter, rolling in the saddle of his pelvis. Sweat shone between her breasts and her mouth was slightly parted, sucking air. Beneath her, Anse was small and square, his body blistered with hard little muscles built in barns and paddocks and corrals.

He was the old jockey, but in bed their roles were reversed. Here she spurred and heeled the fury from him, and he was close now, the flat tiles of his belly converging toward his navel, his eyes mashed shut, his blood rising, flushing his skin. Matilda, the former circus elephant, trumpeted over the grounds.

"God," said Anse.

Tyler popped free of him. He jerked and pumped beneath her, sprouting a white tree of jelly over his stomach.

"God," he said. "God."

He lay there slack-mouthed. Tyler smiled, watching him. She wished he would stay that way awhile. Emptied out, calmed.

Instead he coughed and rose and walked his bowlegged walk to the bathroom, the trailer rattling slightly beneath him. The monkeys screeched in the distance, fighting over their daily ration of fruit. Anse wet a hand towel under the faucet and swiped his belly clean, digging at his shallow navel. When he turned to the toilet, she saw the white chevron of scars clawed into his back. The marks of the lioness.

A green burn in her gut, like swallowed absinthe.

How could she compete with that?

Henrietta was dead, killed in Anse's arms. But even veterinarian Tyler, who believed in love as a mainly physiochemical phenomenon—the product of certain doses of certain neurotransmitters flaring between synapses—knew that no creature died completely. Reflections of them were carried in the very cells of their loved ones, in clusters of neurons in their brains. There was the way the light of a golden lioness imprinted itself on the retina on a Sunday evening at feeding time, when she lifted her face to the falling sun and licked her teeth, or when, on a Christmas morning, she pawed a new twenty-inch Boomer Ball tossed into her enclosure. The way she rolled in the grass to scratch her back, or came bounding to the fence, chuffing like a tiger. These images burned like chemical fires in the dark of a man's brain, and they were a long time in burning out.

That was okay. Tyler could wait. She'd waited so long already.

Little Eden. The place had been built in the 1950s, a roadside zoo that attracted passing families in their overloaded station wagons as they sped down the coastal highway for the beaches of Florida. Coming through Georgia, southbound vacationers crossed salt marshes and passed rickety stands selling PEECHES and P-NUTS—some hosting Razzle-Dazzle and other illegal games of chance in windowless sheds out back. They blasted through tunnels of slash pine and passed motor inns nestled beneath heavy oaks and crossed rivers that bristled with the outriggers of trawling fleets. They passed Little Eden, which advertised 100 SPECIES OF WILD ANIMAL. Here the children bawled to stop, if only to walk beneath the white fangs of the roaring lion whose throat held the entrance door.

Tyler had been one of these children. In 1970, five years old, she'd stood beneath the ribbed red mouth of the lion, waiting, bobbing with anticipation. When her father opened the door, the blast of hay and dung and animal sweat was her kind of heaven. Inside, monkeys swung from a steel jungle gym and parrots cawed. An ostrich pecked corn thrown by children and peacocks roamed freely, fanning their iridescent trains. An elephant bathed itself from a green plastic pool and a maneless lion paced back and forth, his body striped with the shadows of iron bars.

When the interstate was completed a few years later, the river of station wagons was diverted inland, along the new superhighway, and too few people walked through the lion's jaws. It starved. The animals were sold to zoos or private collectors; kudzu covered the cages and enclosures. The roof of the giraffe hangar caved. Storm-felled oaks crushed sections of the corrugated tin walls. Snakes rattled the grass and squirrels skated along the monkey bars in nervy commerce. Roaches scuttled about, the native hordes.

Then came Anderson Caulfield—Anse—who bought the place to turn into an exotic wildlife rescue. A sanctuary. He rebuilt the walls and enclosures and cut back the vines and man-tall weeds. He donned climbing spurs and ascended trees to trim dangerous overhangs, his chainsaw dangling from a length of rope. He pressure-washed the algal film from the lion's fangs and cleaned and stocked the gift shop and got his permits in order. He saved a six-thousand-pound elephant from a bankrupt carnival circus, her body scarred from trainers' bullhooks, and an arthritic white tiger from a defunct Las Vegas magic show who'd leapt through a thousand rings of fire, circus hoops wrapped in kerosene-soaked rags. He brought in animals from failed private zoos or police seizures or illegal backyard pens. The aged and orphaned and neglected.

People had a lot of reasons for why Anse bought the sanctuary. Some said a quarter horse had died between his knees, gigged by his heels, the animal's heart exploding like an over-inflated balloon. They said the trampling hooves of the other horses missed him—a miracle—and he believed there must be a reason why. Others said it was his service in Vietnam, when he watched a tiger run from a napalm strike, trailing long tongues of flame. No, said others, it was his time in the Selous Scouts, in the Rhodesian Bush War, when he wore a steely osprey pinned to his black beret and hunted men like game.

A few, in whisper, said Anse knew the end of man was coming, and he wanted Little Eden to re-seed the continent. He wanted lone tigers to slink narrow-ribbed through the green explosion of old rest stops and lion prides to sun themselves in the weedy craters of Walmart parking lots. He wanted leopards to leap from highway overpasses onto trains of cattle grown long-horned and feral as the ancient aurochs of Eurasia, and ocelots to play dead on the graveled roofs of gas stations, poked by monkeys with sticks until the bravest of them got too close.

Tyler, of course, knew it was simpler than that.

His heart was broken.

"Who wants to pet a tiger today?" she asked them.

A number of them, the boys mainly, raised their hands. The little girls had more sense.

"Okay," she said. "Now we know who the crazies are." The schoolchildren giggled while the boys blushed and lowered their hands. She couldn't remember how old they were. Eight, nine? Their school bus was sitting out in the parking lot, the Plexiglas windows scratched with elementary cave art, curses and crosses and arrow-pinned hearts.

"We have a no-touch policy here at Little Eden," she told them. "These animals are not pets. They're wild animals, and should be treated as such. As a nonprofit wildlife sanctuary, we follow certain guidelines that private zoos do not. We never breed or sell our animals, nor do we allow direct contact with the public. The animals' welfare is paramount."

One of the boys raised his hand—or did he never lower it? He was shorter than the others, squarer. He had the face of an old man. Churchill, maybe, lumped and concentrated. Tyler looked at him.

"Yes?"

"Where do you buy the animals?"

"We don't. They're rescues."

"Rescues from where?"

"Some come from people who try to keep them as pets. Some from breeders in the exotic animal trade or cub-petting parks, where they euthanize or sell off the cubs once they're too big to handle. Some we get from roadside zoos or sanctuaries forced to close due to financial hardship." She knew she needed to simplify her language for these field trips, but she couldn't seem to help herself. "Two of our tigers were found crossing the highway outside of Atlanta."

"So you're like the pound?"

"We're better than the pound."

"Do the animals ever get out?"

Tyler stopped herself. She thought of Henrietta.

"Yes," she said.

Sometimes, when they were making love, Tyler would forget and touch the scars that ribbed Anse's back. They were keloid tissue, thick and fibrous as worms. Anse would shudder, squirming under her touch. Sometimes he even softened between her legs. Then his brow would darken with shame and the jigsaw lines of his face no longer fit. Sometimes Tyler imagined a war inside him. She imagined his lungs as airships, floating in a red-dark sky, his blood shunting trains to the front, the small explosions rumbling in his temples and jaws. At these times, she wished she could reach inside him, like Henrietta did, her hands cool and white, and calm the storm of his heart.

When Henrietta got loose, search parties formed all across the county, small knots of men and women in uniform, clutching their shotguns and rifles with both hands. They roved the tall grasses of empty lots, the treed edges of baseball diamonds. They peeked inside the barrel slides of playgrounds. They stayed as close to their trucks as they could.

Tyler was one of the first on the scene when Henrietta was killed. It was one of the zombie neighborhoods along the river, a scrollwork of curbed streets studded with fire hydrants and street signs and a single model home built the year before the housing market collapsed. The lots were waist-high with weeds and grasses, and Henrietta lay dead in the driveway of the empty house. Red roots of blood had bloomed from the hole in her chest, inching their way across the white pavement, sliding sideways through the joints. Anse lay embraced in her forelegs, her claws set in the meat of his back like grappling hooks. His face was smeared with blood, silvered with tears.

The ambulance lights whirled across the scene, red and white. The emergency workers had just rolled up. They stood stunned, unsure how to proceed. The man who'd shot her—a firefighter searching with Anse—was standing by the porch steps. A rifle hung from his hands.

"He wouldn't get back on the porch," he said. "She charged him."

Later, Anse would maintain that Henrietta was only running into his arms.

"But her claws were protracted," said Tyler.

Anse frowned and spat.

"You never did trust her."

It wasn't that. He'd been too close to her. He would go inside her enclosure. Play with her, feed her by hand. Direct breaches of sanctuary policy. This wasn't some cub hand-raised from birth. Henrietta had been wild once, a young lion bounding and tumbling amid the yellow grasslands of Africa, eating from the bloody hulls of wildebeests or zebras her pride had felled. Maybe that was why he loved her so much. She was fiercer than the others. Wilder. Her eyes had not always been fenced, their orbits defined by men. You could see it in the way she moved, the arrogant slink. How to love a creature of such majesty, and not want to feel its power beneath your hand?

They lifted Anse onto a stretcher, belly-down, and the wheels snapped flat as they loaded him into the ambulance. One of the EMS workers cut down the back of his safari shirt with a pair of trauma shears and peeled back the fabric, revealing Anse's slashed shoulder blades. The workers produced their swabs and antiseptics, and Tyler turned away, enlisting a group of idle firefighters to lift Henrietta's body into the bed of her truck. Afterward, she looked at the scene. A frantic brushwork on the white pavement, scraped and smeared by the boots of emergency workers.

A heart undone.

"He wouldn't listen," said the fireman with the rifle. "He wouldn't listen."

Tyler showed the kids Snow and Fire, the tiger siblings found crossing the highway outside of Atlanta. A placard on their enclosure stated various "Tiger Facts":

A tiger's roar can be heard more than two miles away.
A tiger's night vision is six times better than a human's.
Wild tigers have been known to swim distances of 18
  miles...

Snow Tiger was lying beside her water trough, licking the inside of her paw like an enormous housecat, while Fire Tiger paced back and forth along the fence, watching the troop of young, nose-picking monkeys who might or might not be destined for his belly. Tyler stood before them, hands wide, as if showing the size of a fish.

"Today there are more captive tigers in the state of Texas alone than in the wild in the whole rest of the world," she told them. Their eyes widened. "America is full of them. Thousands. They're bred for the exotic pet trade. For the entertainment industry and pay-to-play parks." The words came by rote almost, a homily said a thousand times. She had to fight this, summoning the power they deserved. "They're kept in cages built for dogs a quarter their size, fed spoiled meat and kibble. Often, their fangs and claws are extracted—taken out."

"What kind are they?" asked the little boy with the old man's face.

"Crossbreeds. Mongrels. The breeders don't care about their species. Some of them, their parents are brother and sister. Many are killed when they get too big, or sold to China for their parts."

This revelation sent tiny hands clapping over tiny mouths and the children's eyes crowded with tears. Tyler always felt guilty at this, but they must know.

"We believe these two were trained as circus tigers, then sold as pets when the circus folded. They were found half starved, chain collars embedded in their necks."

The children were starting to sniffle and hum, mere seconds from open crying.

"Who's that for?" asked the same little boy, pointing to a small, square cage directly across from the tigers' enclosure. Similar ones, empty, were scattered about the sanctuary grounds.

Safety cages.

"Us," said Tyler. "In case one of the cats gets out."

A wail broke from the rank of children.

Just then, Anse's big dually truck appeared on the path, rounding the bend between enclosures. It came grumbling toward them, crunching rocks and dirt clods beneath its six tires, then squeaked to a halt alongside the pen. The children looked up wide-eyed, their tears forgotten. In the truck bed, a plastic bucket bristled with tawny shoots of deer legs, each capped with a polished black hoof. Anse jumped down from the cab—hardly taller than the schoolchildren—and walked to the back of the truck, his square jaw jutting beneath his bush hat. He dropped the tailgate and pulled the bucket to the edge, the hooves rocking like the blooms of some evil houseplant.

"Tiger food," he said.

The kids stood open-mouthed before the sight, forgetting their tears. Anse had them in thrall. Tyler realized she was still talking, telling them about the weekly enrichment they did with the tigers. How they would give them perfumed phone books to shred or Boomer Balls to paw. How they would dress up in costumes or blow bubbles through the fence. Anything to stimulate the tigers, to curb the neuroses of captivity. Otherwise they would rub the fur from their coats, sliding their ribs back and forth along the chain link, back and forth, like inmates rattling their cups.

But the children weren't listening. They were watching Anse, who drew a pair of shanks from the bucket and walked his bandy-legged walk to the fence, his big howdah pistol wiggling under one arm. A large-diameter PVC pipe dropped like a playground slide through the chain link. Snow and Fire were prancing with anticipation, twisting and turning, waiting for their supper to slide through the chute. Anse watched them, jaw muscles rippling like tiny explosions beneath the skin. Tyler opened her mouth. This man, how she longed to be between his ribs, where the thunder lived. How she longed to be there, close to his heart—or else spill him like Henrietta did.

Her words came fast, without thought, springing through her teeth.

"People say the lion is king of the jungle," she said. "They are wrong."

The children swung their heads toward her, round-eyed, and Anse looked up.

Tyler inhaled, swelling her chest.

"Lions don't live in the jungle," she said. "They live on the savannah, the vast grasslands of Africa."

The children looked stunned. Here was a break in testament, in all they were taught.

"But tigers," said Tyler, "tigers are ambush predators, built for the thickest jungles in the world."

Anse was watching her. His face hard, showing nothing.

Tyler straightened her spine. She was long and powerful. She could feel the hard muscles that corded her arms, the sharpness of her teeth. She pointed at the tigers. "Look at them. Look how slim they are, how narrow their ribs and hips." The children looked. "Built narrow," she said, "so they can cut through the jungle like machetes."

Anse had lowered the deer leg. It hung dripping from his hand. His mouth was half open now, watching her. Tyler slid her tongue across her teeth.

"See their foreheads," she said. She touched the fence, lightly, and the tigers turned to look, their heads hovering over the grass. The children squinted at them. Even Anse. The animals bore similar black markings over their eyes, like calligraphy done with brush and ink.

"All tigers have similar patterns on their foreheads, three horizontal stripes and a single vertical one. This marking closely resembles the Chinese character Wang, where the horizontal strokes symbolize earth, man, and heaven, and the vertical stroke unites them." Her shadow danced over the faces of the children. "Do you know what this character means?"

They shook their heads. Their mouths were hanging open, as if waiting to be filled.

"In Chinese, the mark of Wang means *king.*"

Twenty little eyes widened beneath her, and Tyler licked her lips. Her words were like hot stones on her tongue now burning with power.

"So the tiger has *king* emblazoned on its forehead, embedded in its skin. Shave a tiger's coat, and the mark will remain, as if tattooed on its head." She looked across her gathered flock. "So tell me, who's king of the jungle *now?*"

The group hummed with awe, and Tyler looked to Anse. His bush hat was pushed back on his forehead, his battled cheeks zigzagged with tears. Now he blinked hard, as if remembering something, and dropped the clubs of meat through the chute. The tigers pounced on the meal with their heavy paws and teeth. The children watched. Their mouths hung slack and round, filled already with the words they would repeat again and again, like the verses of some new faith. Tyler looked again to Anse. The old jockey had pulled his hat brim low. His tears weren't for her, she knew. They were for these wild old kings, caged like the broken meat of his heart.

CHAPTER 4

PHANTOM CAT

Malaya was at the store, buying milk. The jugs stood like white artillery shells behind the glass, uniform and inspected, ready to boom whistling into enemy country. Her thumb kneaded the door handle—lately, her mind turned everything into a bomb. The avocados had the rough green skin of grenades. The soda cans had the heft of flashbangs. The bricks of ground meat, shrink-wrapped and pliable, could be blocks of plastic explosive.

She opened the cold case, a cool hiss, and grabbed a half-gallon jug of skim milk. At the register, she sorted through crimped, linty bills, flattening them beneath the joyless smack of the cashier's gum. Malaya's nails were chipped and the purple streak of dye in her hair was twisted, frayed. The register sang open, slammed closed, and the cashier dropped the change into Malaya's palm, careful their hands didn't touch.

The AC units rattled overhead, blasting cold air through the ducts, fogging the store windows against the midday sun. Through them, the parking lot looked bleary, water-colored. Malaya jammed the change into her pocket and took the jug under one arm and walked through the sliding doors. It was like walking into a mouth, the wet heat of June. Like walking down the throat of that lion, long-fanged, which roared over the door of the old roadside zoo off the highway.

In her car was a plastic bottle of Aristocrat vodka. One hundred–proof, like a punishment. She mixed equal parts vodka and milk in the thermos, which went nearly everywhere with her now, the insides sticky like old glue, and she glugged and glugged. She must stay like that store, she thought, fogged against the hell of the world. She must stay cold.

She was there again, in the dark country of dream, and the rhino came sliding through the purple waves of grass like a destroyer. The river divided them, the moon puddled on its surface, and Malaya's rifle was chambered, trained on the line of bobbing human heads that pursued the creature through the grass.

Poachers.

She blinked. Now they were on the riverbank, arrayed like pieces cut from onyx and stone. There was the rhino, armored and gentle, bending his head to drink, blades of grass fuzzing his chin, and the poachers kneeling before him, raising their weapons. She could feel her unit fanned behind her, silent in the trees. Then the White Wolf, his breath tickling the back of her neck.

"Don't. They must be first to engage."

Malaya watched the lead poacher level his rifle.

She'd found so many of these creatures blood-blasted in the veld, like wrecked semi-trucks, highway accidents where someone died. Their faces mutilated, their calves nosing them again and again, squealing, trying to make them rise. She'd found too many, too late. She must be the leopard badged over her heart. The killer. She must deliver her teeth at the steely point of a scream.

"Stand down," said Jaager. "That is an order."

Malaya's index finger moved to the fire selector, snapping off the safety. The lead poacher steadied his barrel, threading his finger over the trigger. Malaya held her breath.

"Please——" said Jaager.

Her bullet shrieked across the river.

A spurt of sand at the man's feet.

The poachers turned to run, like Malaya knew they would. All but one. The lead poacher dropped to one knee and turned his rifle across the river, bravely, to cover his comrades' retreat. His weapon flashed in the night, a starry fire, and Malaya waited for a white bolt of power to burn through her skull, to open her mind into the night. Instead she felt a round snap past her ear, the hot pulse against her cheek, and the poacher's head jerked, his body dropping limp on the sand. Now other shots, a staccato burst from the woods, and the rest of the poachers were crumpling in place, as by her own trigger or command. Malaya opened her mouth, wishing to call back the muzzle fire spitting from the trees, but her dream-tongue was silent, as if someone had hold of her throat.

Malaya woke boiling in her own sweat, her chest heaving. She pulled the door latch and spilled from her car, landing on the bank of the Satilla River—a secluded place where she came sometimes to sit and drink, watching the dark water slide past, listening to the *whoosh* of log trucks passing through the pines and over the bridge downstream.

Now she lay on the bank. Her eyes itched and her face was webbed in slime. Her calf burned, still raw from two nights ago when she'd tried to scrub the black leopard spots from her skin, as if that would absolve her guilt. Her thermos lay there beside her, bubbling like a baby's mouth. She leaned and vomited, her stomach laddering with muscle beneath her rumpled T-shirt.

This is your fault.

That's what Jaager had said, surveying the bodies of the poachers on the riverbank. Men stricken, crumpled in knots of limbs. Some countries had adopted controversial shoot-to-kill policies for poachers. *Green militarization.* Not here.

Jaager had taken her by the back of the neck.

"You were not cleared to engage."

Malaya thought of a lone bull rhino, bobbing alone through the bush. Unhurt.

"They were going to kill him," she said.

Jaager's hand tightened on her neck.

"You were not cleared—"

"You do nothing," she said. "But watch. Your country watches while others shoot."

Jaager bent closer, so close his lips brushed her ear.

"*Ja*," he said. "*My* country, which you will be lucky now to escape."

Malaya jerked against him.

"You didn't have to kill the rest of them."

Jaager pressed his thumb into the base of her skull, same as when she was flat beneath him in his hut, her face driven into the pillow.

"They could have been caught at the border," he said. "And spoken against you." His thumb pressed harder, as if seeking the space between vertebrae. His voice quivered with faith.

"Don't you see? *I saved you.*"

Now Malaya crawled for the Satilla River, the blackwater slink where, as a child, she'd set trotlines with her grandfather. The old man had spent his summers at the veterans lodge in nearby Kingsland—home of the Kings Bay submarine base. When his granddaughter came to visit, he would sit in the back of the johnboat, smoking cigarettes and pointing out ospreys and eagles and swallow-tailed kites that wheeled and soared over the river. They would catch trophy-sized redbreast and channel cats with the wide, whiskery mouths of old men. Though they rarely saw them, her grandfather told of armored hulks that roamed the darker fathoms of the river, sturgeon and alligator gar, like living relics from another age.

Malaya kept crawling for the river. The surface was sun-scaled, shimmering with heat, but she knew it was slow and dark and cool in the depths. She thought of those early life-forms that had come belly-crawling from the waters of creation and branched a hundred million times over the millennia, forming the Tree of Life. Her species—man—had scrambled to the very top of the crown, from which point he could look down upon the rest of the animal kingdom. He was lord and master, he thought. The world belonged to him. Meanwhile, his history read like a catalogue of waste, devastation, and war. Malaya felt no better, spotted with sin. Perhaps she should no longer climb, she thought. Perhaps she should crawl back into the primordial waters, turning balloonish and blue, gentle as a whale, innocent as something that could be caught on a hook.

She was nearly there, dragging her aching body the last few feet, ready to slide into the cooling depths, when her hand found a strange depression in the bank. When she looked down, her heart jumped hard against her ribs.

A watery paw print, big as her palm, gleamed under the sun. Could it be? Surely not.

A big cat.

Malaya blinked. She was in South Georgia, where no such creature still roamed. But here was the evidence, glaring in the muck. She wondered what it could be. A big Florida panther, perhaps, said to be nearly extinct, or an escaped lion or tiger. Even an oversized leopard, like the one inked on her chest.

She'd heard of big cats sighted far beyond their ancestral lands, surviving in the shadows of modern cities and towns and parks. Fugitives from zoos or circuses, stalking the thin wilds of the Americas, living by stealth and wile. *Phantom cats*. Shadowy prowlers reported across the nation, crossing rural highways or suburban backyards, stealing pets or livestock. Mystery cats caught on motion-triggered trail cams in the country darkness, their eyes flaring bright.

Malaya looked out at the river, the angry shimmer of sunlight. Now back at the print.

A sign.

Some phantom afoot.

Some ghost.

Before she knew it, she was up off her belly, moving on hands and knees, crawling from one pugmark to the next, following the narrow slink of the cat, a string of silvery crowns left along the riverbank. Then she was on her feet, crouched low to the ground, moving like Big John had taught her on the reserve. At the tree line, she slipped through a narrow crease in the understory, following the trail of the cat. The world darkened, cooled, and the canopy glowed yellow-green above her, diffusing the sun. The light fell slanted through the pines, puzzling the shade, and her gaze leapt from sign to sign. Sheared fronds, creased leaves, faint marks in the dirt.

Malaya followed, moving through slim corridors in the forest, her steps soft on the downy floor of leaves and straw. She was not afraid. There was even a kind of joy rising in her chest as she strung together sign after sign, following the very steps of the creature, tracing its history. She wondered if a rare Florida panther could have veered this far north—a lone male, perhaps, seeking a mate. He would move mainly at night, crossing golf courses and quiet city streets. A creature whose ancestors stalked the Everglades long before the Seminole, before the superhighways and casinos and patio homes.

But no, she thought—these paws were too large, and this cat walked a straighter line than any wild panther would, shouldering unafraid through the bush. She thought of the old roadside zoo, Little Eden, now a sanctuary for exotic wildlife. There had been stories of beasts escaping, their eyes burning through the lowcountry nights, trailing stray dogs or pond ducks or little girls who should have been home at nine.

Malaya had seen her first leopard there as a child. Her grandfather took her, pointing through the iron bars of the cage, telling her of the Visayan leopard cat—a species known only in the Philippine islands of his birth. The mothers bore their young in sugarcane fields, under the hacking machetes of the workers, and hunted the rodents and other pests from the farms. After boot camp, Malaya had the face of a leopard tattooed over her

heart. A tribute to her grandfather, who'd hunted Japanese officers like rats.

She squinted now, as if she might see the phantom cat slinking through the green fans of palmetto before her. A killer with
lean hips and swaying tail, prowling sharp-shouldered through
the bush. He would be a god in his mind, a beast without rival.
But his brain was too ancient, Malaya knew. It hadn't evolved
as quickly as man's. It couldn't comprehend the gleaming hulks
that raced back and forth through the old glades, crushing his
kind under their wheels, nor the steely hornets that men sent
screaming through the pines. It would be like her grandfather
in his last days of senility, when he still carried his commando
knife under his shirt. A man deadlier than ever, because he no
longer understood his world.

Malaya quickened her pace. She must find this creature. She
must save him.

She tracked and tracked, her arms latticed with burning
scratches and cuts. The light slanted deeper through the trees,
the air thick in her lungs. Her car was far behind her now, the
door ajar, the spilled milk souring in the sun. Somewhere, far
across the ocean, a lone bull rhino was rumbling under the
moon.

She'd thought of applying for work at the sanctuary, but
couldn't bring herself to walk through the lion's mouth of the
entrance door. She felt tainted, unworthy even to shovel shit
or butcher deer. But there was no sin here in the wild, she
thought. No guilt. There was only hunger and lust and the
love of mothers for their young. There was the way a yellow
leopard slunk proud-spotted through the ticking green bomb
of summer, his form truer than any word, or the way a southern white rhino dipped his head to drink, his tufted tail flicking his rump. The way her grandfather, gone wild himself,
had drawn his commando knife in the middle of a Southern
heritage parade in the town square. He must have thought
the cavalry riders were the Japanese officers of old, who cut

the heads from his comrades during the forced march out of Bataan in '42.

The knife winked in his hand, flashing before the walleyed faces of the horses, and Malaya was running for him, her plaid school skirt chafing her thighs, when the shot boomed across the square and everyone fell flat to the ground save for her grandfather, who clung to the bridle of the nearest horse. After a moment, he fell to his knees with a crack, the bloody knife clanging to the pavement beside him. The rider, dressed as a colonel, held a smoking revolver in his hand, his thigh slashed through his trousers. The saddest look on his face, like Jesus on the cross. Her grandfather held his hands to the wound in his chest, as if to keep his heart from bubbling out.

"'And for this Yankee nation,'" he sang, "'I do not give a damn.'"

He died in the ambulance on the way to Satilla Regional. The paramedics said he sang rebel hymns until the moment his heart stopped. This man born in the Visayan Islands in 1923, who came to America only after the defeat of the Japanese Empire. A man from the *South* Pacific. The *Southern* Hemisphere. Who used to say that, in *his* South, toilets and typhoons turned clockwise, and the rebels won. This man whose mind went wild, spanning centuries and continents, and she could not save him.

The sunlight lay long across the forest now, dimming, and her eyes were strained. The signs had grown murky, unreal. Sometimes she followed but hunches or stabs of inspiration. Dusk was welling up like dark puddles from the earth, tainting the fronds and leaves. The whole forest was purpling, shifting, and the smell of pine was sharp in her nose. Malaya worried she was losing him, her phantom cat. She imagined his spots growing liquid with the dusk, oozing, bleeding into the sleek black coat of a panther, a creature of night.

Her breath was coming hard now, her cuts burning with vodka-sweat. She knew there must be men roving the alleys and

empty lots, the quiet cul-de-sacs, small knots of them bristling
with hunting rifles and shotguns, their knuckles bleached
white. The doors of homes dead-bolted while patrol cars prowled
the neighborhood streets, their spotlights glaring across neatly
cropped hedges and lawns, searching for the fugitive, catching
the eyeshine of ferals and strays.

Malaya thought of the lions of the Baghdad Zoo, who'd escaped their enclosure during the fighting and gone streaking
through the havoc, bolting between bomb craters and killed
animals and the armored personnel carriers of the 3rd Infantry
Division. A tiny pride, starving and lean and desperate. The soldiers in the sector tried to corral them, but four of the lions had
to be shot. One of them, a lioness, was killed right in front of the
tiger's cage. He was her mate, they later learned—the pair had
bonded after a breeding experiment.

Malaya had felt the hurt of the incident ripple through
the whole body of her company, causing men to suck down
whole packs of Marlboros among the crushed battlements of
thousand-year-old roofs, as if pain could be exhaled into the
desert air. These were hardened veterans, some of them, bred
to kill, and yet.

When Jaager walked her to the gate at King Shaka International Airport, in Durban, he kept his hand clamped to the back
of her neck, as on the riverbank. As if his hand were a collar, his
arm a leash. This man who'd been her lover, who'd called her *my
luiperd*—my leopard—the two of them twisted tight as rope in
her platform tent, breathing into each other's mouth. He sent
her home on a commercial flight, the same way she'd returned
from Iraq. To fly through the night, against the stars, and wake
in a land of strangers, who know nothing of the beasts that beat
themselves against the cage of your breast, the spots that burn
like sins on your flesh.

She had to quicken her pace. The search parties were out
there, the men with guns. Her lungs were searing, her finger-
tips numb. There were white gobs of spit in the corners of her

mouth. She tripped on a root and stumbled headlong into a palmetto thicket, falling bloody and gasping in the green bed of blades. The sky was the deepest purple, the trees bowed and black. She had to get up. She rose, reeled, fell. Her eyes closed.

She was perched in the black crown of an acacia tree, high over the country of dream, and she could hear the distant thunder of artillery. She could see a river winding under the moon, emptying its mouth into the sea. Out there, off the coast, floated a warship painted the brightest white, like some fairy-tale castle risen from the black depths of the sea. The big five-inch naval guns were booming, coughing fire into the night, their projectiles whistling through the sky.

Now Malaya saw the beasts of the field below her, so many arrayed in their kind. She could see great herds of elephant, big as boulders in the night, and the stony hulks of rhinoceros. Leopards walked among them, their spots ticking through the reeds, and lions stalked the high grasses in their prides, watching herds of antelope bound across the night. All these creatures so long in the making, honed for ten thousand millennia to quivering perfection, the swell of their ribs purer than any poem. They would be burned up in the coming fire, in an instant.

The first shell struck home, rocking Malaya's tree, but there was no fire or scream of shrapnel. Instead, a pale column of spray roared upward from the earth, geyser-like, leaving a small, milky puddle in its wake. Now other shells landed, white-bursting in their salvos, leaving pale pools in the cratered ground, and the animals were gathering, bending their heads to drink. The milky pap steamed at their hooves and paws, as if bubbling up from the earth.

The distant guns sounded almost sonorous now, thundering offshore, until a rifle cracked through the dream-dark, louder than any dream. Malaya was ripped awake, her vision shattered, and she knew then, sure as a slug in the chest, that the wild thing she sought was dead. The phantom cat. It had been killed, gunned down in some parking lot, some playground or ballfield or driveway.

Her spots were cold as stone against her skin, as insignia. Malaya rose and began moving toward the distant shot, blindly, as if called.

CHAPTER 5

SABER-TOOTH

When the girl first walked through the doors of the wildlife sanctuary, Anse Caulfield's claw wounds were still raw and unscabbed. The bandages had to be removed twice a day, the lacerations seared clean with alcohol and swabbed.

"I'd like to work here," she said. "Or volunteer, if that's all I can."

Anse was dusting the skull of a Smilodon, a saber-toothed cat, when she walked in. The skull was a replica, cast from polyurethane resin, based on a specimen found across the street from the La Brea Tar Pits in the 1930s, where a bank now stood. The canine teeth were more than ten inches long, curved like something worn in scabbards or sheaths. The eye sockets were wide and deep, like portholes into the creature's mind. Sometimes such a beast stalked through Anse's dreams at night—perhaps the spirit of this very cat.

"Come again?" he said.

The girl shifted her weight, foot to foot. She looked slightly Asian, he thought. Crow-black hair, almond-shaped eyes. He thought of the dark-eyed village girls of Vietnam—the ones he'd been ordered to train his rifle on in case they were strapped with hidden bombs or live grenades.

She looked at the skull, the webbed hole of the nasal cavity. "I heard what happened here," she said. "I want to work."

She wore cutoff jean shorts, her hard gold legs tattooed with spots and scales.

"What did you hear?" asked Anse.

"Lion got out. Attacked you before they put her down."

The wounds flared in Anse's back, as if newly made. He looked at the ancient crania lining the shelves—three-toed horses, woolly mammoths, ground sloths—a catalog of what lay brainless in the earth. They seemed to be waiting, watching.

"What do you want to do?" he asked.

"Anything."

"What are your qualifications?"

"Third Infantry, two tours in Iraq. Honorable discharge. Then I contracted in South Africa, tracking ivory and rhino poachers."

"You catch any of them?"

She uncrossed her arms, buried her hands in the pockets of her shorts. Anse could see her knuckles ridged hard against the denim.

"Yes," she said.

That night, Anse lay facedown in his trailer, shirtless, while Tyler straddled his rump, dousing a cotton swab with alcohol. He could see her long, sun-weathered form reflected in the vanity across the room, the red dust of freckles across her shoulders and chest.

"She didn't attack me," he said. "She was coming to my call."

Tyler said nothing. She ran the swab through the deepest of his wounds.

Anse's breath caught.

She swabbed the next gash. The wounds were wet and bright, as if Anse breathed through them, some gilled prototype crawled newly from the waters of creation.

"I heard we hired somebody new today," she said.

Anse spoke through his teeth.

"That's right."

"I heard she was pretty."

"She's qualified," said Anse.

The girl was ex-army, Tyler knew. A veteran of the rhino and ivory wars. She swabbed the next wound in Anse's back.

"Qualified for what?"

Anse gritted his teeth, pushing his forehead hard into the pillow.

He didn't say.

Twenty minutes later, he was asleep, heavy-browed and jerking, as if creatures warred behind the wall of his chest.

Smilodon hears the trumpet blasts of a stricken mammoth. They pierce the wet fog of the forest, caroming off the red towers of cypress. Saliva rushes to the giant cat's tongue. He turns in the direction of the sound, padding broad-shouldered through the fronds of understory. His saber-teeth hang huge and yellow from his mouth, sharp as the icicles that grow in the white time of year, hanging over the forest paths. His coat is pale-powdered from his ten winters, and his sabers are no longer twins, each chipped and scored by old combats. Still, they are long enough to mine the deep bloodlines of the mastodon, the ground sloth, the mammoth—to spring the red life from those bully throats.

The mammoth is mired, writhing in tar, her great tusks tearing gouts from the morass. Her ribs swell, her body pulsing with effort, but she only sinks deeper into the muck. Smilodon watches from the bank, crouched beneath bluish shoots of juniper, waiting. Soon the cow will tire. He looks out across the tar pits, which bubble and steam. So many carcasses swim in the depths of this mire, those of the scrub-ox and the camelops and the long-horned bison, the tusked mammoth and mastodon. So much wasted flesh. He will plunge his sabers into the neck of this cow, then tear the red layers of power from her shoulders and haunches. He will feast on the tender meat that sheathes her ribs, leaving little but bones for the pit.

He lifts his head, his old fang-nocked ears swiveling for sound.

He must hope the dire wolf does not catch the mammoth's dying trumpets on the wind.

"Where is it you're from?" asked Anse.

They were riding in his big dually truck, touring the grounds.

"West Georgia," said Malaya. "Outside Columbus."

Anse looked at her.

"My grandparents were Filipino," she said. "My grandfather was a Philippine Scout, came to America after the war."

Anse nodded. "Hard ones, them."

"He was," she said.

"And you wanted to be like him?"

"Always."

Malaya meant *freedom* in Tagalog, she said. She rode shotgun in the big Ford—sunglasses on, elbow out the window—while Anse drove from enclosure to enclosure, introducing her to the denizens of Little Eden. There was Trooper, the three-toed sloth, hanging from a forked tree in the center of his pen, and Matilda, the six-thousand-pound elephant saved from a circus troupe. The trunked giant rocked straight-legged toward the fence, as if her joints were fused.

"Arthritis," said Anse. "They made her do handstands for the crowds."

"Handstands?"

Anse nodded. "They used an ankus," he said. "Elephant goad. Looks like a boathook. She's got scars behind her ears, across the backs of her legs."

Malaya's nostrils flared, as if venting smoke.

There was the troop of vervet monkeys saved from a roadside zoo in Florida, where they'd lived on nothing but peanuts sold in overpriced bags to the visitors, who never tired of throwing them at their evolutionary inferiors, trying to peg them between the eyes. But the place was mainly for wild cats. There were the former circus tigers, Snow and Fire, and a motley string of tigers from breeders and menageries and police seizures, some of them bowlegged or cross-eyed from inbreeding. Some declawed, missing their final knuckles, so that their front paws flopped like clown shoes, or defanged, their canine teeth ground down to the gums. They prowled around their enclosures, pawing Boomer Balls or splashing in giant tubs of water, chuffing at Anse when he stepped down from the truck to greet them.

There were smaller cats, too. Servals, caracals, ocelots. Chain-link fences were draped and folded over the tops of their enclosures like ragged circus tops in order to keep the agile cats from climbing out. Fast-growing kudzu and vines snarled through the wire walls, behind which stood custom-built arrays of platforms and catwalks and tunnels. The servals were leggy and yellow, spotted like pint-sized cheetahs.

"Fastest paw strike of any cat," said Anse, hands on his hips. "One-sixtieth of a second, they say. Faster than a king cobra."

One of them, a tomcat named Bowie, had been left on the sanctuary's doorstep in a dog carrier with a note: *This is Major Tom to Ground Control, I'm stepping through the door.*

There were a pair of tufted-eared caracals—"Little Lions"—that could leap more than ten feet in the air, catching birds on the wing. Anse said the ancient Egyptians had tamed them for hunting. Then there was Lady, the black-spotted ocelot, who looked like a thirty-pound miniature leopard.

"God damn," said Malaya. "She's beautiful."

Anse nodded. "People used to call them dwarf leopards. Mainstay of the fur trade. Takes thirty-five pelts to make a single lady's coat. Costs forty thousand dollars."

Malaya crossed her arms, as if to protect her chest.

"Jesus Christ."

"People try keeping them as pets. Can't imagine why. Their scent-marks have to survive in the rainforest. Smell about like a skunk. But Salvador Dali had one. Gram Parsons, too."

"She was one?"

Anse nodded. "Escaped from a makeshift pen in suburban Atlanta, killed a German shepherd that cornered her before Animal Control arrived." Anse licked his lips. "Dog was eighty pounds, four times her size. He must of thought she was just another housecat."

Wetness in his eyes, as for a pair of star-crossed lovers.

They stood in front of the empty enclosure where Henrietta had lived. It was bigger than any of the others, the hurricane fence erected straight and true. There was a large wooden shelter, built doorless with a tarpaper roof, where she could take shelter from sun and rain. There were groves of saw palmetto and bamboo, which she'd used as cover to stalk sanctuary visitors, and logs where she'd lain in the sun. The enclosure was littered with old toys, Boomer Balls and perfumed phone books and shredded cardboard boxes once full of treats.

Anse breathed through his teeth. His heart was punching his sternum, again and again, like a set of bloodied knuckles. The girl stared straight ahead, through the fence wire.

"You loved her," she said.

Anse licked his lips.

"I did."

"How'd she get out?"

Anse looked at the gate latch. He scratched the back of his neck.

"I don't know."

The girl breathed in, out, steadying herself.

"You know I got into some trouble in Africa."

"Figured as much, you end up here."

"It was over a rhino." She interlaced her fingers, twisting her hands together. Her knuckles cracked. "I fired on a poacher I wasn't supposed to."

"You hit him?"

"No."

Anse nodded, spat between his boots.

"Too bad."

That night, Anse couldn't sleep. His wounds, beginning to scab, itched incessantly, and a feverish loop of memory played in his mind. The same scenes, again and again, like a movie he couldn't stop. Tyler lay next to him, dead asleep. Anse slipped from bed and out the door of the trailer, padding barefoot down the steps. The night was black and strange. There were the native sounds, bullfrogs and cicada and the bellowing croak of an alligator. In the distance, the hoot of a barred owl. But other sounds, too. Exotic. The rumble of Matilda plodding about her enclosure, rumbling like a distant thunderhead. The drowsy slink of the tigers crisscrossing their enclosure, their stripes rattling the fronds.

Anse headed for the monkeys.

He kept thinking of a night in Africa, in the late seventies, when he served in the Selous Scouts—a soldier of fortune. He and a force of seven Scouts had crossed the border into Mozambique at dusk, stepping through the rusty strings of barbwire like men entering a prizefight. They were dressed in the uniforms of their enemy, FRELIMO—*Frente de Libertação de Moçambique*, the Mozambique Liberation Front. Anse was the only white. Since his skin would give them away, he was smeared with what the Scouts called "black-is-beautiful"—a foul-smelling camouflage cream that darkened his face and hands. The other Scouts grinned every time he had to reapply the cream, chuckling through reams of dagga smoke.

They were looking for Mr. X, a Mozambican local who'd been helping enemy guerrillas cross the border into Rhodesia. Their cover was that they were freedom fighters seeking safe passage. Anse stood far away, laced in moon shadow, while two of the Scouts negotiated with a local chieftain. The man was savvy, skeptical of their claims. If they were true liberators, he said, they would save his village from the troop of baboons decimating their maize fields. Then, surely, he would remember the name of the man they sought.

There was a rickety watchtower built high over the fields. Anse, the best shot, chose himself and one other Scout for the job. There was no ladder so they scaled the latticework exterior board by board. The planks groaned beneath their hands, the whole structure rocking like a ship's mast in the breeze. They crouched on the upper platform, their weapons steadied on the edge, and waited. The moon was high and fat, glaring down on the maize. The black cream bled from Anse's forehead, burning his eyes.

Sometime after midnight, the baboons appeared. Dozens of them, loose-limbed and silver-furred, bouncing through the cornrows. Infants rode on some of their backs. They began ripping the cobs from the stalks, huddling slope-shouldered over their prizes, their ridged heads pulsing as they chewed.

"Pick your targets," whispered Anse.

The other Scout nodded. His barrel moved in a careful pendulum, target to target.

"Ready," he said.

"On three," whispered Anse.

They walked the field at dawn. After the first shot, the whole unit had opened up, raking the maize with automatic fire. They had to give the chieftain a show. Several baboons lay dead in the cornstalks, curled into themselves, holding their wounds like secrets they were trying to hide. Anse stood amid the bloodied stalks, his breath coming fast and ragged from his throat. One of the Scouts appeared next to him.

"Sergeant Major, you must come see."

He led Anse toward the center of the field.

It was a lion, a lone male. He had the lean angularity of a nomad, with a broad black mane. A stray round had entered one eye. The blasted socket had wept down his face, and crusted, and his blackened head rested on his forepaws, as if arranged for viewing. He lay in a circle of flattened stalks, where he had whirled and thrashed in terror, blinded, before sinking to his belly, calmly, to die.

"He was hunting the baboons," said the Scout. "He might have done our job for us."

Anse spun on his heel, surveying the damage. The dead baboons, each the size of a child, and the shredded cornstalks. The sightless lion, jeweled with flies. The world seemed to spin on and on. He could feel the untethered roll of the earth through space. He wanted to sink to his knees, to grab fistfuls of stalks to keep from being hurled from the face of the world.

"Sergeant Major," said the Scout. "What should we do?"

Anse looked up, blinking to focus. The others stood around him, waiting.

He spat through his teeth.

"Tell the chieftain we want Mr. X. Or, under this moon, we might mistake him for another baboon."

The mammoth has tired. She is all but dead. Smilodon stands on her back, a woolly mound in the steaming lake of tar. He can feel the guttural rumble of her lungs, those great hollows mucked black. Her trunk strains to stand free of the surface. He watches its desperate dance, so much like one of the great, ribbed constrictors of the caves, which crush the bone-cages of lesser creatures.

His claws clutch the cow's hide. Hardly a quiver. His eyes rove her contours, the hills and swales, looking for the blood-river that keeps her warm. His ancestors tell him where the hidden blood pulses, deep through the meat of her neck. His jaws open wide, his great sabers gleaming. He is Smilodon, built to loose blood from flesh.

His ears jerk upright—sounds, the thud of paws.

Smilodon wheels on the spine of his prey.

Dire wolves. A rout of them, they break dark-furred and snarling from the forest. These fearsome dogs, the bane of his kind. Smilodon is larger, stronger. His teeth dwarf their own. But there are so many of them. He crouches over his prey, belly low, paws wide, and shows them the double sabers he carries. The wolves whirl and growl, pacing the bank, flashing their white fangs. The first, the bravest, steps across the fleshy bridge of the mammoth's rump.

Smilodon will slash them, swat them yelping into the pit. He will fight them until he, too, enters the black, or else stands triumphant, bloodied on his mound of flesh.

He lifts his head, swelling his chest.

A roar. Anse came fast awake from the dream, coated in sweat.

The monkeys were squatting on their platforms, watching him, incurious as they munched their seeds. As if none of them had heard the sound.

Had he?

The sun was rising. Dawn light seeping along the grounds, crawling through the enclosures like glowing vines. Anse's eyes were burning. Tears or sweat or camouflage cream. He wiped them, stood. He wanted to apologize to the monkeys, but he didn't know the tongue. Instead, he cast an extra fistful of feed through the chute, as if that would help. All the while he was listening, listening, as if Henrietta's death were but a dream. As if she would roar again.

"I let her out," said Anse.

The girl looked up. She was dusting a skull.

"What?"

"Henrietta. The lion. I let her out myself."

Malaya held up the feather duster she'd been using.

"The hell would you do that for?"

Anse bent, looking into the skull of *Mammuthus columbi*. A Columbian mammoth, the ten-ton ancestor of the Asian elephant. The skull stood on a display pedestal, the seven-foot tusks curved like a pair of giant sickles, the eyeless sockets staring back at him. Absently, he scratched the base of his throat with his thumb. Behind the mammoth, a display discussed the Pleistocene extinction event, ten thousand years ago, when the megafauna vanished. Placards for various hypotheses: climate change, disease, overhunting by prehistoric humans.

"Just out of her enclosure," he said. "I don't know how she got out of the sanctuary." He squinted into the empty eyes of the mammoth, as if they might tell him. "You're the only one that knows."

"You haven't told me why."

Anse blinked. His eyes burned. He thought of Henrietta,

maneless and svelte, her high shoulders burling through the grass. He wiped his eyes with the back of his forearm.

"I wanted to see her free."

Anse lay facedown on the bed that evening, shirtless. His scabs were finally beginning to peel away, leaving pink stripes of scar that itched. Tyler straddled him, squeezing the anti-itch ointment from a tube.

"All I'm saying is this. A lion—or any cat, for that matter—keeps her claws retracted until she's ready to use them. Henrietta's were out."

Anse squeezed shut his eyes. He thought of Henri dead in the driveway of that empty house. Her heart exploded, oozing over the pavement. Her claws buried in his back. He turned his head, speaking from the side of his mouth.

"Automatic response when the bullet hit her," he said. "Her claws coming out."

Tyler shook her head. "Couldn't be, Anse. *Primary flaccidity*—an animal's muscles relax instantly at the moment of death."

Anse turned his head, winding one eye up at her.

"They teach you that up at Cornell?"

Tyler leaned over him, her breasts brushing his back. Her lips grazed his ear.

"No," she said. "You did."

Anse mashed his forehead into the mattress, growled.

Tyler bent closer.

"It's better this way, don't you see?" Her lips chased his ear. "She died *wild*."

At the word, a tingle ran up Anse's spine. A drove of tiny beasts uncaged by her voice, loosed under his skin. His blood flew. Anse turned over beneath her. He buried his thumbs in the hollows of her thighs, smiling.

"Come here, you."

"I know," said Malaya.

Anse had strung a whitetail doe from an iron gambrel in the butcher shed. He stood before it, scraping a stone across the blade of his knife.

"You know what?"

Malaya was leaning against the doorframe of the shed, arms crossed, watching him. He was supposed to be teaching her the art of making tiger food.

"I found a report of an ocelot that killed a German shepherd outside Atlanta a few years ago. She was scheduled to be euthanized by the local Animal Control."

"So?"

"So she disappeared from the facility three days before her euthanization date."

The butcher's knife hung loosely from Anse's hand. He didn't say anything.

Malaya scratched her elbow. Her nails were black, freshly painted.

"You said you got Henrietta after the DEA raided some cocaine lord's house, right? Somebody who kept her as a pet?"

Anse's knuckles shifted on the handle of the knife.

"That's right."

"Three years ago, the Miami police found this cartel bigwig passed out in his front yard. He had a tranquilizer dart in his ass, a kilo of Colombian white tucked under his head for a pillow. People said he kept a lioness in his backyard. Her chain was broken, like she'd escaped."

"There are thought to be more than two thousand captive lions in the United—"

"I made a couple calls, Anse. In both cases, a playing card was found at the scene. It was an ace of spades, like the Air Cavalry used to leave for the Viet Cong. The back side was black, with a pair of white thunderbolts crossed under the skull of a saber-tooth tiger."

"Cat," said Anse.

"What?"

"Saber-tooth *cat*. Separate evolutionary lineage from the tiger."

Malaya smiled. "Who else knows about this?"

Anse looked at the gutted doe. He would shear her forelegs first, laying them in the deep freezer like the cached rifles of a rebel force. Remnant blood would patter about the steel drain on the floor, flecking his boots and pants.

"No one," he said.

"Not even Tyler?"

"Not even Tyler." He kept looking at the doe, so tawny and lean. "What do you want?"

Malaya stepped forward, uncrossing her arms. She held out her hand for the knife.

"In."

Smilodon is striped with blood, his hide torn ragged by wolf teeth. Still he crouches atop the mountain of flesh. His sabers gleam red, his claws; the tar squeals and boils beneath him, a black mania of paws and tails and gnashing teeth—wolves he has sent yelping into the pit, who will never escape.

Still more of them come, these white-fanged beasts endless as the bald apes that wear the furs and skins of the creatures they kill, harrying him with the cold stone of their spears. He is Smilodon, the saber-toothed, and yet he is only a single creature, alone. It has been two winters since he has scented another of his kind, four since he thrust himself into the hot vent of that old single-sabered dam, caging her neck in his teeth.

He is, perhaps, the last of his line.

Now comes another snarling of wolves, three of them. They leap together onto the mammoth's rump, the dark wedge of them arrayed before him like a single three-headed beast. Their black hackles are spiked, their red mouths slung with white ropes of saliva, and Smilodon sees his fate unfolding. Three dire wolves locked snarling to his neck, and he will rise roaring atop his woolly mountain, wearing their furred forms like a mane, and together they will fall toppling into the pit. He will drown, sink. His bones will be shed of his flesh, freed, his eyeless skull floating in the black night of tar.

He is Smilodon, born to die.

Let them come.

BOOK II

CHAPTER 6
THE LITTLE AMAZON

Malaya sat in the fork of a riverine oak, glassing the shrimp trawler with a pair of high-power binoculars. It was fifty feet long, the white hull scabbed with rust. The outriggers stood like folded wings, their green nets ragged and mossy, insufficient for flight. The whole boat listed slightly at the dock, surely sprung with leaks. The name of the vessel had been hand-painted along the bow, the letters faded, bleeding down the hull: THE CATBIRD SEAT.

Malaya had been watching the boat after work for a week, by order of Anse. Long hours behind the binoculars or spotting scope, watching from various hides, recording the comings and goings of the crew. Each morning, in the sanctuary's butcher shed, she provided Anse a full report of the previous day's surveillance: movements, times, habits. Anse would frown, making notes or asking questions. Then she would consult the task board in the sanctuary office, completing her regular work for the day, which might include cleaning enclosures, butchering deer, or feeding various animals. After work, she would head back to the river, change into the camouflage clothes she kept in her trunk, and slither into a new blind or hide, surveilling the boat until well after dark.

The first day, Anse had given her the location of the boat but no idea of what she would find. It was moored to a private dock on a backwater creek near the mouth of the Altamaha River— the "Little Amazon" of the South. Rigging, rust-brown, lay in the uncut grass of the bank, alongside winches and turnbuckles and coils of rotten line. A diesel marine engine, painted pea-green, sat keeled in a bed of sea oats. There was a utility shed that looked hammered together on a whim. The only mark of care was the iron-barred security door that stood in the middle of the dock, flanked by a wide shield of wooden planks and razor wire.

She expected a vessel exporting farm-raised tigers or black bears to the Far East, where they could fetch handsome sums for their parts, or importing black-market ivory or game trophies. Instead, crab traps were stacked high on the deck, boxy and salt-rimmed, squawking and flapping with parrots of every color and size. Macaws with cobalt wings and lemon bellies, their dusty beaks hooked like linoleum knives, or scarlet macaws with yellow coverts at their shoulders, worn like the epaulettes of a colonial army. Nanday parakeets, Patagonian conures, Brazilian aratingas. Yellow-headed amazons, some of them Magnas— magnum breeds sold in pairs, which could command two thousand dollars a head.

Stray cats strode atop the makeshift birdcages like prison guards, now and again striking through the wire, while the birds screeched beneath them, outraged, their wings rattling the traps. Layers of molted feathers and droppings lay beneath their perches.

"They smuggle them in from Central America," Anse told her. "Feed them tequila to shut them up, tape their beaks. Been known to poke holes in their eyes, keep them from singing to the light. Hide them in thermoses, toilet paper rolls, spare-tire wells. Babies still got those pinfeathers, filled with blood. Bleed out from the rough handling. They say only one in four makes the trip."

Malaya had expected sexier assignments, but she hid her disappointment, her face a cold mask beneath Anse's hard, iron-flecked eyes. She lifted her chin half an inch.

"I can stake the place all day on my days off."

Now, as she watched, the triple deadbolts of the dock's security door snapped open and the door swung wide. Out stepped the married couple who ran the operation. The woman's face was the shape and texture of brick, flushed with sun or spite. The spaghetti strings of her halter top cut grooves in her fleshy shoulders. Her words carried on the breeze.

"You put millet on the list? We need 'least five sprigs for the macaws. Like cotton candy to them greedy scarlets."

Her husband, half her size, nodded.

"They on there," he said.

"What about extra sunflower seeds? You remember them this time? Them parrotlets need the extra fat. They don't put on weight like their mamas do."

Her husband nodded again. His chin seemed superglued to his chest.

"It's on the list, Berta."

"Better be. Can't have so many dying like last time."

"That wasn't my fault."

"Hell it wasn't. What about spirulina for their feathers? These people don't want some dull-ass parrots. Color's the reason they buy the things. Them last parakeets looked like damn bunches of old bananas."

She walked ahead of him, her pink sandals squashed beneath the white cows of her feet. The planks of the dock were warped and rickety, but Malaya knew they would hold.

There was never enough justice in the world.

The couple loaded themselves into a battered minivan for their weekly run down the coast, raiding the big pet stores over the state line. Malaya watched the vehicle grumble out of the drive, then raised the antenna of the ancient cellular phone Anse had given her.

"We're on," she said.

The days spent watching the birds had put Malaya in mind of her grandfather. When she was five, her father had been killed in a helicopter crash at Fort Benning and her mother had gone to work double-time, managing the local dollar store. That's when her grandfather had moved in with them, bringing only a single battered suitcase and a trunkful of Marlboro cartons, as if he'd robbed a cigarette truck. He drove a mile-long black Mercury coupe whose motor growled like a demon under the hood, and Malaya would ride shotgun around town, lifting herself with both hands to see out the window.

"They used to call him the Pigeon Man," she said.

Anse was threading his arms through the sleeves of his wet-suit. His shoulders were small and hard as baseballs, stitched with old scars. Downstream, the shrimp boat thumped against the rubber tires of the dock.

"Who?" he asked.

"My grandfather." She zipped up the back of her wetsuit, bought from a local thrift store for the occasion. "He'd pick up one of those three-foot loaves of French bread from the Winn-Dixie and take it down to the park. Find himself a bench. Plant himself there for hours, casting shreds for the birds."

She could remember him sitting there, his shoulders set so straight and square beneath one of the polyester bowling shirts he'd owned since the 1950s, an aged Filipino man chain-smoking Marlboro Reds behind a pair of green-lensed Ray-Bans, his hard brown hands tearing off crusts of bread. Soon whole blizzards of pigeons would cloud about him, squabbling and flapping. This man who'd seen his friends beheaded by the samurai swords of Japanese officers and hunted down several of those same officers after his escape, wielding the selfsame commando knife he still carried under his shirt. This man they called an aswang, a werebeast capable of shifting shape in the night, becoming a dog or bat, boar or bird or large black cat. Creatures fast and silent, said to steal their victims in the night and replace them with tree trunks.

Malaya shook her head, thinking of the birds swirling around her grandfather's bench.

"All those damn pigeons, they never shat on him. Not once."

They slipped into the water upstream of the boat, their fins cycling beneath the surface. Their gear trailed them in a floating dry bag leashed to Anse's wrist. When they reached the vessel, they held themselves against the current, finning, while Anse lifted a boarding pole from the water, securing the double-pronged hook over the gunwale.

Malaya went first. She removed her fins and clipped them to her belt, then ascended the side of the hull, the ladder twisting and swaying beneath her. At the top she hooked her heel over the edge and hauled herself aboard. Stray cats darted from her, taking up defensive positions behind old winches and coils of line. Anse followed. They squatted on the deck and opened the gear-bag, rifling through the contents, removing gloves and wire cutters and surgical masks. They were breathing hard from the swim, the climb, the sense of being inside enemy walls. The wire fortress loomed over them, squawking and rattling.

Malaya donned a mask and gloves and began climbing the crude scaffolding that attended the traps. The birds watched her strangely as she climbed, cocking their bodies sideways and swiveling their heads. Their movements were jerky, animatronic. Some opened their beaks and Malaya half expected them to speak, to shout expletives or biblical pronouncements. Instead they screeched. Several lay dead beneath their perches, their feathers fading to dusty hues. The smell from the traps reached right through the mask, gagging Malaya's throat.

The topmost row of cages held scarlet macaws from the jungles of South America. Giant rainforest birds, long-feathered and vibrant, sized like the war plumes of medieval knights.

They clutched the wire in their claws and cocked their heads sideways, holding Malaya in the tiny yellow sunflowers of their eyes. Their scaly dark tongues wiggled at her, bone-pronged for jabbing into the fleshy innards of palm and jocote fruit. Some screamed.

Little Eden had no aviary. Anse had called the avian rescues up and down the coast—none had capacity for such a flock. Wildlife officers, if notified, would be forced to destroy the birds, most likely. Malaya looked down at Anse, who nodded from the deck. She held her breath and released the catch on the nearest cage and pulled open the top. A scarlet macaw burst forth from the trap, stretching its wings blood-red against the blue sky, then turned wheeling and cawing for the trees. Now the others, loosed, lifted from their cages, blistering the sky with color, with flames of blue and lime and bloodiest red, bright as chemical fires, as the weather of rapture.

Malaya was in third grade the day the boys from Fort Benning came to the park. They were teenagers fresh out of the Army Infantry School, their hair cut high and tight, their cheeks hardened by hunger and fatigue and the incessant insults of drill sergeants. Their fists held grease-spotted bags of fast food and they sucked Cokes through straws, their necks pulsing. One of them kept spinning a small blue box between his hands, catching it against his chest.

Alka-Seltzer.

They sat in a half circle in the grass. Soon the pigeons were hopping and flapping about them, greedy for scraps. Malaya was sitting a little ways from her grandfather's bench, cross-legged, arranging a green company of plastic army soldiers, copying the formations diagrammed in the pocket-sized *Ranger Handbook* she'd found on her father's bookshelf. She looked at her grandfather but could not tell if he paid the young grunts any mind. His eyes were hidden beneath the sea-green lenses of his Ray-

Bans, his face masklike, set rigid beneath the gray flapping of pigeon wings.

The grunts had taken off their shirts. Their bodies were hard, hammered into shape by thousands of push-ups and ruck marches, their stomachs scaled like snake bellies. The boy with the Alka-Seltzer, who seemed their leader, didn't eat. Instead he watched the pigeons hopping about his legs. His head was swiveling back and forth, tracking them like a weapons system.

"Rats with wings," he said.

One of the others spoke through a mouth of burger.

"You think it'll explode 'em, Mackey? Like with seagulls?"

Mackey rattled the box.

"One way to find out."

He tore open the top and flicked a white tablet of antacid into the grass. A trio of pigeons descended, pecking it apart.

Malaya's grandfather rose from the bench and straightened his shirt, his palms sliding over his flat belly. He began walking toward the trio of grunts, a straight-backed old man heralded by a dirty cloud of pigeons. Malaya scooped up her army men, hurriedly, shoveling them into the pockets of her plaid school skirt, and followed after him.

The old man stood before the boys. The one named Mackey squinted up at him.

"Need something, grandpa?"

"Your Alka-Seltzer."

"Indigestion?"

"Yes."

"Don't you got some herbs or something for that?"

Mackey's eyes flicked to his buddies, eliciting chuckles.

"Please."

"Don't you mean *p-wease*?"

At this, Malaya's grandfather made a come-here motion with his hand—a gesture reserved only for dogs in the nation of his birth. When the young infantryman looked confused, the old man hawked and spat a long worm of phlegm across the boy's face.

An international gesture.

Malaya could never really decipher what happened next. It was too fast, a flash and a roar. When it was over, three pigeons lay bloated in the grass, dead, and an army infantryman was curled in a ball, holding his groin and mouth, while his friends stared wide-eyed. A former Philippine Scout, seventy-some years old, was leading his granddaughter back to the car, holding her hand. A commando knife rode under his shirt, untouched. A box of antacid tablets rattled in his pocket.

Malaya stood high atop the emptied fortress of wire, watching the sky burn with color. The birds were alighting in the trees, bright-bellied among the branches. She thought of odd equatorial birds being reported along the coast, as if the Tropic of Cancer were moving northward, the torrid zone fattening around the equator. It seemed hot and steamy enough here. No wonder the army had prepared soldiers for Vietnam in the Deep South, in places called Tigerland and Fayettenam. She could imagine tigers or leopards stalking the banks of this very river, weaving in and out of the trees, while parrots cawed.

Malaya looked down to see if Anse was watching the birds. Instead, the old man was kneeling over a line of crab traps on the deck, snipping holes in their galvanized wire. He lifted one he'd finished and tossed it overboard.

"What you doing down there?"

Anse cocked his jaw over his shoulder.

"Don't want ghost traps," he said.

Malaya climbed down, squatting next to him.

"Ghost traps?"

Anse nodded. "An unchecked crab trap. It can trap crab after crab after crab—hundreds over time, each one attracted to the starved corpse of the one before it. *Ghost trap.*"

The old jockey knelt before another trap, shoulders hunched, straining both-handed to cut holes in the rusty wire. Malaya could almost see the claw scars that ribbed his back, striping beneath the black neoprene of the wetsuit. She lifted her hand, as if to touch his shoulder, but didn't. She reached into the bag for the second pair of cutters.

CHAPTER 7

AURORA

"What do you mean you won't see him?"

Anse growled through his teeth.

"Just what I said. I won't."

"He's come to apologize," said Tyler.

"He doesn't owe me an apology. He did what he thought was right."

"Look at him, Anse."

Anse leaned slightly forward, glancing down the hall to the glass doors of the sanctuary. Larell Pope, the firefighter who'd shot Henrietta, was sitting on his motorcycle before the lion fangs of the entrance. His head was down, his hands crossed over his helmet. His shoulders were sloped.

"You aren't doing this for yourself, Anse. You're doing it for him."

Anse was standing over a glass display case of prehistoric sharks' teeth, big as arrowheads. He growled.

"All right, goddammit. Send him in."

Tyler leaned against the wall, sipping her tea.

"I'm not your fucking secretary, Anse."

Anse came around the display case and clopped his way down the hall, his legs bowed like someone who'd spent too much time on a horse. His bootheels rang like rifle shots. He banged open the glass door.

"What?"

Lope looked up, startled.

"Mr. Anse," he said.

"What do you want?"

"I want to talk."

"Fine," said Anse. "But I have to feed the tigers. You'll have to come along."

Lope swung his long legs from the saddle of the superbike, which resembled a diving bird of prey, long and furrowed and beaked.

"What do you feed them?" he asked.

Anse was already turning, walking back through the door.

"You, if you get in my way."

Lope followed Anse down the short hallway, the walls painted like the throat of a lion. It opened into what seemed an exhibit from a museum of natural history. The skulls of extinct beasts stared from banks of glass cases, each fanged or tusked. Placards described their range and habitat, their diet and social behavior, their geologic era and the time of their extinction—obituaries for entire species that once roamed the earth. The skull of a mammoth, big as a boulder, sat on a pedestal on one side, bearing wide snarls of tusk. On the other, a cash register and gift shop, replete with hats and koozies and bumper stickers. There was a rack of T-shirts, each bearing the roaring mouth of a lion, along with the name of the place:

LITTLE EDEN WILDLIFE RESCUE
SATILLA, GEORGIA
SANCTUARY FOR EXOTICS OF ALL BREEDS

Anse crossed the room without slowing, his bootheels ringing in the hollows of the skulls. Lope passed the tall woman, Tyler, who'd invited him to come. They'd met at the scene of the shooting, after he'd killed the charging lioness. He'd been standing there, the heavy rifle hanging across the tops of his thighs like a barbell, his chest rising and falling without his control. There had been so much blood on the pavement, slashed like characters in a language he didn't know.

The woman had stood beside him, her wheaty hair spilling from beneath a rumpled ballcap that read LITTLE EDEN. Her face was hard, unbroken by the scene. A moon-colored pendant hung from her throat. She'd set her hand on the bony knob of his shoulder and squeezed.

"Thank you," she'd said.

The words had entered his blood like a drug, soothing him.

Now, as Lope followed Anse through the gift shop, Tyler winked at him over the top of her mug, as if to say: *Don't worry about that old son-of-a-bitch, you're doing right.*

Anse pushed through the rear doors, dropping the three steps into his domain. It was, to Lope, like entering a whole other world—some land older, more exotic than the one he knew. The fences of enclosures rose through pines that seemed taller than any beyond the high metal walls of the place. The crowns of giant palms stood like green explosions against the sky, their trunks all spiked. Dragonflies zipped past him, glassy-winged, and several peacocks roamed freely over the grounds, fanning their eye-spotted trains.

They climbed into Anse's big dually truck—the same one he'd driven to the firehouse the day the lion escaped, when they'd gone on their strange safari through the zombie neighborhoods along the river, searching for the lioness among the high weeds of empty lots. The bed was full of five-gallon plastic buckets, each sprung with shorn deer legs. Lope stared.

"Tiger food," said Anse, seeing his face.

He cranked the big diesel engine and they went rumbling along the dirt drive between enclosures, the truck swaying and rocking over the ruts. Lope's window was down. He spied a spotted cat—a small leopard, perhaps—standing on the crossbeam of a giant cat tree, a jumble of platforms and stepladders and balance beams built among the ferns and bushes of the enclosure. She seemed female to him, her giant, amber eyes tracking him through the diamond mesh of her cage.

Lope thought Anse might explain the story of this animal or the others he saw darting through the understory or eyeing him from perches or hides, but the old man said nothing. Even when they passed the enclosure of an elephant that moved in a stilted, rocking fashion—more like a Disney animatron than a live animal—he remained silent.

Lope cleared his throat.

"I wanted to tell you I was sorry about Henrietta. About what I did."

Anse's hands twisted on the wheel, as if revving a throttle.

"You only done what you thought was right."

"I can't quit thinking about it," said Lope. "I gone over it in my head a thousand times. The way she stood there, swishing her tail. The look in her eyes. How her muscles jumped when she charged. I don't know if it was right."

Anse ground his teeth.

"Thinking it over and over won't help. Trust me. That'll eat you down to the bone, ruin your life. It don't matter if it was right or not. You thought it was right at the time." Anse's fists swelled hard on the wheel, his knuckles knobby and scarred. "I done some things I knew they were evil and I done them anyway. That's worth burning up over. Not this."

Lope drove his thumb inside his fist, squeezing.

"You really think she was just coming to your call? She wasn't gonna attack?"

Anse spat out the window.

"I don't know, Lope. I think I just wanted to know either way, even if it meant her claws. I wanted to save her. But there's no telling. She was a wild thing—"

"If I hadn't shot—"

"If you hadn't shot, I might be dead." Anse looked at him. "Don't hate yourself over this, okay? If anything, hate me for letting her out."

"You let her out?"

Anse cut his eyes out the window.

"You know what I mean."

The tigers stalked back and forth on their side of the fence, crisscrossing, their striped coats flickering through the brush. Crackling. They seemed dangerous even here, like flames waiting to be loosed over the land, sparking wildfires. Anse had slid the bucket of deer legs to the edge of the tailgate. He took one dripping in each hand and approached the feeding chute. Across from the tiger enclosure lay a man-made pond covered in a green carpet of algae, encircled with a high chain-link fence. An elevated viewing platform stood on the bank, perched on heavy posts.

"What you got over there?" asked Lope.

Anse stopped, the clubs of meat dripping at his sides.

"Old gator pit," he said. "From the zoo era. They tossed live chickens in the pond at chowtime for people to watch. Big hit in the old days."

"What's in there now?"

"Nothing," said Anse. "That I know of." He lifted the meat to the lip of the chute. "But I'd double-check my life insurance policy before going for a swim."

Lope looked at the pond. The thin layer of scum looked firm enough to walk on—a trap that could suck you into waters thick and black as tar. He wondered what monsters could be living down there, waiting.

"Drones?" Anse's face was twisted, as if the word offended him.

They were sitting on the tailgate of Anse's truck, their foreheads shiny with sweat, drinking Coca-Cola from the can. For the past two weeks, Lope had been coming on his days off to help around the sanctuary. It was late afternoon now, the sunlight spreading whiskey-gold over the grounds.

"Drones," said Lope. "That's right. They're becoming a problem for air traffic controllers and law enforcement. Government is hiring falconers to take them down."

"What do you know about falconry?"

"My uncle Delk, he's a master falconer, flies raptors at a couple of the beach resorts, keeps the gulls from pooping in the piña coladas. I worked for him every summer growing up. I still have my license, just haven't kept a bird since I started with the fire department. But I'm qualified, Mr. Anse. I can do this."

"What is it you want from me?"

"For now, I'm still at the firehouse ten shifts a month. I need somewhere to build a better outdoor perch and mews—raptor barn—and someone to feed her the days I'm at work. I could train Malaya to do it, if you don't want to. I'd give you ten percent of the business in return. It's a good deal, Anse."

Anse rubbed the stubbly brick of his chin.

"You sure there's enough business in nuisance drones?"

"Yes, sir. They got issues with them flying over government facilities, restricted sites. European police started the trend, using eagles to take them down. The Kings Bay sub base is looking for a falconer—they already reached out to my uncle. It's a lucrative contract. And I'd train her for bird control, too. Uncle Delk is retiring soon. He wants to pass on the resort contracts, the one at the local airport, too. He wants somebody to take over the business. I got that little one at home. I got to think about the future now."

Anse nodded, squinting across the sanctuary grounds.

"You already got the bird?"

"My uncle has one for me. A golden eagle, Aurora."

"You flown her before?"

"Many times."

"And you think she'll attack drones?"

Lope leaned back, crossed his arms.

"Like God's own hammer, sir."

Anse nodded faintly, his mouth crackling into a grin.

Lope looked out toward the old alligator pond.

"Maybe I could set up on the feeding platform of the pond?"

Anse's eyes cut that direction, iron-hard.

"Not there," he said. "I got plans for that."

"Another gator?"

The old man sniffed.

"Something like that."

Anse set him up with the old giraffe enclosure on the edge of the sanctuary—another relic of the zoo days, when a giraffe named Hightower had leaned his long neck over gathered knots of Florida-bound vacationers, chewing his cud and eyeing them for handouts. The giraffe house still stood in one corner of the place, a corrugated-steel hangar built double-tall and narrow.

Lope started coming whenever he could, transforming the structure into a raptor barn. He built perches and a two-door entry system and an outdoor weathering yard. He hammered iron hooks into one section, draping leather jesses and hoods and bells along the walls. The eagle, Aurora, would be free-lofted— allowed to roam untethered about the barn, picking her perches.

She was the color of dark chocolate, with white epaulettes on her shoulders, and weighed nearly fifteen pounds, with a wing- span of seven feet. Lope could be seen long into the afternoon, flying her at baits he swung from the end of a leather leash. The bird would orbit high above, as if awaiting orders, then dive for the earth, popping her wings like a parachute, high-arched, to strike the bait from midair.

"You think we can trust him?" asked Malaya.

They were sitting on the tailgate of Anse's truck, watching.

"He doesn't know."

"Neither does Tyler, but we can trust her."

Anse looked at the firefighter standing in the ankle-high grass of the enclosure, the hooded raptor riding the fist of his leather gauntlet. He wore a SATILLA FIRE & RESCUE shirt, which bore a pair of crossed fire axes, and a green boonie hat to shade his face, the strap hanging against his chest. His Hayabusa sport bike was parked just outside the fence, with its fierce

beak and oversized rear tire. Saddlebags hung from the tail of
the machine, bulging with supplies.

A quadcopter hovered over the enclosure. Anse squinted at
the tiny flier, the rotors whispering against the sky, buzzing
like insect wings. The landing skids, lean and black, made him
think of other skies, older, when he rode in the open doors of helicopter gunships. When the tongue of his best friend—a dog—
flapped in the wind.

Sometimes he could feel the untethered wheel of the earth
again, same as he'd felt that night in the Mozambican maize field.
The seasons cycling on, and the world growing ever stranger,
ever more overrun by machine facsimiles of the animals. Great
herds of automobiles rumbling down the interstates, endless as
the buffalo of old, and bearded men clad in leather chaps, riding horses of steel and chrome across the prairies. Migratory jet-
birds, white-winged, cutting contrails through the heavens, and
the oceans patrolled by black killer whales with atomic hearts,
their blowholes capable of launching city-killing warheads. Robotic pack-mules that walked on all fours, hauling the gear of
commando patrols high into the mountains, watched by predatory drones that could see from twenty thousand feet the ghost-
heat of enemy bootprints on the black scar of a footpath.

All this in a century. In less.

This man-made dragonfly hovering before them, it would
evolve. Its descendants would patrol fences or inspect power
plants or spy on illicit lovers through bedroom windows. Drones
would wash the windows of skyscrapers and herd cattle and deliver packages to doors. They might buzz about truck stops,
washing windshields and checking tire pressures, or serve as
first responders, hovering over accident scenes with red flashers,
delivering medical aid or instructions before the paramedics
could arrive. Whole swarms of robotic fliers, serving mankind.

As they watched, the eagle lifted from her master's fist, her
wings thumping the air. Anse slurped from his can of Coke and
thumbed back the brim of his bush hat.

"Lope says the Mongols used them to hunt wolves."

"Eagles?"

Anse nodded. "There were special grounds on the steppe where only the khans could hunt, marked out with stones. There's still pictures of wolf skins draped from the houses of Kazakh hunters, wolves killed by golden eagles."

"How can an eagle take down a wolf?"

"Diving strike to the back of the head, severing the brainstem. In the eighties some goldens went on a tear in New Mexico, injured or killed some fifty head of domestic cattle."

"Jesus."

They watched the eagle ascend, her form darkening against the white face of the sun. There she would hide, cloaked in fire, waiting to strike. She was descended from the feathered dinosaurs of prehistory, Anse knew, nothing left of the lesser iterations but skeletal impressions in bellies of rock, like the hidden art of God. Anse wondered how long until this raptor, too, would be outmoded, obsolete. A relic of blood and feather, preserved only in photographs, in the stories of men. He looked into the blind eye of the sun. Waiting, waiting, for the bird to strike.

CHAPTER 8

WOLFMAN

Dawn, the pines etched like dog ears against an aluminum sky. Horn walked along the backyard path to the enclosure. He was barefoot, like always, his soles callused so hard and unfeeling he could walk on noontime asphalt and broken glass. His bare torso shone, sweat-wrung with the five hundred push-ups he did every morning, hardening his chest like an armor breastplate. His hair was pulled high from his head, sprouted black and bushy as a wolf's tail, and he wore a bleached pair of canine teeth through the lobes of his ears. Black writing slithered beneath his skin, the words of poets and bards and madmen. Scrolled like a necklace beneath his collarbones, a line from *Henry VI*:

THOU WOLF IN SHEEP'S ARRAY

The wolf pack paced back and forth on their side of the fence, crisscrossing, waiting for him. They were pure-bloods, gray and timber wolves, their coats swimming black and silver through the dawn. The chain-link fence was ten feet high, angled inward at the top and strung with electric wire. A four-foot length of ground mesh extended into the enclosure, topped with rocks and logs and paving stones to keep the animals from digging out. The entrance was a double gate, latched and padlocked.

Horn took the key from a thong on his neck and let himself through the first gate, locking it behind him, then opened the second. The wolves swarmed him, bounding to touch their noses to his, to lick the teeth of their alpha. He ignored them, striding into the enclosure as if unaware of their affections.

Disregard, the ultimate mark of power.

The wolves only worked harder for his attention, torqueing themselves high into the air, seeking his mouth. He carried on toward their shelter, a flat-topped shed on which they liked to stand perched in the afternoons, looking down on the world like cats. Their bodies whirled and smoked about him as he walked, a storm that enveloped him, conjured as if by the black words written beneath his skin. Their white teeth flashed.

He climbed the steps of the shelter and sat cross-legged on the roof, limber as a yogi, his hands on his knees. The sun, streaking down through the pines, found the wolf pack paying tribute to their alpha, staring into his black eyes and nibbling his bottom lip, feathering his skin with their tails. All this until Horn made a diagonal slash of one arm, shoulder to hip, and the beasts fled the platform at once, leaving him sitting in lotus pose, his body glistening with the work of their tongues.

The pures were Horn's retinue, the furred engines of his empire. They sired his kennel of wolf dogs, crossbreeds that sold for five hundred dollars a head to people who wanted them as pets. There were new age Vermont and Colorado spinsters who believed in the wolf as their power animal or spiritual totem, and there were lovers of the arctic breeds, the Siberian husky and malamute and Samoyed, who wished to own an animal of even higher, wilder blood. There were men who wanted to wield the beasts like weapons at the end of a chain, and owners who were exceedingly protective of their property and kept the hybrids as guard dogs. There were families with the time and money and dedication to care for such animals, and those without. Horn vetted the new owners as best he could. He ran their names through a background-check service and made them complete a questionnaire by mail, giving proof of address. Still, the lives of the animals beyond his care were largely unknown.

Horn's were high-content hybrids, more than three-quarter wolf. Unlike the pures, the wolf dogs lived in kennels, a series of four-by-eight boxes with six-by-ten runs. They ate kibble instead of raw meat and rarely tasted the roadkill that Horn purchased from a mainland contractor in charge of pickup and disposal, nor the whole bison shanks and shoulders bought from a bison ranch along the old coastal highway. He could only afford so much.

A litter of three hybrid pups, pulled from their mother fourteen days after birth, tumbled over his knees while he fed them formula from a baby bottle. His refrigerator was loaded with neat rows of these bottles, each containing a whipped concoction of goat's milk and egg yolks and Karo syrup spiked with the amino acid arginine to prevent cataracts. He warmed the milk in an electric bottle warmer before feeding time.

The pups chewed on the plastic nipples, their throats pumping, their oversized paws trying to grip the bottle, as if they had thumbs. In two weeks, he would begin feeding them formula-soaked kibble. In another three, they would be on solid food. At four weeks, their brains would already be as big as those of the largest dogs, constantly analyzing the world for opportunity, weakness. The limp of an injured animal, the strained lungs of an aging pack mate. They would test every lock and vent. They would try to climb and dig. Some could chew through eleven-gauge fence. Still, they were harmless compared to the creatures that lurked elsewhere in the compound, hidden, crackling like secret fire through the brush.

The sun was hovering over the trees. The pups were fed. Horn stood in the medical shed with his hands on his hips. Mystic Tiger lay before him, dead. The tiger had passed in the night—

surely as a consequence of the maltreatment he'd endured at the hands of his previous owner, which Horn had tried so hard to reverse.

Horn had taken him from the backyard of a private owner who'd been posting ads in a trade magazine dedicated to exotic animal ownership. The house was a neat doublewide with a paved driveway and man-made trout pond. A giant pickup was parked slantwise in the yard, sky-jacked on mud tires, flying the flags of the local high school team, the Golden Tigers. A For Sale sign had been tucked beneath the windshield wipers.

The owner had fallen on hard times since the mascot clawed a varsity cheerleader during a pep rally, which led to a lawsuit. Mystic lived in a ten-by-ten cage in the sideyard, fed on dog food and table scraps since the incident. No longer would the high school sponsor an annual hog-hunt to fill the county's deep freezers with the four thousand pounds of meat the animal ate each year. No longer would the tiger be trotted out for halftime shows and pep rallies and homecoming parades. Soon the animal would be surrendered to the state, his fate unknown.

Mystic Tiger was starving when Horn found him, thin as a knife. His cage reeked, uncleaned. When the wind was right, the odor could be smelled from the main road. Still, the big cat's pride was unbroken. He was nearly lame from refusing to lie down in his own excrement, which carpeted the cage.

Horn loved him for this.

Under cover of night, he darted the tiger and cut the locks of the cage and loaded him into the back of his cargo van. Then, with the claw-shaped karambit he carried at the small of his back, he slashed the big truck's mud tires and squeezed the contents of a glucose drip bag into the fuel tank. The next time the owner started the truck, the sugar solution would caramelize inside the cylinders, causing the engine to seize. When Horn returned to his van, Mystic Tiger was breathing softly on his litter, tranquilized.

Horn spent weeks nursing the big cat back to health, rolling ball after ball of hand-warmed hamburger meat through his feeding chute, some of them loaded with capsules of glucosamine or fish oil or even Valium to help him rest. After two months, Mystic Tiger's health appeared drastically improved. He no longer limped, and the fire had returned to his coat. He looked hard and angular and strong, ready to hunt, kill, mate. Then, this morning, he hadn't woken up. His death had been painless, at least—a quiet passing in the night.

Horn washed the tiger's body with moist towelettes, tracing the inky black blades of his stripes, making them gleam. The stripes broke up the creature's silhouette in long grass or dense jungle, though this tiger, born captive, had never stalked such landscapes. Horn cleaned the webbed spaces between the tiger's toes and the white tuft of his beard, kissing him on the broad bridge between the eyes.

He could not help but think of his mother, dead when he was eight. She'd made crafts and jewelry, which she sold through the local gift shops. Necklaces of sharks' teeth and abalone spike earrings and gun-barrel rings with points of crystal snared in copper wire—rose quartz or blue lapis or black tourmaline. She hadn't cut her hair since her teens, so the dark waterfall of locks nearly touched the floor. Mainly she kept the black tresses wound up in large buns, perched high atop her head and pinned with wooden knitting needles. She had sharp little teeth, like a wolf pup, and she always smelled faintly of blood and milk, so that little Horn's stomach would growl in her presence and he would long to eat.

One morning just after his eighth birthday, she did not come from her room for breakfast. As always, his father had left for work before dawn, gone before anyone woke. Horn ate his cereal alone, slurping the milk from the bowl, then jumped down from the chair, his bare soles slapping the linoleum. He found his mother still in bed, buried in the dark nest of her own hair. Her cheek was cold. He crawled on top of her, shaking her, lifting one lid to find the white of her eye gone red, a world aswim in blood. Aneurysm, they would later say. Little Horn spent hours bawling into the crooks of her, her armpits and elbows, screaming

for her to rise. He bit blue horseshoes in her cold skin, as if the
pain might call her back. He straddled and hammered her chest
with the heels of his fists, glazing her nightgown with snot and
tears.

Here his father found him when he came home from his
shift on the road crew. Horn went wild when the man tried to
pull him from his mother. He ripped her nightgown trying to
cling to the cold country of her body, splaying her breasts flat
and wide across her bony rib cage, and his father slapped him
hard across the face. Horn attacked him, clawing and biting and
kicking like a creature gone rabid, his eyes red-blazed with fury.
He ripped antlers and driftwood and feathered dream catchers
from the walls. He howled.

That was the first night his father locked him in the dog box.

All day, Horn worked over the raised bier of the medical table
with his karambit and skinning knife and a hand-chipped ob-
sidian blade, dressing the animal, saving the bones and claws
and tiger-striped hide, which he fleshed and salted and hung
to dry. When he finished, the sun was low over the trees, the
sky darkening. The hour between the dog and the wolf, when
darkness whelmed and shapes shifted strangely into night.
The tiger's remains had lain upwind of the wolves all day, the
red scent curling invisibly through the fence, entering the wet
cages of their jaws. Now Horn loaded the meat and organs, near
boneless, into a large washtub, which he set on a handcart and
wheeled over the path toward the high fence of the enclosure.
He entered the double gates for the second time today.

The wolves circled, circled, whining with desire. Only his
favorite, Onyx, refused to duck his head in submission. The black
beta wolf strutted beyond the ring of beggars, flashing the white
barbs of his smile. He would make a play for alpha soon. His yellow eyes never left his leader, the sharp black arrow of his mind
hunting for any sign of weakness, any hitch or opportunity.
Horn would be ready. He had ten years of experience training
animals for the circus—wolves and tigers, mainly—and more

than twenty victories in the cage, applying the ancient arts of leverage and limb in which he was trained. This would not be the first wolf that challenged his power, that he would have to roll and stare blaze-eyed into submission, or else.

When he was fifteen, his first love, Jessie-Ray Long, had cheated on him with an upperclassman football player, blowing the boy in the cab of his pickup truck in the school parking lot. Teenaged Horn could not quit crying. Sobs racked him for forty-eight hours, like all the hurt in the world was in her mouth, on the slick of her tongue. He lay curled in a ball on his bed, his cries muffled by his pillow. He could not let his father hear. He must not show weakness. But his pain pulsed through the sheetrock of the house. After two days, his father had had enough. He burst in and took Horn by the back of the neck and ran him down the hall and into the yard. He meant to force the boy into the dog box—the first time in two years.

Unbeknownst to his father, Horn had been training at an underground gym after school since the age of twelve, learning jujitsu in return for mopping floors and cleaning lockers. Without thought, he wheeled and leapt high-kneed for his father's head, locking his legs around the bigger man's neck—a flying triangle choke. His thighs applied pressure to his father's carotid artery, cutting off the blood supply to his brain. They stared into each other's face for ten long seconds, Horn hanging like a monkey from the bigger man's neck. He watched his father's eyes soften, as with love. The man melted to his knees with a thump, then crumpled to the earth. Horn held the blood-choke for a long, quivering minute. Then he tied his father to the ten-foot lead of the dog run and broke his thumbs so that when he awoke, he could only paw blubbering at the knot.

The cell at the juvenile detention center was ten times the size of a dog box. From then on, jail cells were always too big to bother him.

The wolves swirled beneath him, their ribs rattling against the clapboard of the shed. He had not given them the command to rise. They rumbled slink-shouldered, slack-tongued, a vortex of desire. Before him lay the red flesh of the tiger, hauled onto the flat altar of the roof with a block and tackle. As he'd heaved the thick rope of the pulley, sweat spilled and veins lurched from his skin, making the words on one forearm gleam.

THY DESIRES ARE WOLFISH, BLOODY, STARV'D AND RAVENOUS

Now Horn descended the steps and loosed the wolves with an upward slash of his arm. They bounded straight up the vertical walls of the shed and fell upon the carcass. In the morning, the meat would be gone, heavy in the bellies of wolves, and Horn would sit cross-legged in place of the beast. He strode out of the enclosure, locking the gates behind him, and up the path to the tiny house at the front of the property. There he would sleep, curled in a room hardly bigger than a dog box, dreaming of running wild and dark beneath the moon.

CHAPTER 9

TREMBLING EARTH

The pair of them lay hidden high in a grove of saw palmetto, shoulder to shoulder. Sweat crawled beneath their shirts and pants, tickling like ants, beading at the points of their noses and earlobes and chins. Mosquitos whined in their ears and beetles trundled over the folds of their camouflage fatigues. Red bugs the size of freckles burrowed under their skin, leaving hives of irritation in their wake.

Malaya felt better than she had in weeks.

She lifted the binoculars to her eyes, scanning the property. They were on the edge of the Okefenokee Swamp—"Land of the Trembling Earth"—where isolated pockets of swampers had used words like *ere* and *oft* and *yon* well into the 1900s. A land peaty and old, slashed with black creeks and abandoned rail lines, rumored to harbor the Georgia Pig Man and the Florida Skunk Ape—Southern bigfoots, muddy and foul-smelling, said to haunt the swamps and glades, ever fleeing the sight of men.

Through the binoculars, Malaya spotted a wire corncrib. It resembled an enormous birdcage—round with wire walls and a conical tin roof, set on the floating platform of an old barge. Inside were stacks of cages and crates, which contained a whole menagerie of swampland fauna, both furred and scaled. Otters, raccoons, tortoises, even water moccasins.

The smell reached them from fifty yards. It reminded Malaya of Baghdad, the back alleys where people had lived like animals, driven from the bombed ruins of their homes. She breathed in, out, telling herself she was in South Georgia, lying on the raw edge of the swamp. She was not passing the backstreets of Baghdad, perched high in a Humvee, her turret gun charged.

She licked her lips.

"Why?"

Anse ground his teeth beneath his bush hat.

"I ain't for sure on that. They've got some end-time notions, I think."

Malaya glassed the main house, a porched cabin perched on skinny stilts. The roof was rusty tin, the windows cracked. An airboat sat moored on a dark creek behind the house, powered by a giant propeller. Alligator skins were pegged against the porch walls, star-shaped, like the kill marks stamped on old fighter planes.

In front of the house, inside a shallow pit of bricks, lay the lone exotic: a giant Nile crocodile in a thick leather collar, chained to an iron post driven in the ground. Unlike the blunt nose of an American alligator, its snout formed a daggerlike point.

"*Crocodylus niloticus,*" said Anse. "Nile croc, same's the ones that take antelope and Cape buffalo in Africa, even lions."

A wooden sign had been wired to the post: MIGHTY MO.

The reptile's hide was grayish-green, striped with camouflage, and he was missing one of his hind legs, a yellowish bulb of stump. Rumor said the owners pitted the creature against native alligators for sport, saurian wars fought in backyard mudholes to the screaming glee of men in green and white rubber boots, waving twenties like pennants at a ballgame.

Malaya had balked at first, looking at a photograph of the croc.

"I thought we were mainly a big-cat rescue."

"You got something against cold-bloods?"

"Hell, look at the fucker."

Anse sucked on his cigarette.

"What, only the pretty ones matter?"

"That isn't what I said, Anse."

The old jockey shrugged.

"He might surprise you yet."

She remembered a fight she'd seen once in the reserve, a Nile croc defending an elephant carcass from a trio of lionesses. That crocodile had been more than fourteen feet long, with the camouflaged hide of a Panzer tank. It wheeled and hissed, brandishing its eighty-odd teeth, but the lions were too quick. They pounced from three angles at once.

Now, looking at Mighty Mo, Malaya felt something akin to awe for the old battler—a creature largely unchanged since the time of the dinosaur, built like a prehistoric warship. She remembered the Sunday school stories of her Catholic upbringing, when Moses commanded his brother, Aaron, to cast down his staff before Pharaoh, who wished to see a miracle, some evidence of the power of the Hebrew God. Aaron's rod had transformed into a giant serpent—some said a crocodile—and devoured a knot of snakes born from the staffs of Pharaoh's court sorcerers.

"You heard about the Battle of Ramree Island?" asked Anse.

"Should I have?"

"Ramree is in the Bay of Bengal, off the coast of Burma. In 1945, British Royal Marines flushed a thousand Japanese troops from their base there. Tried to get them to surrender, but instead the Japanese decided to make a break across the island, crossing the interior swamps to join up with a battalion on the far side. Middle of the night, all these terrible screams started coming from the swamp. Hundreds of them, and gunfire, the crack of bones. British troops on patrol said it was like standing at the edge of hell, listening to the agonies of the damned."

"Crocodiles?"

Anse nodded. "They moved in with the ebb tide. Hundreds, crushing men in their jaws, death-rolling them down into the black, ripping limbs from sockets. Come morning, the sky stayed dark, so clouded was it with carrion birds. They say only twenty of the one thousand lived."

"Goddamn."

"Worst human massacre by animals in history. Worse even than the sinking of the USS *Indianapolis,* that inspired *Jaws.*"

"That supposed to make me want to save the son-of-a-bitch?"

Anse shrugged. "Drop in the bucket compared to what men done to men in a single day, in a single second. Hiroshima, Nagasaki, the Somme. Then there's the American bison, the Barbary lion, the northern white rhino."

"Fair enough," said Malaya.

"Some say we killed off the saber-tooth and the mastodon, too, at the end of the Pleistocene era. Human hunting pressure."

"Hell, maybe we all ought to just shoot ourselves, let the lions and crocs run the world."

Anse spat and grinned.

"It's a thought."

The sun was noon-high, an angry boil in the sky, when a pair of swampers in white rubber boots came tromping down the porch steps into the yard. They wore tatty tank tops and canvas trousers tucked into their boots. One was older, with a chinstrap beard and the stud of a diamond earring. He yawned and scratched his armpits, then lit a cigarette between cupped hands. His knuckles were tattooed, the letters illegible as bruises from this range. Malaya zoomed in with the spotting scope, squinting at his cupped fists.

BORN FREE

The younger swamper's skin was unblemished. He carried a bangstick, a long spearlike device for dispatching alligators and other dangerous game at close range. At contact, it could fire a Magnum slug into the base of an animal's skull.

"Is it gator season?" asked Malaya.

"Started August first," said Anse.

The boy with the bangstick was maybe seventeen. He had pale pink lips, an angel face. His hair, white-blond, was pulled back from his face, tied in a long sliver of ponytail. He'd begun twirling the silver bangstick around his body, whirling it like a mace, displaying a mastery of drum-major flourishes. The finger roll and prop spin, where the staff whirred propeller-like through his hands, and the palm spin, where it thundered flat over his head like the rotors of a helicopter like it could lift him out of this place. Now he was whipping the staff around his wrists and elbows, passing it hand to hand, behind his back and around his neck, slashing silver arcs from the fast-spinning stick. The boy lifted his boots high from the ground, marching in place, twirling the staff this way and that. Then the older man—his brother—wheeled and kicked the bangstick hard from the boy's hands. It clattered to the ground a few feet away.

"Sissy," said the man. He spat at the boy's feet.

Malaya tensed. She felt an urge to pounce from this hide, to fall upon the older man and give him a dose of his own medicine.

The boy stood there a moment, hands empty, then bent down to recover the bangstick. The older man was already walking the zigzag of duckboards that led to the airboat, his belt-knife clapping against his thigh. The boy took a brass shell from his pocket and loaded the firing mechanism at the end of the spear, then followed his brother to the dock, using the long bangstick like a hiking staff. They unmoored the boat and mounted the side-by-side seats, raised high as bar stools from the deck. The boy set the bangstick in a holder between them and donned a heavy pair of earmuffs as his brother fired the engine. The big propeller kicked over amid a cloud of smoke, spooling up. Soon they were roaring away from the dock, tearing a ragged chevron in the creek, the trees shivering as they passed.

Malaya looked at Anse. His eyeglasses were slightly fogged, the lenses perched small and round on his nose like the pince-nez of Teddy Roosevelt. He might be a miniature version of the man they called "the Lion," his battered bush hat perched on his head like a Rough Rider's. He lay next to a long catchpole tipped with a noose of steel cable. He pulled the instrument close as the sound of the airboat faded.

"Showtime."

They rose from their hide and approached the brick pit. The killing mouth of the reptile turned toward them, crowded with crooked teeth. Anse held the catchpole before him. The steel loop of the snare floated through the scattered sunlight, halo or noose. Thunder rumbled from the crocodile's belly, making the ground tremble beneath their bootsoles. Malaya looked at the yellowy knob of the missing foot. She'd asked Anse why they couldn't just cut the creature loose into the swamp.

"Any alligator fed by humans becomes a danger," he'd told her. "State policy is for it to be harvested."

"But it's a crocodile, not an alligator."

"Same problem."

"What if these swampers hear about a three-footed alligator at a sanctuary up in Georgia and decide to come after you?"

Anse had squinted out the window of the butcher shed a long moment, as if waiting, watching them come.

"Let them."

"Whoa boy," said Anse.

The crocodile was straining against the end of his chain, hissing and bellowing. Yellowish scars covered his hide, each a mark of some previous battle.

"Watch it," said Anse.

The tail swept across the ground, dull-spiked like a heavy war club. Malaya knew the reptile could wheel in a flash, whipping that long tail far beyond the outer limit of the chain, snapping femurs and buckling joints, blasting shards of bone through arteries. The yellow knob of foot scraped the earth for traction, pocking the dirt. The reptile's eyes, turning their way, looked like a pair of alien planets, swampy and primeval. Malaya thought of the vast histories eyes like those must have witnessed, ages when flying lizards screamed through the heavens or saber-tooth cats prowled the riverbanks, ambushing three-toed horses or mastodons. No wonder the Old Testament God would transform Aaron's rod into a saurian destroyer, showing what he thought of Pharaoh's small-time court sorcery.

The noose of the catchpole floated before the creature's snout. The inhabitants of the corncrib squeaked and scratched at their cages, hearing the war-bellows of the croc. Anse lunged, snaring Mighty Mo in the noose. The creature thundered and shook, as if shot or speared, slapping the earth with his tail, hissing and death-rolling. Anse held fast. His muscles blistered beneath his shirt, his forearms strung with effort. Malaya swooped in and set the chain in the iron beak of the bolt cutters, snapping the links.

When the crocodile had drained itself of fight, they cinched its jaws with duct tape and bound its legs behind its back with flexi-cuffs. Malaya stared at the binds. Her heart beat hotter, faster. The words came before she could stop them.

"Let's just let him go, Anse. Nobody will know."

"He'll come back here to be fed. They'll just catch him again."

"We're taking him off a chain and putting him in a cage."

"*Enclosure*," said Anse. "He'll have a whole pond to himself. He won't have to fight."

Malaya looked at the battle-scarred hulk, so like some battered warship of old.

"Maybe he likes to fight," she said.

Anse unhinged his jaw to reply, but the roar of an engine filled his mouth.

They stood two against two, the crocodile bound between them. Anse held the catchpole in both hands, slightly canted, while the angel-faced boy slowly twirled the bangstick, letting it flash about the axle of his wrist. Behind him, the airboat floated at the end of the dock. The boy seemed strangely undisturbed at their presence, even as his tattooed brother shook with fury, palming the end of his belt-knife.

"The fuck you think you're doing?"

"Fish and Wildlife called us in," said Anse. "Said there was a nuisance crocodile for removal here."

"Nuisance? He was on a fucking chain."

"Somebody must of called the state hotline," said Anse. "Anything over four feet could be deemed a nuisance if it's believed to pose a threat to people, pets, or property."

"You got a warrant?"

"Permit," said Anse. "It's up in the truck."

"Ain't that convenient."

Anse's hands knuckled slightly on the handle of the snare. The curled grip of the howdah pistol hung against his side ribs.

"Complainant must of granted legal access to the property," he said. "Else the state wouldn't of issued the permit."

The swamper turned, glaring at the angel-faced boy.

"You done this?"

The boy didn't look back at him. He was staring at Malaya. His eyes were bright blue, as if filled with sky. Somehow he seemed older than before, harder.

"Sissy-boy," said the older brother. "You listening to me?"

Still the boy said nothing. Malaya thought the older man might lunge for him, throttle him, but he didn't. The man seemed terror-struck, paralyzed by the strangers in his midst. His knife stayed glued inside the sheath even as his hand flexed on the handle. He appeared shorter than before, cowed. His eyes kept flicking to the bound crocodile. The power dynamic had shifted, realized Malaya. The man was afraid of the strangers—of what they could do—but the boy was not. He seemed taller now, surer, as if he were drawing power up from the ground, absorbing what bled from his brother. His hand snapped closed, catching the bangstick vertical in his fist—a rod designed to smite monsters, turning rivers to blood.

"Take him," he said.

"What?" said his brother.

"Take him," said the boy. "He wasn't ever meant for the ark. Too big."

"Ark?" said Malaya.

The boy tipped his staff toward the barge.

"We'll save them when the waters rise."

"Hang on," said the older swamper. "They can't just take him."

"Watch them, brother."

The man was sweating profusely now; it blistered his face like a plague.

"I won't have it. I'm the one bought Mo from that gator park. He's mine."

"He's fought well for you," said the boy. "It's time."

The man was shaking visibly now. His voice was a strangled whisper.

"Don't let them take him," he said. "Please."

The boy stood with the long rod of the bangstick held upright in his hand, his eyes calm and blue. He was in charge now. Unafraid of the strangers, or the world that sent them.

"Take him," he said.

Malaya and Anse looked at each other, then bent toward the bound reptile. The older swamper quivered in place, as if bound by some paralyzing spell. He was staring at Mighty Mo, this three-footed lizard king, and Malaya saw a wild love in his eyes. The spell broke and his body flooded into action. He lunged at them, drawing his knife.

"No!"

The bangstick flashed in the boy's hand, wheeling outward to strike the man's wrist with a crack. The knife was knocked from his hand, flashing into the dirt, and then the staff reversed direction, slung around the boy's body at a diagonal, striking the older swamper behind the knees. He buckled to the dirt, as if receiving grace, his injured hand clutched to his chest. Again the staff whipped about the boy's body and drove the man into the ground, the powerhead placed against his heart. A little pressure and a round of .357 Magnum would discharge into his chest.

"I told you about calling me sissy," said the boy.

The man's whole body was clenched, as if skewered. His eyes were wide.

"Please," he croaked.

The boy spoke to Malaya and Anse, not turning his head.

"Take the crocodile," he said. "And don't ever come back."

They bent and took a rope hitched under the croc's forelegs. The knot veed outward, giving them each a length of towline. They slung the lines over their shoulders and began hauling the reptile from the clearing, heavy as a beached boat. Their heads were bent, their chins low. Each listening for the sound of a shot, like the first crack of a coming storm.

CHAPTER 10

THUNDER BOY

"How do you afford it?" asked Malaya.

They were working in the butcher shed, quartering chickens for the smaller cats. A few of the birds they set aside whole, reserved for the mighty jaws of the sanctuary's new crocodile.

Anse didn't take his eyes from the cutting board. He positioned his chicken with the breast side up, pulling one leg away from the body.

"Afford what?"

"All of it," said Malaya. "The tigers each eat ten pounds of meat a day. I did the math. Even at two bucks a pound, that's over seven grand a year apiece just in meat. Multiply that by all the other animals you got here."

Anse sliced the web of skin at the animal's hip to reveal the socket, then cut through the ball of joint, freeing the leg.

"The others don't eat as much."

"The hell they don't. It adds up. Plus the vet bills, the mortgage."

"There's no mortgage. I bought the place outright."

"Still," said Malaya.

"There's tours, merchandise sales. Tyler runs fund-raising campaigns."

"Don't give me that shit, Anse. Nobody ever comes for the tours, and you never charge for the field trips. I don't think anybody's bought a T-shirt since I've been here. If there were big donors, they'd be coming around to visit."

Anse felt for the knot of cartilage at the center of the chicken's breast, then positioned the blade slightly to the side.

"I have money," he said.

He cut through the ribs on either side of the knot, freeing each assembly of muscle and wing. Tiny engines of flesh, so neat they could be factory-made.

Malaya watched him.

"Money from what?"

Anse thought of the day he rode Thunder Boy, a miracle of a horse, and he could not die.

"I don't like to talk about it," he said. He used the flat side of the cleaver to scrape the four pieces of chicken into the cooler at the end of the table. "Besides, it's rude to ask people about their finances."

"It's rude to trespass on private property and steal somebody's pet crocodile, too."

"*Rescue*," said Anse.

Malaya leaned forward.

"Tell me."

That night Anse drove the backroads, his headlights igniting starry pairs of wild eyes. He knew people saw his big truck cruising the roads and whispered that he was collecting strays to feed his pride of cats. Truth was, he never knew what he was searching for out here, not exactly. Now less than ever. Since Henrietta's death, his heart felt fissured, shattered into a hundred bloody nomads, each fled fugitive from the cage of his chest. He was driven out of bed, into the night-lands, the dark wilds of slash pine and swamp. Searching, searching. Perhaps he was trying to find them, those lost fragments. To round them up before they were lost.

He thought of the story he'd told Malaya that afternoon. The same story he'd told Tyler, years ago, and no one else. It was the truth, as best as he could remember it. But like so much of his past, it seemed more akin to some painful dream.

"I was a jockey in my teens," he told her. "Went back to racing after I came home from overseas."

"From Vietnam?"

"Africa."

In 1981, he'd gone to Ruidoso Downs for the All American Futurity—the richest quarter-horse race in the world. He was there to ride a string of lesser horses, the small-money races of a journeyman jockey. After a race, in the locker room, he was approached to ride a horse called Thunder Boy. A horse known to win. A favorite.

"I took the ride, even though it smelled. You don't turn down a ride like that."

The night before the race, he was intercepted at his motel. There were two of them, hired thugs in white shirts and black gambler hats and flashy silver bolo ties. They had the asymmetric faces of cavemen, shaped as if by club and stone. Their muscles bucked beneath the starch of their shirts. Seeing them, he knew why the original jockey had taken "sick." Why he, a mere journeyman, had been given a ride so good.

They cornered him in the vending room, where he'd come for ice. They knew he would suck on the cubes instead of eating that night, dipping them in a tumbler of bourbon, savoring the burn. In the quarter mile, every ounce could count.

"You will not win this race," said one. The snack machine buzzed in the small room. Their boots were sharp-toed and black, polished like knives. "You will not."

"The fuck I won't," said Anse. He muscled between them, scooping his brass bucket full of ice. The hired guns turned to watch him. Their hands were crossed over their belt buckles, like men at church.

"Thunder Boy wins this race, you will be gelded," said one, snipping his fingers.

"Then shot," said the other.

Anse looked at them over the ice bucket hugged full against his chest.

"Clip me, I'll still have more balls than you two mariachis."

He made to push between them, out of the room, when his knees buckled beneath him, stomped in. Blades appeared at his chin, his groin.

"You no listen," said one of the men.

Anse glanced down at the knives. Stilettos. One blade rubbed up and down his zipper. The other scratched the stubble at his throat.

"How much?" he asked.

Thunder Boy was a wonder of a horse, a storm-gray stallion, bouldered with power. His shoulders and haunches pulsed like thunderclouds. His hooves gleamed as if shoeshined. His black eyes, long-lashed, looked Anse up and down, taking in his racing silks, his visored helmet, his five-ounce cheater boots. Anse touched the horse's neck, fingering the veins there, the great rivers of blood. The horse nuzzled him in the crook of his neck, telling him he would run. He would run as hard and long as necessary. He would run his heart out.

Soon Anse was crouched in the stirrups, waiting for the gates to open. He felt like a god, poised on a horse made of cloud and fire, when the gates slammed open and Thunder Boy exploded from the chute, striking to the head of the field. The horse detonated between his heels, again and again, and Anse cared for nothing but the surge of blood, the storm of hooves. He was thundering high over the Mekong Delta again, riding in the door of a helicopter gunship. He was galloping over the silver sage of Little Bighorn, charging into the singing arrows and rifles of the Lakota, the Cheyenne, the Arapaho. He could hear the war-cries of Crazy Horse, rearing his painted stallion, a yellow lightning bolt flashing on his cheek.

"Hóka-héy! Hóka-héy!"

Today is a good day to die.

Anse forgot about the men from the hotel, the deal. His past was dead, his tomorrows unborn. There was only the thundering of blood, the crashing of the hooves.

Now, now, now.

He would ride this thunder into the earth.

He would win.

He whipped the horse for speed, merciless. The animal charged and charged, as if into battle, his black blinkers bearing the white blaze of a thunderbolt. The lesser horses fell away and Thunder Boy's hooves struck the earth like cannon fire, again and again, hard enough he might break from the ground and roar into the sky.

They were ahead by two lengths, an unbeatable margin. The terraced screams of the grandstands whipped past them and the high windows of the Billy the Kid Casino and Anse lashed the horse's rump for power, drinking the wind in his mouth.

The thunder was everything. There was nothing else.

To this day, he thought he could feel the animal's heart break beneath him, like the crack of split stone. Thunder Boy's legs folded and his chest plowed into the dirt and Anse was thrown from the stirrups, sent cartwheeling down the track. He felt ribs snapping inside him, joints wrecked, and then the ten-horse field was upon him, a barrage of iron-hoofed cannons firing on every side of his head, staving the earth at his temples, at his arms and hands and legs and feet. He would be stove-in, ridden down like Custer's men, riddled like the boys in Vietnam, in Rhodesia and Mozambique. Like the baboons, the lions, the elephants.

He would have what he deserved.

Then they were gone, a passed storm. Anse lay sprawled on the track, his body wreathed in hoofprints, a cloud of crescent moons stamped in the dirt. One lay in the pocket of his armpit, another between his legs. A pair crowned his head. Any might have killed him.

There must be a reason why.

Thunder Boy lay behind him, a little to one side, the track torn and pocked in the wake of his fall. His neck was broken, his head curled strangely beneath the gray heap of his body, as if he were hiding in embarrassment. The thunderbolt on his blinkers was dirt-smeared, extinguished.

Anse was discharged from the hospital three days later, arrayed in plaster casts and slings. He opened the door of his motel room to find a gray leather duffel bag set neatly on the center of the bed. Inside were columns of stacked bills, sealed in cellophane.

"They thought I'd done it on purpose," said Anse. "Gone over and above. Maybe that's why they left the note."

"Note?" asked Malaya.

"Yellow Post-it note, stuck on the bills. Said a little oil company to invest in." Anse twitched his nose. "Ain't so little no more."

"You two have been spending a lot of time together," said Tyler.

They were lying in bed in Anse's trailer, spent.

"She's learning the ropes," said Anse. "Nobody to teach her but me."

Outside, his truck was still ticking, cooling from his long drive through the country midnight, the black sea of pines. He'd been thinking of how he was cruising along the ancient seabed. Sixty million years ago, there were no glaciers at the poles and the lower half of the state was covered in a vast sea, warm and shallow, rife with corals and arthropods, megasharks and thirty-foot crocodilians whose tooth-marks had been found in the bones of tyrannosaurs. Sometimes he would park his truck and lie in the bed and imagine their silhouettes swimming through the skies overhead—creatures the size of attack helicopters and business jets.

"You all were a long time picking up that croc from the DNR last week," said Tyler. "All day. It's not like you had to wrangle it yourself."

Anse squinted up at the ceiling fan, so much like the spinning propeller of an airboat. His hands were laced across his chest.

"I told you there was complications."

Tyler rolled up on her elbow.

"If you fuck her, just tell me, okay?"

"Hell, she ain't half my age."

"As if that ever stopped anyone."

"You like her so much, why don't you fuck her?"

Tyler flinched, her eyes sudden-wet. She turned onto her back, staring through the ceiling.

"You know what your problem is, Anse? You only love the wild ones, the ones that don't love you back."

Anse mashed shut his eyes. He wanted to argue but couldn't find the words. Instead he growled and rolled onto his side, welcoming the world of his old saber cat. Smilodon, a winter king facing down his last rout of wolves.

A creature savage, untamed.

Malaya strode down the aisles of the store, her grocery basket hanging from one arm. She wore a tank top to let her new tattoo breathe. A flaming tropical bird, still puffy, lifting from the perch of her shoulder blade. She tested avocados with her thumb, placing three in a bag, and selected a green bunch of bananas. She walked through the dairy section, enjoying the cool hum of the shelves, the eggs cradled in their paper or Styrofoam cartons. The milk jugs stood in their rows, innocent, no longer screaming to be weaponized with 100-proof vodka.

She turned up the baking aisle, then quickly doubled back— she'd forgotten the Greek yogurt she liked. Rounding the corner of the aisle, she nearly bumped into the cart of another shopper. The man's face was hard and lean, as if stone-chipped, and a black spray of hair stood high from his head, banded into a ponytail. Tattoos sped down his forearms, rooted in the oversized knuckles of his hands. She wondered if he might be a rescue swimmer or frogman stationed at the submarine base, but he looked too wild for government service, too feral.

"Excuse me," she said, casting her eyes at his cart. She saw carton after carton of Grade A jumbo eggs, neatly stacked, along with trays of chicken necks and ground beef and a fifty-pound sack of dog food on the bottom shelf.

She looked up. "Paleo diet?"

The man grinned, revealing large white canine teeth.

"Something like that."

Malaya felt a warmth rise in her cheeks. When she opened her mouth, she found a rare hollow where her words should be. She cleared her throat.

"Well, don't let me stand in your way." She edged aside.

The man nodded, politely, and Malaya walked on with her grocery basket, trying to remember why she'd doubled back in the first place.

"I'm ready for a big cat," she said.

Malaya was riding in the bed of Anse's pickup, one elbow on the toolbox, talking to him through the rear window of the cab. Buckets of quartered chicken and deer legs flanked her, the upturned hooves swaying in the breeze.

"I know you've been scouting one, those nights people see you out cruising the roads."

It was true. He'd found something just over the state line.

He leaned his head out the window, spat.

"You ain't ready yet."

"The fuck I'm not, old man. I was born ready."

Anse glanced at her in the rearview mirror. In the past two months, the bruiselike bags had vanished from the girl's eyes. Her black hair was combed now, washed. The once-bitten squares of her nails had lengthened, sharpened, painted black or charcoal or chocolate-brown depending on the week. Her breath no longer smelled like sour milk.

Anse kept his eyes on the rearview mirror, watching her from beneath his hat brim.

"I got a question," he said.

"What?"

"That rhino poacher, the one you missed. You wish you'd hit him?"

She turned her head. Her eyes went narrow, sighting far beyond the trees.

"Somebody did."

"That ain't what I asked."

Now she crossed her arms atop the toolbox and stared back at him in the mirror.

"I don't know," she said.

Anse nodded, looking back to the road.

She was ready.

That night it stormed. Anse sat on the stoop of his trailer in his skivvies, protected by the tin awning that covered the door, and smoked a cigarette. The rain rattled the awning above his head, hard and metallic, like brass shell casings raining from a gunship. A bolt of lightning fissured the night, followed by a sharp crack of thunder, as if the sky were breaking, busting at the seams.

He thought of all the broken hearts. Malaya, Tyler, Lope. Henrietta and Thunder Boy and a scout dog named Huey, from his days in Vietnam. Anse had his bare feet curled one atop the other, his bush hat pushed far back on his head. He put the cigarette to his lips and sucked deep. Sometimes he longed for the lands of prehistory—a world before cages or bombs, when titans roamed. A world before sin. Sometimes he wished the rain would fall and fall, drowning the histories of men, letting the world begin anew.

Anse shook his head, blowing smoke.

Too easy, he knew.

CHAPTER 11

PANTHERESS

They crossed the Savannah River at noon, high over the city's port and riverfront, then dropped into the lowcountry of South Carolina. It had rained that morning and the pavement was still slick, blued like a gun barrel. Their tires hissed along the old coastal highway, the world steaming from the roadsides. They passed the strip clubs and fruit stands set in the marshy no-man's-land between states, then entered the shady tunnels of oak and pine where Pentecostal churches and cinderblock nightclubs squatted beneath the moss. Hand-painted street signs loomed from the trees and they passed a junkyard with a Dumpster of used tires out front, the cars hunkered like beetles in the weeds.

They drove north on the backroads, turning onto smaller highways where broad tracts of slash pine grew spindly and frayed, destined for the sawmills. Anse wheeled onto an old two-lane, cracked and scarred, covered in tar-snakes that gleamed like hatchlings beneath their wheels. Malaya watched his jaw muscles flicker and pulse, as if chewing on curses or fighting words. A wonder he had any teeth left.

The house was set far back from the road, the rickety mansion of a turn-of-the-century timber baron. A man who'd made his money in virgin pine and naval stores, whose workers had lived in canvas tents, wielding axes and crosscut saws. The white facade had turned greenish, as if left underwater, the windows filmy and opaque. The surrounding acres had been sold off to the state. Anse drove past the house and turned down the dirt road of the wildlife management area that now adjoined the property.

They parked at an old turnout littered with ancient beer cans and busted glass and the black ruin of a torched car. They were dressed as hog hunters—camouflage overalls and ballcaps and heavy boots. Malaya dropped the trailer gate for Anse, who backed the sanctuary's buggy down the ramp. It was a gas-powered 4×4 with off-road tires and side-by-side seats, like an oversize golf cart. He'd taped over the Little Eden decals and fitted an exhaust silencer designed for hunters who didn't want to spook their trophy bucks. The bed was scrubbed clean and cushioned with foam mats. They started down a trail through the woods, the wheel springs creaking over the roots.

Malaya rode with a jabstick propped at her heel. It was long as a lance, designed to inject a dose of tranquilizer from a safe distance. Anse had taught her to use the pole-length syringe on a sack of feed, plunging the hypodermic needle through the burlap. At the time, she couldn't help but think of the swamp boy's bangstick, which injected a Magnum-sized slug instead.

Later she used the jabstick to sedate one of the sanctuary's tigers for his annual medical examination. Anse and Tyler first lured the animal into a narrow chute attached to the enclosure, coaxing him with hunks of store-bought beef. Meanwhile, Malaya crouched alongside the fence. She slid the lance through a diamond of chain link, aiming for the high, angular plane of the tiger's rump.

She was kneeling there, about to plunge the syringe, when her hair stood on end, like someone had breathed on the back of her neck. She looked back over her shoulder, as if a pair of eyes might hang there, watching. A wolf or other predator. There was nothing, only the pines swaying on the other side of the sanctuary fence.

She turned back to the tiger and steadied her aim.

They parked the buggy and crawled into a hide of holly shrubs, pausing to scope the old mansion. There had been a fancy garden behind the house, but weeds had sprung through the place, strangling flowerpots and slithering across walking paths. The concrete statuary was drowning. Gargoyles ensnared in weeds, angels garroted by creeper vines. The whole place lay beneath a twilight of heavy oaks, their branches spread in strange, gnarled rafters.

Malaya's elbows were propped on the ground, steadying her binoculars. The house itself was tall and narrow, weathered greenish-gray, the chimney pocked with missing bricks. The roof over the upper porch was steeply gabled, the pediment window broken. Anse said bats roosted in the attic—he'd seen them come pouring out at dusk. She swept the binoculars to the base of the house, where an ancient cattle trailer sat on dry-rotted tires. Behind the iron bars lay a large black cat, poised sphinx-like beneath a metallic cloud of flies. Malaya could see hotspots on the animal's elbows, puffy with infection. A pale crisscross of scars on her nose.

The animal seemed incognizant of these miseries. She was watching the minute workings of the garden. Her green eyes flicked here and there, tracking the dart and hover of dragonflies, the *tick* of beetles through the grass. The fireflies would be out soon, sparking from the weeds.

Malaya shook her head, her mouth slightly parted.

"You never said she was a black panther."

Anse growled. "I said she was a leopard, which she is. No such thing as a black panther. There's melanistic jaguars and melanistic leopards. Cats born with extra black pigment, *melanin*. Advantageous trait in dense, lowlight jungles. Black panthers don't exist."

"Well, *melanistic leopard* doesn't have quite the same ring, now does it?"

The old jockey grunted beneath his bush hat.

"Truth rarely does."

Malaya rocked on her elbows, trying not to grin.

"What about the Beast of Bladenboro—you heard of that one? In the fifties, a large black cat laid waste to a string of dogs and goats and hogs in eastern North Carolina. Multiple witnesses, including police, reported a black cat at least five feet in length."

Anse sniffed.

"I heard they never caught it. Probably a rabid black dog or some such."

"What about the Carrabelle Cat—black panther said to roam Tate's Hell State Forest down in Florida. Phantom cat. So many sightings the city commissioners sent down a team of biologists to investigate."

"And I bet they ain't found a damn thing," said Anse. "Whatever name you want to give it—panther, painter, cougar, mountain lion, catamount—they're all the same. *Puma concolor.* And there's never been a single documented case of a black one caught or killed in this country. Until I see a body, I ain't believing."

But sightings of black panthers were still rampant, Malaya knew—especially in the Deep South. Reports of such prowlers stretched from deep swamps to suburban shopping malls. Witnesses told of shadowy panthers skulking through backyards or darting across expressways, stalking the Croatan of North Carolina or the Great Smokies of Tennessee, the North Georgia foothills or the swamp pine of the Florida Panhandle. Some said they were the escapees of private owners. Others, apex predators living in the shadows of civilization, perfectly camouflaged. Skeptics claimed they were outsized housecats or mere delusions.

Shadow populations, in which people had little faith.

Malaya licked her lips, gazing at the cat.

"She's all panther to me."

The sun hovered in the topmost branches of the trees, shotgunning the garden with slanted rays of light. Malaya looked at Anse. His shirt was plastered against his back, a dark Rorschach of sweat.

"How much longer?" she asked.

"Not long."

The owners were a middle-aged couple who'd bought the place as a foreclosure. They'd intended to restore the house themselves, but the husband, a successful long-haul trucker, had injured his back in an accident, which changed their financial situation drastically. They'd been forced to sell the rig and collect disability. Now they spent most of their time watching television from their La-Z-Boys in the great room, which gave a view onto the cattle trailer and garden. According to Anse, the man visited the cat each summer evening around dark, feeding her leftovers before bed.

"Pot roast, country-fried steak. Wonder she don't look like a damn wrecking ball."

The pantheress had remained svelte, though her overlarge paws, which hung through the bars of the trailer, shone like weighted boxing gloves. Zooming in, Malaya could see the animal was not solid black. Her spots were just visible—a pattern of darker rosettes clouded her coat. *Ghost spots*, only visible in certain lights.

Anse nudged her with his elbow.

"Here we go."

A man stepped out of the house. He was shirtless, wearing only sweatpants and rubber sandals, with a large belly and scraggly gray beard. A dark mole on his cheek. He waddled carefully across the yard, carrying a casserole dish. Grimaces slipped through the fog of his pain medication. When he turned, Malaya saw the long white zipper of scar that ran the length of his spine, crosshatched with suture marks. He stood before the cattle trailer and began hand-feeding the panther. He held chunks of meat through the bars, which she snapped hungrily from his fingers. Meanwhile, he talked to her, lips puckered, speaking in coos and clucks.

Malaya shook her head.

"She could strike through those bars, dump his intestines right between his feet."

"Reckon he trusts her," said Anse.

Malaya narrowed her eyes at the old jockey.

"Trusts her? It's like somebody said when that Siegfried and Roy tiger attacked his trainer on stage. That tiger didn't go crazy—that tiger *went tiger.* It's their nature, born killers. What else could you expect from them?"

Anse had not taken his gaze from the man and panther. Now he blinked, quickly, and Malaya thought she saw a teary light behind his glasses. A wet sting, like she'd just jabbed him in the side. She knew he was thinking of Henrietta—a story that ended nearly so bad.

The old jockey gasped a deep lungful of breath, as if surfacing for air.

"Nothing, I reckon. Can't expect nothing but blood."

It was nearly nine when the lights went out in the house. They shimmied from their hide and approached the garden on foot. The summer dusk lay heavy over the land, the first few stars pricking the violet sky. They passed the statue of a three-headed hound that guarded the garden gate and their boots crackled lightly on the shell paths of the place. Concrete statuary reared from the weeds on every side of them, pale against the falling dark. Sphinxes, centaurs, gargoyles. Fire-tongued dragons and winged lion-birds, their beaks screaming from snarled manes of creeper vines. A whole gauntlet of talons and teeth and wings and claws, lunging for them. Malaya looked into the face of a chimera, a lion-headed beast with a scaly tail that terminated in the fanged mouth of a viper. She nodded to the creature, then moved on.

They squatted before the cattle trailer. The pantheress seemed unconcerned. Her green-glowing eyes scalped the shadows from them, cutting their shapes from the dusk, their every detail, so that Malaya felt jacklit, exposed. She swallowed the sensation and looked at Anse, who nodded. Slowly, so as not to spook the animal, she unslung the jabstick from her back. The syringe was loaded with a premixed dose of ketamine, a preferred tranquilizer for big cats.

Malaya had come across "Special K" in the army, when ex-junkie recruits whispered of euphoria, out-of-body experiences, even astral travel from the drug. She'd seen it once at an off-base party—a nineteen-year-old rifleman struck comatose in a clawfoot bathtub, bliss-eyed and vacant, his friends slapping his cheeks to return him to this galaxy or dimension or eon.

Malaya flicked the reservoir, then set the jabstick over one knee and threaded the shaft through her fingers like a pool cue, aiming for the thick muscle of the animal's rump. A bead of fluid formed at the very tip of the needle. She wondered whether the panther would harbor some inborn dread of spears, some fear long buried in her genes. After all, the bones of her ancestors had been found in the trash heaps of Paleolithic clans—animals surely trapped and speared. But the cat betrayed no anxiety until the needle pierced her skin. Then she leapt, hissing, twisting her body to lick at the injection site.

Anse tapped his watch and flashed the number five with his hand.

Five minutes for the tranquilizer to take effect.

The hardest part, Malaya knew. Waiting. Fear rose in the void of action. It was the worst in Iraq, when her supply convoy would stop in the middle of a city block already pocked and black-blasted from previous firefights, waiting while an ordnance team was called in to investigate a suspected IED. A suspicious trash can or animal carcass, which could hide a command-wired artillery shell or improvised land mine. Waiting, waiting, while insurgents could be creeping across roofs or slinking through alleyways with rockets on their backs. The heat fuming like spilled gasoline across the dirty streets and sidewalks—one spark from going boom.

Malaya looked at her watch: four minutes.

In Africa, it seemed they were always too late. They would discover the sunken carcasses of poached elephants littering the bush like wrecked hot-air balloons, their tusks sawed from their heads, or else they would find only the animals' bones, the meat stripped by hungry villagers, the tusks shipped abroad. With the rhinos, it was worse. Organized gangs and heliborne poachers, choppering the still-bloody horns straight to ships anchored in the Indian Ocean, ready to make steam for China or Vietnam. She and the rest of the rangers were always waiting for that call on the radio, waiting—another animal killed.

Three minutes.

Malaya breathed in through her nose, out through her mouth. Slow the breath, slow the heart. She looked to the old house. This close, the signs of disrepair were even more evident. Torn window screens and unpruned creeper vines. Dead leaves gathered in doorframes, loose shingles curling from the roof. Overburdened gutters, sprouting their own ferns. A yellow-green film of pollen and mildew over the whole facade.

She wanted to be angry at the owners of the place but couldn't summon the spark—even as she saw the condition of the animal, the raw patches and scars. Their dreams had run aground here in the woods, grown filmy and opaque, foggy with pain and age. Perhaps their own pain normalized them to the pain of others—perhaps they were doing the best they could. Perhaps the panther gave them purpose or hope. Perhaps a sense of power like a Mustang or Firebird kept in the garage. Perhaps, perhaps.

Two minutes.

Malaya's gaze went to the busted window under the eave. She wondered if the bats were coming awake in there, chittering and shifting their wings, making ready to rise from the attic, to pour like smoke into the night. Beside her, the pantheress began to lie down. Her legs were melting beneath her, curling under her belly. The drug was going to work. She had calmed, settled. Her breath had slowed, her pupils gone round, as if sighting distant worlds. Her mouth hung slightly agape now, a pink glimpse of tongue. Almost like a panting dog.

One minute.

Surely the panther's heart was drumming loud and slow inside her now. Surely she could feel her form growing strange, vague, her body lengthening into the shadows, her coat bleeding into the shades. Her tongue dry, her eyelids heavy. Soon she would be weightless, airy as smoke. She would be the dusk, falling across the land. She would be the shadows, slinking through the iron bars. She would be the bats, tattering the moon.

"Her name is Midnight," said Anse.

They watched the pantheress slink through a patch of wiregrass, exploring her new enclosure. It had been the home of the white tiger, Polara, dead of kidney failure years ago. Tyler— who believed the panther had come from Animal Control—had placed her under a thirty-day quarantine, during which time she would be checked for signs of infection, parasites, lameness. Tyler had given her an antibiotic shot for her skin infections and prescribed antifungal tablets to combat ringworm. She found the cat had hind-limb paresis from a substandard diet and showed signs of neurotic behavior—tail-chewing and toe-biting, common to caged big cats.

"Midnight?" said Malaya. "It said Noira on her collar."

Anse hawked and spat, as if to rid himself of the name.

Malaya walked to the fence, hooking her fingers in the diamonds of link.

Her voice was soft: "Midnight."

The pantheress paused and looked in their direction. Malaya felt the leopard over her heart purr, as if seeing its shadow. She leaned into the fence, letting the links waffle her belly. She glanced over her shoulder at Anse.

"How come you didn't put her in Henrietta's old enclosure? Heaven for a panther."

Anse looked toward the lion enclosure at the heart of the sanctuary—so huge and vacant. Then he looked back at her, his face strangely boyish. His eyes were silvery, wet.

"Her name is Midnight," he said. "She's a leopard."

BOOK III

CHAPTER 12

MOSI

Mosi is born in caul, a cub curled in a ghostly white veil. He doesn't know he has entered the world of light, of men. His eyes are closed. He believes he swims yet in the warm sea of his mother's womb, and he might stay here, never waking, passing from birth to death within the same shroud, but the birth of his sister wakes him. She comes curling from his mother's vent, slick with blood and afterbirth, and her furred haunches bump him to life. Tiny white splinters of claw emerge from his paws and he cuts through the thin membrane that binds him against the world, emerging into air and light.

He is blind at first, like all cubs. He lives in the warm, furry tumble of his siblings. He feels the rough, possessive tongue of his mother, cleaning him, and unravels the sweet white string of her milk. His world is hillocks of fur and the gravel of tiny throats, and hunger. Already he knows it, this ringing hollow in his belly for milk and blood. He cannot be sated, but he tries and tries, sucking at the teat. His mother carries him by the scruff of his neck, a trophy dangling from the protective cage of her teeth.

He is her firstborn, after all, born in his gossamer bubble. In other parts of the world, in other species, the midwives might find his birth significant. They say a caul-child will love water and never drown. They say he will see the world beyond the world, past the veil of our unknowing, and see death hover like a black shroud over those whose time is near.

But Mosi is still blind when the pair of hands descend to tear him from his mother. He's placed in a pen among cubs of many other litters. Here is the heady sting of urine, the pervasive reek of shit. The odor of coughed-up milk souring in the sun. He knows the scent of his three sisters, though he cannot see them. In the morning, he finds one of them gone cold. He nudges her in the ribs with his nose. She is useless. The ghost that warmed her has vanished. To where, he doesn't wonder. Who wonders where a single fire has gone?

"He's so cute," she says. "Look at the size of his paws!"

She isn't heavy, this woman, but her cheeks are round as plums beneath the floppy brim of her straw hat. Her eyes are tiny, bird-bright. She's running her lacquered nails through Mosi's coat, scratching him between the ears. Surely she has cats at home, fat tabbies that slink along molded baseboards, doze on the backs of white couches, curl themselves in warm bars of sunlight. Surely she loves them.

"His fur is so soft," she says. "It's like flour in your fingers."

Her hat is broad and white, big as a wading bird.

"Feel him, Jud."

Jud indulges her, roughing Mosi's head, tugging the scruff of his neck. He's a dog man, it's clear. He has square, whiskey-browned teeth and a hard potbelly. His safari pants, outfitted with various zippers and cargo pockets, were purchased just for this trip. It was his wife's idea to come to Africa. Two weeks of game drives and bush lodges, drinking chipped-ice cocktails in the beds of tour trucks and eating dinner beneath the torchlight of open-air *bomas*, where they chat with Texans and Germans on safari. The women are giddy, recalling the nearness of the beasts that approached the truck that afternoon—lions or elephants or Cape buffalo—while the men sit sipping their scotch or bourbon, as if unfazed by the day's events.

Now, at the lion park, they have the opportunity to play with a cub.

"Don't you just want one?" asks the woman.

Jud only grunts.

"Judson has never been a cat person," she tells the park-keeper. "What's his name?"

The keeper is clad in khaki, top to bottom. A block-faced woman, with fine threads of green under her fingernails.

"Mosi," she says. "Means *firstborn* in Swahili. Would you like to feed him?"

"Can we?"

The keeper retrieves a baby bottle from her pack.

Mosi holds the soft white flesh of the woman's arm in his overlarge paws, sucking at the amber nipple. The milk is slightly alien. Too cool and bland, missing the warm glow of his mother's teats. Still he bites and sucks, for here is life, drawn greedily into his belly.

"How long are they like this?" asks the woman.

"About six months."

"And then what happens?"

"Then they want meat."

Jud's wife looks around the lion park, sees only cubs tumbling behind the chain link of the playpens.

"I mean what happens to the cubs?"

"Oh. We sell them to parks and zoos around the world."

Jud's wife looks across the hillocks of fur, so many of them. Too many.

Her eyes narrow.

That night, they eat heavy kudu steaks on ceramic plates while the torchfires lick across the woven trunks of the dining *boma,* built like a giant nest behind the lodge. They hardly talk. Jud's wife is distant, chewing on more than her food. In their room, she sits on the edge of the bed, removing her earrings. Jud slides his hand up the oiled trophy of her calf.

"I can't quit thinking of all those cubs," she says, setting her earrings on the side table. "Surely there isn't enough demand for the grown ones from zoos and parks. Where do they go?"

Jud parts her knees slightly, dips his head to kiss the skin that caps them.

"Forget it," he says, speaking to her knees. "There are laws about such things."

"It doesn't make sense."

"It's our last night, honey." He's moving up her thighs, his face halved by the hem of her skirt. "Forget it."

She leans back on the pillow, closes her eyes.

She forgets.

Mosi isn't like the other cubs. He grows faster than the others, stronger, and he sees things they do not. They come to play-fight with him, often in pairs and threes, their tiny throats rattling. He lets them climb over his back, paw at his throat and haunches and ears. He lies like a statue, tolerant, watching the tumble and pounce of the other cubs. Every so often he swats one of his playmates so hard they yelp or else pins them screeching to the turf with his teeth. Soon he will kill. He knows he was born to this, to swallow the fire of life in his throat.

He tolerates the petting hands that feed him his milk. The visitors coo and gabble, their fingers knuckled with bands and stones. Mosi misses the rough scrape of his mother's tongue. In the evenings, he patrols the metal thicket that keeps him caged, looking for slits or tears. If he walks fast enough, the diamonds of fence wire blur, vanishing before his eyes, as if he roams free through the veld.

Mosi grows larger, stronger. Soon he can feel the first spikes of a mane, rising dark from the field of his fur, and he wants meat. The keepers cut him from the litter and lead him into the belly of a great, wheeled beast that rumbles across the earth. He watches the country bleed yellow and green through the iron ribs of the cage.

Mosi turns two years old, three, in this new place. His mane grows full, ringing him with authority. He lies on a wooden platform raised over the burnt grass of the enclosure, watching the lesser lions flick the flies from their rumps. Their meals arrive through metal chutes, headless chickens rimed in ice. Only then do they rise, like stoked flames.

In this place, no one comes to pet them. Men come to rub their chins and cock their heads and point at this lion or that, and sometimes Mosi can see a shadow clinging to a certain member of the pride. In the morning, that lion will be gone, cut from the others and hauled away. To where, Mosi doesn't know. Loosed, perhaps, into the yellow kingdom beyond the fence wire. Then he'll hear a single crack of thunder, though there is no storm.

One day three men stand at the fence. They squint and point. Mosi feels their nervy, glittering eyes, which rove him. His high haunches and sharp spine, his black mane.

"Perfect specimen," says one. "Not a scratch or scar. And you know what they say. Darker the mane, stronger the lion."

The others nod.

"Of course, there is a price for such perfection."

"Of course."

They throw numbers back and forth—amounts that could buy a car.

Later, Mosi is led out of his enclosure, into the belly of the ribbed beast that delivered him here. He's been chosen, he thinks. His freedom is near.

He wakes groggy, slowed by some alien weight in the blood. There's a stinging pain in his rump, as from a thorn, and the world is strange. He sees a fence but no other lions. The bush is alive around him, throaty and thick. He can hear adders whispering through the dry grass, their tongues forking, scenting the air for shrews or rats, and terrapins dragging their hard domes through the brambles. The trees are abuzz with termites and wasp nests. Little bee-eaters swirl overhead, clipping insects from the air. Mosi feels a tickle and swings his head to look. A skink leaps from his belly, where it's been sifting his pale belly-fur for parasites. Mosi tries to swat the lizard, but his movements are slow, drunken. The skink is gone, rattling into the weeds.

Mosi stands, swaying on his four wobbly legs. The acacia trees purr above him, sun-shot, and he's dappled with light. His stomach is a resounding hollow; his mouth is dry. He moves slowly, as if his blood were the sticky red sap of a rain tree. Still, he is unafraid, his pride unshaken. There is confusion, but no fear. He is born of a ten-thousand-millennia bloodline. His ancestors outlasted the saber- and scimitar- and dirk-toothed cats. His whole life has led to this. He weaves through the veld, his massive paws pancaking beneath his weight. His claws are hooked like the beaks of fish eagles, his mighty bone-house clad in muscle.

A troop of baboons squats in the snaggled crown of a lead-wood tree, chattering among themselves, and a mongoose spears through the brush, pursuing the green luster of a longhorn beetle. A pair of blaze-bucks raise their heads from a clearing, their horns twinned high and sharp over their white-painted faces. They wheel and flee, bounding high through the grass. Desire rises in Mosi's throat. He would tear the saddle-fur from those narrow, bouncing rumps and lap the red tang of blood from their flesh. He lurches, giving chase, only to trip over the shed limb of an acacia tree, tumbling through a thorny bush. He rises red-torn and bleeding, breathing through his jaws, his ribs swelling against the torn flesh of his hide.

Mosi is descended of the savannah kings. He knows this, certain as the wheeling fire of the sun. And yet here he stands, his tongue dry, his lungs burning like trees of fire. His kingdom shaky now beneath his paws.

Winter Melton sits on a high bench in the bed of an open-air safari truck, surrounded by a protective frame of two-inch pipe. Between his knees stands a Ruger No. 1 rifle, a hammerless brute chambered in .458 Winchester Mag. His two South African guides sit in the front of the truck, clad in camouflage. Their rifles stand in special mounts bolted between the front seats. They wear walkie-talkies on their belts, large revolvers under their arms. The Rover creaks to a halt before the twenty-foot hurricane fence of the enclosure while one of the guides steps down from the open cab and ambles to the gate. His boots are swollen and warped, his belly large. He squints a long moment into the bush, then unlatches the gate. They rumble inside the multi-acre pen, where the black-maned lion has been loosed.

Winter rides high in the bucking truck, as if on a royal litter, conveyed on the sweating backs of men. He's a man of means after all. He owns fifty-seven truck stops across the South. Their signs soar over the sleepless highways day and night, advertising cheap gas, clean restrooms, free Wi-Fi. Some of the stops are paired with fast-food franchises; others offer dog parks, car washes, overnight parking for RVs and semi-trucks. Winter has read Hemingway. He thinks of his truck stops as clean, well-lighted places. There is the steam of coffee, the crunch of corn nuts, the gleaming haloes of toilet seats swiped clean every hour.

He lives with his dog, an arthritic Labrador retriever named Sadie. His house echoes loudly whenever he removes his shoes at the door. He shuffles sock-footed through his home, an ice cream—eating haunt, and there is only the stilted click of Sadie's nails on the varnished floors. The false eyes of his trophies, black and gleaming, watch him from the walls. The 202-inch mule deer from Colorado, the sharp-tusked javelina from West Texas, the blondish grizzly sow from the Klondike. He loves these creatures he has killed, their skulls full of foam and wire. Each is a story, telling him he has lived.

He's come to Africa to kill a lion, to mount its roaring head over the fieldstone hearth of his great room. His hands are greasy on the foregrip of his rifle. Every now and again he catches a whiff of himself, a nervous odor crawling from his armpits. He thinks of poor Francis Macomber, Hemingway's American boy-man who shows himself a coward before his wife and guide and gun-bearers when he flees the charge of a wounded lion.

Winter, too, is afraid, but not of the lion.

An American dentist shot a famous lion in Zimbabwe and the world bared its teeth. The man's practice was boycotted, his family threatened. Animal rights activists called for him to hang. Winter had already booked his flight, his trophy hunt, and his accommodations. He'd put down his deposit. Now he thinks of protesters strung in front of his truck stops, blocking the pumps, their hand-painted signs calling for his blood. He thinks of the clucks of his employees, ready for any reason to hate him, and the glass eyes of his trophies turned against him, bright with malice. He thinks of everything he has built, his empire, crumbled by a single shot.

He lifts an arm, swabbing the sweat from his brow, and smells himself again. He prays that he is strong enough to face the roaring pink mouth of his fear, to put a 500-grain bullet through its heart.

Mosi smells blood on the wind. His bones feel willow-soft and his tongue is dry, scaly as snakeskin. He's been rumbling all day through the bush, his belly growling with hunger. Now his meal must have arrived. He turns upwind, tracking the red string of scent. Drool hangs in tassels from his bottom jaw. His heart blares, driving him on.

In the distance, a flock of starlings explodes to flight, shrilling in alarm. Their cries chase after him, hounding his nerves, but Mosi is no creature of doubt. He presses on. His ancestors tore gladiators limb from limb, spilling them beneath the red throats of the crowds. His form has emblazoned the shields of kings, rampant, his tongue bared bright as a flame. No beast has a blacker mane than he.

The blood is close.

Mosi breaks from the trees on a low bluff over a green jag of creek water. The bloody hull of a skinned impala hangs from an acacia tree, dizzied by flies, while vultures wheel slowly against the sky. Mosi doesn't wonder who has left him such a boon—his meals have always appeared this way, dropped as if from the sky. Surely this is how kings are fed.

First he descends the bluff to lap from the stream. He can taste distant green mountains on his tongue, thunderheads big as nations. He can taste his old enemy the crocodile, who lies yellow-eyed and grinning in the darkness, watching the world from below, and he can taste the many tongues of the land, those of the impala and the zebra and the Cape buffalo, whose multitudes long sustained his kind. His pride swells against his ribs, his heart huge and ripe. He is where he was born to be.

Eden.

He looks down at the water. The tongued surface slowly calms, smoothing into a mirror. There stands a great lion reflected, a wavy ghost-king, and Mosi sees, with the vision of his birth, that the great black mane is not his halo but his shroud. His doom. Death wreathes him, heavy as a cloak, ready to snuff his fire.

Mosi lifts his great head in defiance.

He roars.

Winter descends to one knee, as if genuflecting, and brings the heavy rifle to his shoulder. The lion's mane is angular and black, broad as a shield. Winter floats the crosshairs just back of the beast's shoulder, seeking the hidden red apple of the heart, when the lion lifts his head from the stream. Silver blades of water flash from his jaws. He rocks heavenward, poised proud and rampant upon the shore, and his throat booms like a cannon across the veld.

Winter lowers his gun. He is awed, outdone.

He doesn't wish to kill a creature of such majesty.

He wishes to own it.

"You want to what?" says the guide.

Jud and his wife take the next off-ramp from the interstate. They need to gas up and pee, to grab a fresh pair of coffees and a new roll of Life Savers for the road. They're stopping just outside of Savannah, Georgia, on their way down to a five-hundred-room beach resort in Palm Beach.

The summer sky is full of swift, dark clouds that shudder and pulse, threatening storm. Jud, driving, squints at the emblems of gas stations and truck stops thrust high against the darkening heavens, a glowing medley of shells and chevrons and hearts. So many to choose from . . .

"That one," says his wife. "Look what it says!"

She's pointing to the yellow paw of Lion Gas, erected slightly higher than the rest. Beneath the emblem, a display with the price for each fuel grade, and a small billboard:

COME SEE OUR
RESCUED AFRICAN
LION!

Jud swings the white Cadillac SUV beneath the fluorescent canopy that shelters the pumps. Next to the main building is an enclosure the size of a batting cage, steel-barred with a corrugated-tin roof. A lion lies on a wooden platform, his head collared in a heavy black mane. The ground beneath him is littered with child-thrown sundries. Gumballs and Popsicle sticks and dirty pennies—anything to court his attention. A half-eaten lollipop hangs matted in his mane, a pink knot of chewing gum.

There's a large information plaque mounted on the side of the enclosure, a story of the lion's rescue from a canned hunt in Africa. Jud's wife can't read the details from where she stands. She starts toward the cage but a thunderclap splits the sky and the rain comes hissing down in slanted silver spears. It rattles marble-hard against the canopy, the pavement, the tin roof of the enclosure. Jud's wife stands at the edge of the concrete apron, sheltered beneath the floodlights, and squints through the assault. She calls back over her shoulder.

"Judson, do you remember that time on our safari trip, when we got to feed that lion cub from a baby bottle?"

Jud is rattling the fuel nozzle into the gas tank. He cracks a Life Saver between his teeth.

"Vaguely."

"What was the cub's name, do you remember?"

Jud sighs. The trigger catch on the pump is broken—he'll have to hold the pump for all twenty-six gallons.

"What?"

"I think it started with an *M*," says his wife.

She runs names through her head—*Musa, Musi, Mosul?*—trying to remember.

She can't.

Mosi watches the endless herds that slash back and forth through the gathering dark. Some of them peel off from the rest, stopping at his watering hole to drink. Here comes another one, hulking like a rhino. A woman emerges, standing before the shiny grimace of the beast, and there is something in the shape of her, the scent. Something from his cubhood. The bright eyes and plummy cheeks, the hat perched stork-large atop her head. Her nipples stand knobbed against her shirt, like his mother's teats, and a warmth begins to pervade Mosi's belly, like swallowed milk.

Now comes a blast of thunder and rain slurs his vision. Mosi looks to the heavens, the dark kingdom that hovers over this little oasis of light, ready to douse it hissing from the earth.

He wonders, like always, if it is only a storm.

CHAPTER 13

THE WHITE WOLF

"What if they all got out?" asked Malaya.

Anse was chewing sunflower seeds. He spat a pair of hulls in the dirt.

"Who?"

"Tyler says there are more tigers in captivity in the state of Texas alone than left in the wild in the rest of the world. What if they all got out?"

Anse shrugged. "Fucking mess."

"You think any would survive?"

Anse bounced his eyeglasses on the bridge of his nose. He thought of three thousand tigers bobbing through the darkness, knifing between rows of tract houses and pausing to stare through kitchen windows, watching families like roasts in the oven. They would flash across the highways of West Texas, passing through the lights of minivans and semi-trucks, then disappear again into the desert night, pursued by the manic sabers of helicopter searchlights. A red wreckage left in their wake, the remains of coyotes and stray dogs and children on trampolines. Nature's serial killers, single-minded and remorseless, released into the night.

"Why," he asked, "you got a ticket to Texas booked?"

"I'm serious, Anse. Whenever she says that, it's all I can think."

Anse looked at Snow and Fire, standing in echelon behind the fence, waiting to be fed.

"They would be hunted down, every one. Shot from helicopters and armored cars, deer blinds and kitchen windows." Anse stepped closer to the fence. "People get riled about zoos, say that caging any wild animal is an injustice. Those fences are there as much to keep people out as to keep animals in. Men'll kill anything, bigger the better."

"You don't think even one would survive? One tiger?"

Anse moved a sunflower seed from one side of his mouth to the other, propping it on the deathbed of his lower molar. What he really wanted now was a Marlboro, the hard burn in his lungs. He was trying to cut down. He needed to be fit for what was coming.

"One might go unaccounted for, I reckon. Disappear. People would report seeing it all over, of course. Far states away, even. A tiger in the night. A ghost. We kill a thing, then can't believe it's dead."

"Like Elvis."

Anse cracked the shell in his back teeth, smiled.

"Like Elvis," he said.

He looked at Snow and Fire, their huge faces and yellow eyes. He thought of the saber cat that roamed his dreams, roaring chip-toothed over the dark tides of wolves and men.

"One day there will be a last one, I reckon. An Elvis tiger. Time's coming. There was this anti-poaching unit in the Russian taiga, Operation Amba, meant to save the Siberian tiger."

"Mamba?"

"*Ahm*-ba," said Anse. "Means *tiger* in the native tongue. Old cultures out there worshipped her as lord of the ginseng, told stories of weretigers that could read men's minds. Wouldn't kill any *amba* but a man-eater, and then with apologies. But poachers went wild after the Iron Curtain fell. Chinese were paying big money for tiger parts—furs, bones, organs. In Siberia, poachers got to calling the tiger 'Toyota'—that's what a single one could buy you. By the mid-nineties, they were hunted near extinct. Then came Operation Amba. Bad mothers, ex–Soviet commandos with SKS carbines and six-wheeled trucks. Men who could read the white book of the winter taiga, tracking anything through the snow."

Anse cracked another seed between his teeth.

"The tiger-unit commander was old-breed, a survivor of the Stalinist era. Cossack by birth, big iron-gray beard. Liked to wear shoulder boards and fur hats. People called him the General. Some journalists come out in the nineties, asked him what, if anything, could save the tiger from extinction."

"What did he say?"

Anse spat a pair of seed hulls in the dirt.

"AIDS."

That night Malaya lay in bed, thinking of her early days in Iraq.

She and the rest of the 3rd Infantry Division were staying at the Al Rashid Hotel, an eighteen-story behemoth that once lodged visiting despots and oil-hungry businessmen. Now the sand-colored walls were pocked and cratered with artillery fire. The five-star rooms, some of the finest in the Middle East, glistened with shattered glass. The plumbing was out and the toilets in each of the 449 rooms were brimming. Humvees and armored personnel carriers and turbine-powered M1 battle tanks were parked helter-skelter about the place, as if awaiting valets. At night, the residents could watch the city flicker and pulse with automatic weapons fire. Tracers soared across the ancient skyline, snuffing themselves against walls or cars or bodies. Parachute flares dangled above domed mosques and spearlike minarets—each a possible sniper perch.

In the morning, she and the rest of the division would file out of the shattered lobby and fire up their hundreds of engines, a rolling thunder of American firepower, and go chewing through the broken streets, along the sludgy meander of the Tigris and past the dawn mania of the looters' bazaars. They would pass palaces built with rape-rooms and torture chambers in their bowels, their upper reaches ravaged by laser-guided bombs and raided by the Special Forces, who'd descended goggled and armored from black helicopters like alien war-gods. The procession would pass the blasted gates of the Baghdad Zoo, like some new portal to hell.

Here the Fedayeen Saddam—Saddam's "Men of Sacrifice"— had taken up defensive positions against the American assault. The place had been bombed and shelled; the surrounding streets twinkled with bullet casings. A stray mortar had blasted a hole in the wall of the lion enclosure and the cats had escaped, a whole pride of them rumbling heavy-shouldered and hungry through the zoo. They stood sun-struck and strange at crosswalks, as if looking for street signs, while assault rifles clattered in the distance and American fighter-bombers carved vapor trails through the sky. Members of the 3rd ID had used their armored personnel carriers to round up as many of the loose cats as they could, but four had to be shot when they couldn't be corralled. Three lionesses and a black-maned male.

A week later, Malaya walked through the wrecked gates of the zoo for the first time, leading a string of goats bought from a back-alley seller. Word had it that only thirty of the original seven hundred animals had survived, and they were starving. Her patrol had rounded up what meat they could, paying for the goats out of their own pockets.

A stench lay heavy on the place, an evil reek of shit and death that threatened to toss her stomach onto the pavement at her feet. Dead animals were everywhere, clad in living shrouds of flies. Here a camel, the ship of the desert, wrecked by mortar fire, its ribs exposed like the timbers of a shattered hull. There an ostrich blown headless, a pink scrawl of neck. Before her, a troop of baboons had been machine-gunned from the branches of a eucalyptus tree. They lay about the trunk like a necklace of death's-heads, rotting, each the size of a child.

Malaya turned her head away, only to see a bear curled in

the corner of an enclosure, trembling, her head buried in her paws, and a long-eared fox shooting from cover to cover, as if pursued by phantoms. There were other animals she could not even identify, their shapes shattered into simple bone and meat. A cast of desert falcons, having fled their aviaries, wheeled high against the sun, as if lasing targets for the gunships, while exotic parrots screamed.

Malaya could hardly breathe. She felt for a moment that she had been transported into the distant past or future, the end of an age. A mass extinction. Behind her, the string of goats moaned like the damned. She was standing there, open-mouthed before the massacre, when she felt the string tugged gently from her fingers. She turned to find a giant of a man standing beside her, holding the rope. Smiling. He was a white man, gray-bearded and wearing a khaki safari shirt. His eyes shone a kind blue beneath a ballcap that read THULA THULA GAME RESERVE.

"Thank you," he said. "You don't know how much this means."

Malaya swallowed. "You must be the Loco Lion Man of Africa. You're the talk of the Al Rashid."

Later he'd become known as the Elephant Whisperer for rescuing a herd of traumatized elephants rampaging across Zululand. He held out his paw-sized hand.

"Lawrence Anthony," he said.

"They say you were the first civilian in, just eight days after the invasion. How did you manage that?"

The big man smiled, his cheeks a jolly pink.

"The head of a bull," he said, knocking two knuckles against his forehead. "And a Kuwaiti rental car."

Anthony led her through the place. There was the Bengal tiger, Malooh, pacing back and forth in his cage, back and forth. A paling specter, meatless, his bones like some intricate coatrack beneath his skin. His stripes were faded, as if his hide had been spread on the floor of a game lodge, tread threadbare beneath a long parade of boots. Still, he snarled yellow-toothed at their passage, his instincts undead.

"He'd bonded with one of the lionesses," said Anthony. "Part of a mating experiment. She was killed in front of his cage." The big man shook his head. "The soldiers did their best to corral the animals. No one knew she was just trying to get back to her mate."

They passed a sounder of Iraqi wild boars, tusked furies that princes once hunted from horseback. A burst water tank had flooded their pen and only a small island of high ground remained. Here the swine had gathered themselves into a mountain of bristly gray misery, their hooves churning for traction in the muck, while dead piglets floated in the cesspool about them.

"Water is still our primary problem," said Anthony. "The pumps are broken. We've been carrying water from the canal in buckets."

They passed a Eurasian lynx who was rattling his ribs against the iron bars of his enclosure, again and again, as if trying to rub the spots from his coat. He had the double-pointed beard of his kind, wizard-like, and black tassels of hair streamed from the tips of his ears. He'd rubbed his skin raw against the bars, his spots bleeding, and Malaya could only imagine what black terror was bolting through the cat's mind, the soul-shattering crash of bombs or mortars or machine guns. The screams of the seven hundred inhabitants of this once-oasis, dying by alien violence. They passed other rows of cages and enclosures with their doors twisted open, as if wrenched from their hinges by an ogre or troll.

"Who did this?" asked Malaya.

Anthony showed his teeth.

"Ali Baba," he said. The Arabic slang for *looters*. "Mobs of them. They come every night. They steal any animal they can for meat. Some are sold for exotic pets." He shook his head. "My opinion, the only good cage is an empty cage. But not like this. The Baghdad Zoo was a jewel of the Middle East."

Malaya stared at the wrecked hinges and twisted bars. She could hardly believe this was the work of human hands. A padlock lay on the ground at her feet, the shackle torqued noodlelike from its tumblers. The barred door hung drunkenly from its latches, iron-built like something to hold Billy the Kid. Malaya imagined the hundreds of hands that must have gripped these bars at once, thousands of pencil-thin hand bones straining beneath the skin. The same power that toppled the bullet-chipped statues of Saddam's regime.

"What lived here?"

"Giraffe," said Anthony. "Someone feasted on the long steaks of her neck." Again, his teeth showed in the hoary gray of his beard. "The only survivors are the animals too deadly or elusive for Ali Baba to catch." He used the name as if the looters were a single beast come in the night. "They come over the walls or the blast-rubble or straight through the front gate. They are hungry, yes, but still. They steal everything, even our fecking water buckets. We can do nothing."

Malaya felt a shadow fall over her. When she looked up, there stood a trio of private security contractors, conjured as from the dust itself. The cowboys of Baghdad, former commando mercenaries who sped through the city in unmarked SUVs, escorting VIPs and protecting civilian convoys. They wore heavy beards and angular sunglasses, baseball caps and rugby jerseys beneath their tactical gear. They carried their M4 carbines high across their chests, black and deadly, and the braids of radio earpieces hung from their ears. Pistols were strapped to their thighs, and rubber tourniquets and packets of QuikClot peeked from pouches in their chest rigs.

The one in the center spoke.

"Lawrence, you should let us smoke a couple of the Ali Babas for you, teach them a lesson." A South African flag was stitched on his tactical vest. "Your problems will be over, man."

Malaya looked at the man. He had a blond dagger of beard, nearly white, and wore a pair of safari shorts that showed the hard little balls of muscle that capped his knees. His legs looked like those of a cyclist—hard-calved and hairless, with sharp shinbones. Malaya's heart was thumping hard against the chest plate of her body armor—surprise or something else.

"I hope you're joking," she said.

A sly cut of grin ran across the man's face and Malaya wished she could see his eyes. She wondered what color they were, what spark of glee or menace they might hold.

Anthony rocked from foot to foot.

"That's very kind of you," he said. "But, as always, I must decline."

The mercenary shrugged.

"It's your funeral, man." The merc turned toward the trio's black SUV, parked just short of the twisted wreck of the enclosure. Malaya could not believe she hadn't heard them roll up, the crunch of glass beneath their run-flat tires.

"Hey," she said, stepping after him. "I hope you're joking about shooting looters."

The man didn't reply. His mates had posted themselves at each corner of the SUV, scanning the zoo grounds for threats, while he raised the rear door of the machine.

"We found something for you in one of the Hussein palaces," he told Anthony.

"Hey," said Malaya. "Who the fuck do you think you are?"

She was about to grab his shoulder when she stopped short, staring at the creature in the cargo bed of the truck.

"*Leeu welpie*," said the mercenary. "He was the only one we could save."

The lion cub lay accordianlike, lank and emaciated on a wool army blanket. His ribs pressed against his skin, fine as harp strings, his paws sized like cartoon mitts. Slowly, he lifted his head to the hand of the mercenary, who scratched him between the ears. Now the man lifted the cub from the blanket, gently, and held him out to Malaya. "Would you like to hold him?"

Malaya's mouth went sudden-dry. She could only nod.

The man handed her the cub, warm against her chest.

"Forgive me," he said. "My name is Jaager de Vaal."

Anse stood in front of the empty lion enclosure. A cold wind was blowing through his chest, and the ground felt spongy beneath his boots, tremulous, as if the world were spinning too fast. Memories, long buried, were rising from their graves. A whole nation of them—so many he felt the urge to run.

It was the questions Malaya asked, he knew, the memories that haunted her—so many that echoed his own. He felt old ghosts quickening inside him. More than once in the past weeks, he thought he'd caught a glint of light in the trees, like the scope of a Viet Cong sniper, or heard the patter of bare feet beneath the pines. He'd felt his neck-hairs stand on end, as if he were being watched. As if something haunted the edges of the sanctuary, circling closer, closer.

That night he lay beside Tyler in bed. They were naked, coated in a saline glaze. Their lovemaking had regained its wildness of late, a desperation that left them panting and spent. They lay tangled now, their skin burning with new scratches and abrasions. Anse pulled a shred of Tyler's hair from his mouth.

"Do you ever think about the last one?"

Tyler rolled up onto an elbow. She wore a moonstone, a lustrous pendant that hung in the sun-wrinkled valley between her breasts.

"The last of what?"

Anse was looking at the ceiling of the trailer. He swallowed.

"I dream of a saber cat sometimes. *Smilodon fatalis*. He's old and gray, with chipped sabers. His joints ache. Winter is always coming for him, and wolves."

"And he's the last of his kind?"

"I think so. Sometimes I see him stalking through the forest, alone. Hungry. Everything bolts from him. He's the prototype of the lion and tiger, too crude to survive. The megafauna are dying out, the mastodons and giant sloths. He can't feed himself." Anse squinted, looking back into his own dreams. "Other times I see him standing atop a fallen mammoth. A real tusker, big as a little planet, her body all mired in tar. And there's wolves coming and men with spears and he can feel his own bones under his skin."

Anse swallowed. Lately he felt a longing to tell Tyler the secret of Little Eden, the one that only Malaya knew—how so many of the animals had passed into his care. How, in the years since opening the rescue, he'd begun taking the mission of the place quite literally, *rescuing* animals from conditions of abuse and neglect. The urge to confess haunted him with the mad little joy of a death wish, like he would rip open the cage of his ribs for her sight. He inhaled.

"Smilodon knows it's his last battle, I think. And he isn't afraid."

Tyler's green eyes roamed his face. She was a woman of hard principle, he knew. Her principles shaped her, sure as the bones of a soul.

"Why isn't he afraid?" she asked.

Anse felt tears swim into his eyes. His heart was punching at his sternum, trying to break out. He chewed his lip.

"Sometimes I think he's just tired. Been fighting his whole life, and he just wants a good death."

Anse thumbed the base of his throat, hard, as if digging for words.

"Other times, I think it's something else."

"What?"

"Sometimes I think he's so lonely, he has no fear of death." He looked at Tyler. "I think he welcomes it."

Tyler's eyes glowed that edenic green, as if she were seeing a world beyond his own. Sometimes he worried it was a paradise he would never know. A peace.

She bent to his ear.

"Roll over."

Her hands found the pale scars that striped his back. She began working in the buttery salve that eased and softened his old wounds. Anse pressed his forehead into the pillow, letting her hands shuttle him, stroke by stroke, into the strange lands of sleep.

Jaager de Vaal, aka the White Wolf of Baghdad. Malaya had heard this name whispered with reverence, even awe, among the 3rd Infantry Division. He was a veteran of the Recces—the South African Special Forces. In his room at the Al Rashid, there was a thumbtacked photograph of him in some jungle hell, wearing the brigade's maroon beret and shoulder badge—a black commando knife wreathed in laurels. He'd come to Baghdad as a diplomatic bodyguard, but the Special Forces soon found other uses for him.

The elite operators of the United States military could be found standing in the man's hotel room at midnight, caparisoned in full war-fighting regalia, complete with green-eyed night-vision goggles and ballistic body armor. They would be tapping their boots and checking their watches while the South African donned his rugby jersey and safari shorts and black Chuck Taylor tennis shoes without socks. Outside, the staccato crack of gunfire, the thud of artillery. These men would wait for the White Wolf because he could find places no one else could. Some said it was his tracking skills, honed in the wilds of Africa. Others said his senses were more highly attuned—that they were superhuman, wolflike.

He found torture rooms hidden beneath the grand palaces of the royal family and secret passages that spread beneath the city like the tunnelwork of ants. He found caches of small arms and supplies intended to sustain the Republican Guard in case of foreign siege. He even found the hidden stables that once housed Saddam Hussein's herd of priceless Arabians— steeds whose bloodlines could be traced back to the warhorses of Saladin himself, the great war king of Islam, who banished the Crusaders with a Damascus steel scimitar sharp enough to slice bolts of falling silk. In the wake of the U.S. invasion, black-marketeers had stolen the herd. Priceless Mesopotamian blood horses, whose ancestors had borne sultans, were rumored to be running weekday heats at the track in Abu Ghraib.

The White Wolf did not find the weapons of mass destruction the coalition forces wanted so badly to find. No vast underground warehouses where bombshells full of anthrax or sarin gas lay cradled like the eggs of some genocidal dragon. He did find, again and again, the private menageries of the ruling class. He found Iraqi brown bears squashed into six-by-six iron crates, living in the evil stench of their own feces, and tigers thin as rails, starving at the end of backyard chains. He found the lions of Saddam's eldest son, Uday Hussein, kept in an iron pen fifty yards long, said to be fed on the bodies of the man's romantic rivals. The White Wolf found the starving lion cub—the one he brought to the zoo—in the basement of another palace, locked in a dog crate. His siblings were dead of thirst, piled about him like discarded toys.

"That little cub survive?" asked Anse.

They were sitting on the tailgate of Anse's truck in the sanctuary's parking lot, waiting for the UPS truck to arrive. A shipment of ADF-16 was scheduled for delivery, a pelleted herbivore diet made from wheat middlings, alfalfa, dehulled-soybean meal, and cane molasses. They would load the fifty-pound sacks straight into the bed of the pickup. Malaya watched a pulpwood truck rattle past on the highway, a quiver of pines.

"He survived," she said. "Thanks to Lawrence Anthony and the Iraqi zoo staff."

"And to the White Wolf," said Anse.

"Yes," said Malaya. "And to *him*." She could not keep the venom from her voice.

Anse leaned over the side of the truck bed and spat a pair of seed hulls into the parking lot.

"Is the White Wolf how you ended up in South Africa?"

Malaya shook her head.

"No. When I got out, I wasn't ready for the States, I couldn't adjust." She spread her hands flat beneath her and leaned on them, pushing herself slightly from her seat. "There were things that . . . *happened,* in-country."

Anse nodded slowly, chewing his seeds.

"So I called Lawrence, who'd become a friend. A mentor, really. He said one of the other game reserves had been hit hard by ivory poachers and was putting together an elephant protection team. He recommended me. Said there was nothing quite as healing as elephants in the bush." She nodded. "I did three years with them and started contracting at some other reserves, helping train rangers. Then one day Jaager called out of the blue, said he'd been made head of security at one of the country's biggest reserves. Said their rhinos were being decimated and he had a spot waiting for me on their anti-poaching unit."

Malaya leaned farther back on her hands and looked up at the sky. Lope's eagle, Aurora, was orbiting high above, riding the wind. She liked to watch him work the bird in the late afternoons, swinging baits aloft for the creature's talons. She found herself attracted to the quiet falconer. Not sexually. But there was a gentleness to the tall man, to the light touch he used with his raptor. So unlike the White Wolf.

"Jaager," she said. "Sometimes I thought he didn't value the animals' lives enough, the rhinos we were trying to protect. That he didn't do enough. Other times, I thought it was human lives he didn't respect. I still don't know whether he sent me home because I fired on that poacher, or because I missed."

Anse nodded, listening, his eyes on the raptor, too. Another pulpwood truck throttled past, bringing them to earth. Malaya watched it go, then looked at the fanged lion that roared over the sanctuary's entrance door.

"I still think about those Baghdad Zoo lions a lot. The first time I saw them, they didn't even look real. They were so thin, all hollows and bone. They could hardly lift their heads from their paws. Their walls were pocked with shrapnel. I thought of the ones that escaped, gone streaking through the park, over the bridges and down the avenues, hounded by tanks and helicopters. The guys that were there, they said the animals never seemed afraid. Alarmed, yes, and angry—but not afraid. And I remember wondering if it was worth it to them. That death. If those were the lucky ones, the ones that didn't go gentle."

She shook her head and cracked her knuckles.

"I mean, if I was going down, I'd rather go with a bang than a whimper, you know? Sometimes, when I'm falling asleep, I think of breaking the latches on every lion and tiger cage in the world. Those cats streaming like fire and lightning into the night. Maybe, if we were forced to feel like prey again, like *animals*, we'd have a little more respect for the rest of the creatures we share the world with."

Anse leaned over the side of the truck and spat.

"Maybe that's why the big man sent down Christ instead of another meteorite. See what it was to be flesh. Prey. See if the rest of us was worth saving."

"You believe that? Heaven and hell and all that?" she asked.

Anse chewed his lip.

"Personally, I never wanted part in a heaven without animals, without dogs or lions or elephants. My opinion, this planet is paradise enough, or should be. And hell? There's nothing in the Bible matches a napalm strike. I believe we have all we need of hell."

Malaya looked out across the roadside pines, a thousand spires glowing in the afternoon sun.

"Amen," she said.

Malaya was in the grocery store checkout line when she saw the long-haired man with the tattoos the second time. He was in the parking lot, standing in front of a black cargo van with wide, meaty tires and smoked rear windows. He wore a thin sweatshirt with a stretched-out collar, like a yogi or surfer might wear, his black hair knotted high atop his head. Despite the overlarge shirt, Malaya could discern a hard precision in his movements, the slide and torque of interlocking muscles. There was something about the man that reminded her of the White Wolf—a jaggedness—but this man seemed darker, stranger. The edges of letters and words crept from his sleeves and collar, as if a whole story were written underneath his clothes.

The cashier was smacking her gum, beeping through bar codes with a limp wrist, operating at the speed of someone underwater. Malaya tapped her foot, bobbing the shieldlike emblem of crocodile scutes inked newly over her kneecap. She already had her money out.

When she looked out the window again, a white pickup truck had parked nose-to-nose with the van. The driver was a big man in tan overalls, high rubber boots, and a waist-length beard. He was squatting before a large perforated dog crate, inspecting whatever lay behind the wire screen of the door. Then he rose and took a fat wad of bills from his back pocket and began counting them off into the palm of the smaller man. By the time Malaya got her change, the buyer was driving off with the plastic crate in the bed of the truck and the tattooed man was squatting on one knee inside the cargo door of his van, locking the cash in a strongbox.

Malaya walked fast across the parking lot, straight toward him.

She wanted to know what words were etched across the hard planes of his chest, arced over the flat tiles of his stomach, trailing the veins down his arms. The desire to know rose like a howl inside her—a longing—but she didn't want to call out, to seem desperate or crazed. Instead, she raised her hand to get his attention. The man looked up, straight in her direction. His eyes, so clear and sharp, nearly stopped her. She felt naked, exposed, as if those eyes knew her already. What mysteries pumped through her heart, under her skin.

The man raised his own hand, as if in greeting, only to grasp the inside handle of the van door and slide it home with a long scrape. The black van growled to life, throaty and low, and crackled out of the parking lot.

Anse lay in bed, cradling Tyler's head against his shoulder. She slept soundly, her brow smooth, unknit. Sometimes she seemed to him some more highly evolved form of the species—a creature from some hopeful future, perhaps, sent back in time to instruct these earlier, cruder forms of men. Sometimes he feared she was simply too good for him, too honest. That she would recoil at the sins lurking in the dark country of his heart. That she would leave him.

Anse swallowed, staring up at the stained ceiling of the trailer. The fan blades wheeled and wheeled. The blood crashed in his chest, thunderlike. Memories were rising, booming under his skin. He blinked, trying to hear the jungle night of the sanctuary, the beasts of Little Eden. He listened for their rustle and chuff, straining his ears, as if he could hear the flicker of their very stripes through the bush, the heavy pump of their hearts.

He feared their kind would be gone too soon, glimpsed only in the corners of man's vision. Myths passing through the woods, spirits a-lurk at the edge of the field. Creatures once worshipped, no more alive than the black beasts of ash scrawled on cave walls.

Anse closed his eyes, bravely, letting the dreams rise.

CHAPTER 14

SCOUT DOG

Private Anderson Caulfield, nineteen years old, watched the elephant grass race five hundred feet beneath his jungle boots. He was riding in the door of a slick, a cicada-green transport ship from the 1st Cavalry's Air Assault Division. The land was dewy with dawn, lush and bright. Rubber plantations lay in vast green polygons, the trees planted in orderly rows, as if the earth had been combed. The waterways shone like hammered metalwork, flowing toward the wet expanse of the Mekong Delta. It looked too pretty a place for men to die.

They had and they would.

Beside Anse lay his partner, an eighty-pound German shepherd of the 34th Scout Dog platoon out of Biên Hòa. The dog's identification number was tattooed on the inside of his left ear: HU421. Anse had named him Huey, same as the UH-1 helicopter gunship in whose open door the dog liked so much to ride, his tongue flapping in the wind. They had been together since handler training at Fort Benning, Georgia, and in-country for six months.

Huey was more tan than black, more pet than wolf, with a white smile ever flashing through the black bandit's mask of his face. Anse ran his hand through the dog's coat, tugging on his ears. Four days ago, a man at the rear of their patrol had stepped on a land mine, a North Vietnamese MD-82, which obliterated his legs. His upper half lay screaming in agony, damning God and Mother and Christ. Since then, Huey hadn't been able to sleep. The dispensary had provided tranquilizers—not uncommon for traumatized scout dogs, creatures strung as if with trip wire. Still, Huey jerked and bucked in his sleep, yelping, as if to warn the man again and again of the mine.

A dirt road, crusted hard and brown, flashed beneath them, heading for the cloud-swirled peak of Nui Ba Den, the "Mountain of the Black Virgin." There a Buddhist princess had cast herself on the rocks instead of marrying the son of a neighboring chieftain. They found one of her legs in a cavern, dragged there by some toothed thing. Her ghost was said to walk the mountain, passing a shrine erected high on the slope in her name.

The 1,100-horsepower turbine whined over their heads, thumping them farther north. The other members of the eight-man patrol sat with their black rifles held between their knees. Their faces were painted black, their camos tiger-striped. They were 1st Cav Rangers, hardly more than boys, their upper lips fuzzed with thin wisps of mustache. Their heads bobbed, each man pumped full of rock and roll, ready to search and destroy. There was Dice, from Detroit, with biceps hard as eight balls, who could cut down trees from fifty yards with his M60 machine gun, and Whoa-Boy, from Texas, a virgin who masturbated into a lucky cheerleading sock his sweetheart sent him, striped blue and yellow.

Their senior noncom, Master Sergeant Wilde, was from Tennessee, a veteran of the long-range reconnaissance patrols, the dreaded "Lurps." He kept his head shaved slick as a cue ball beneath his boonie hat and wore a handlebar mustache and there was gold in his teeth. This was his third tour. He had operated out of small Special Forces bases high on the Laotian border, living behind palisades spiked with the heads of dead Viet Cong, fighting alongside highland tribes and American boys who wore necklaces of shorn human ears. In 1968, his patrol had climbed Dong Tri Mountain, outside Khe Sanh, and there been stalked by a lone Bengal tiger for five straight nights. Unable to break noise discipline, they'd listened to the slow crackle of the beast through the jungle—circling, circling, hour after hour.

Telling the story in their hooch one night, Master Sergeant Wilde had set his beer between his thighs and rubbed his palms together, as if making fire.

"I tell you, kid, I wished so bad right then for my Olde English bulls, Tinker and Ball. Both born out of King Generator, hardest mouth in the South. They would of torn the belly out that fucking tiger and ate her breakfast for dinner."

Days later his team fast-roped onto the peak of Dong Re Lao Mountain, site of a disused French airfield, and established a perimeter under heavy sniper fire, clearing a landing zone from virgin forest with chainsaws and Bangalore torpedoes. The peak, mile-high, was needed as a radio relay station, directing airstrikes to support an eleven-thousand-man air assault of the A Shau Valley.

Wilde smoothed his mustache, the gold shining in his teeth.

"You could see all the way to the South China Sea from up there, warships like toy boats. Skycranes all over the valley, hauling out crippled slicks, while the fast-movers laid napalm along the ridges. Afterwards, you could see the NVA balled up all black and smoking, small as ants. Crispy-crittered."

His eyes were wide and blue as he told this story, as if he were describing a vision of sweeping majesty. His Budweiser sat between his knees, undrunk.

"Come night, the B-52 Arc Lights started rolling in. Three bombers at a time, flying in V formation at thirty thousand feet, running lights like little stars. You could hear them faint, like far-off thunder. I tell you, kid, you ain't known power till you watched an Arc Light strike come down in the night. Sixty thousand pounds of ordnance ripping across the valley floor at five hundred miles per hour. It was like the skull of the world being split open, bleeding fire. I knew God in that moment, kid. The American God. You could feel him in your bones."

Wilde licked his lips, his eyes far-off.

"Come morning, the valley was black, charred like the end of the world. Smoking. Nothing moving. Not a thing." Master Sergeant Wilde rubbed the wet skin of the bottle, shaking his head. "But here's the fuck of it. I'm glassing the valley, and what do I see but a Bengal fucking tiger come trotting along the valley floor, ducking under fallen trees and jumping over bodies."

"No shit," said Anse.

"No fucking shit. How she survived, I don't know. Didn't look to have a scratch on her, like she could live through fire. Like she was made of the stuff."

"What did you do?"

Wilde jammed his thumb into the neck of his beer bottle.

"What my bulls couldn't. Called in the Phantoms, dropped a couple thousand pounds of ordnance on her head. Snake Eye bombs and napalm. *Snake and nape,* motherfucker. Revenge for all those sleepless nights." Wilde sighed. "Turns out, she wasn't so special after all."

The elephant grass swirled and waved beneath the hovering slick. The Rangers leapt from the skids, coming up on their knees, scanning the tree line for movement. Anse watched Huey, the dog's black ears risen sharp as daggers from the grass. The helicopter wheeled and slid off into the sky, and Anse felt the lonesomeness he always felt when the cavalry left them alone in the jungle.

Huey walked point, zigzagging along the trail, sniffing, pausing every few seconds to listen, his ears swiveling for sound. It had been Wilde's idea to attach a scout dog to the patrol. When Anse first showed up at the Rangers' hooch, the sergeant had circled the dog, appraising his every inch.

"Why's his tongue so red? He sick?"

"It's sunburned, Sergeant, So much panting in the heat. They call it *red tongue.*"

Wilde looked skeptical.

"Tell me, Private, why we should have this dog on our team."

Anse straightened, starting his pitch.

"A German shepherd's sense of smell is forty times better than a human's, his hearing twenty times better. He can sniff a gook fart from a thousand yards."

Wilde squatted in front of the dog, head weaving, trying to look the animal in the eyes.

"No, Private. *This* dog, particularly. I want to know why *this* dog is the one."

Anse shifted in his jungle boots.

"He cares, Sergeant."

"*Cares?*"

"He's a shepherd. Thinks we're part of his flock. He'll do anything to keep us alive."

The master sergeant nodded, showing the gold in his teeth. Grimace or grin, Anse couldn't tell.

"Will he fight?"

Anse set his hand between the dog's ears.

"He's not trained for that."

"I didn't ask if he was *trained* to fight, Private. I asked if he would."

"If he has to, I think he would."

Wilde caught Huey's muzzle between his hands, stared into his face. The dog's eyes darted up to Anse, unsure what to do. A growl started low in his throat, but Anse cut it short with a slight twitch of the head.

Wilde was still looking into the dog's eyes.

"There's no time to *think* out there, Private. We fight or die."

"He'll fight," said Anse."

"He fucking better, Private."

They stopped on the trail at noon, chewing chocolate bars and swigging from canteens, watching the trees. Huey came bouncing down the line, sniffing each member of the patrol for wounds. Detroit ignored the dog, staring into the bush, his little biceps balling under his skin, while Whoa-Boy gave the shepherd a few mindless scratches between the ears. Only

Wilde took real notice, squatting in the center of the trail, surrounded by men in striped fatigues—*tiger suits.*

First he scratched Huey's chin, then cradled the dog's jaw muscles in his palms. His fingers burrowed outward to the animal's shoulders, kneading them, then slid down the dog's forelegs, squeezing here and there, as if testing their ripeness. Anse, watching him, felt the high burn of jealousy in his gut. This man touched his animal like he owned him.

Wilde's hands came back to Huey's snout. His thumb lifted a black flap of jowl, revealing the white ranges of teeth. He shook his head.

"Sheepdog," he said. "No match for one of my bulls. Too soft of mouth."

Anse stiffened, full of fire. He would have pit his Huey against both the man's bulldogs, then and there. He ran his tongue along his teeth.

"It ain't his mouth that's keeping us alive out here," he said.

Wilde cut his eyes at him.

"Let's hope not." His gaze ran back over the shepherd, the bright eyes, the black saddle of his coat. "You know Olde English Bulldogges like mine were nearly extinct by the 1940s. It was only in the last few years we started reviving the breed in America, re-creating the English bull-baiters of the early eighteen hundreds."

"Bull-baiters?"

"Dogs bred to bait bulls and bears, even lions. To fight them. Bull was tied to an iron snake, pepper blown up his nose to rile him. Then they loosed the dogs. Outlawed as a blood sport in England in 1835. Breed started to die out."

"'Least they died in peace."

"*Peace,*" said Wilde, as if he'd forgotten the word.

They were five klicks into the bush when Huey raised his nose and started to high-step in a tight circle, prancing like a show horse. Anse raised his fist, halting the patrol. They knelt on either side of the trail, taking defensive positions, while Wilde came ducking up.

"What is it, Private?"

"He's alerting," whispered Anse. Huey's snout jabbed the air, sniffing here and there. Anse's heart thundered with love, fear. "Could be an ambush."

A first *pop*, like a dam breaking, then the air was full of shrieking metal. Tracers zipped across the trail and men fell screaming. Branches dropped from the trees. An enemy machine-gun nest raked fire through the jungle, searching for the soft flesh of the patrol.

Anse found himself on his belly, his serpent brain driving him hard into the dirt, his trained finger snapping rounds toward the nest. They were pinned, automatic fire screaming over their heads. Men lobbed grenades toward the machine gun but they fell short, harmless as fireworks. Curses pierced the air and shrieks and Anse realized he had hold of Huey's collar. He was holding the animal tight against his side.

Protecting him.

Then Master Sergeant Wilde was up and running straight into the flashing muzzle fire of the nest. It seemed impossible that he would not be hit, blown red and broken through the trees, but nothing touched him. He leapt over the berm, his arms held high over his head—a Ka-Bar knife in one hand, a nonissue revolver in the other. The pair of NVA machine-gunners rose against him, and the three of them locked together, fused, pummeling and screaming, a single three-headed beast tearing itself limb from limb. Huey lunged and lunged against Anse's fist, trying to help, to save this gold-toothed Tennessean he thought part of his family, his flock. This man who would pit him against his bulls if he could.

This monster.

Anse loosed the dog.

Huey tore through the bush, driving himself into the fight. Shots, screams, and the dog ripped one of the NVA free of the melee, caging an arm in his jaws. Anse followed, charging toward them, his heart churning with fear. He leapt the berm and there was no time. He saw Wilde and the other soldier grappling over the revolver. The Vietnamese was kinking Wilde's wrist like a duck's head, turning the pistol back on its owner. Meanwhile Huey stood over his enemy, gripped one arm in his teeth while the soldier's other hand drew the black blade of a bayonet from his belt.

Anse drove his rifle like a spear into the chest of Wilde's adversary and pulled the trigger three times, then aimed at the man on the ground. Too late. The soldier's hand was empty, the bayonet plunged to the hilt in Huey's chest. One of the dog's ears had been shot away, a red furrow along his skull. Despite all, the dog had not let go. His teeth were locked in the man's flesh, vising the bones of his forearm.

Anse stood flat-footed, stunned, his weapon forgotten. He could not think what to do. Master Sergeant Wilde stepped forward, revolver in hand, and shot the soldier in the head.

Still Huey didn't let go. His legs began sliding wide beneath him, scissoring open, and he sank to his belly, splayed flat like a spider, the arm held tight in his teeth. The small wooden handle of the bayonet ticked from his chest, prodded again and again by his heart. It might have been an experimental device of some kind, a switch surgically implanted so that men could toggle his modes: detect, pursue, assault.

He looked up at Anse, as if to ask if he was doing right. There was blood along his gums, bubbling between his teeth. A crimson necklace shone between his forelegs. His ribs strained beneath the black saddle of his coat, like the bones of buried wings. A wet sound rattled in his throat.

He was going to die.

Anse fell to his knees, burying his face in the scruff of Huey's neck. He wanted to tell him that he was the best dog that ever lived. The most loyal and brave and strong. That Huey was his heart. His blood. That he loved him. That he was sorry for letting him loose.

Instead he bawled.

He was nineteen years old. He was in a foreign country, and he had just killed one man and seen another killed. His best friend was dying, and he could do nothing but cry. His uniform felt like an oversized costume, something he would wear on Halloween. His boy-sized body quaked beneath the badges, the belts and webbing. He thought Master Sergeant Wilde would tear him from the dog, slap him, tell him to act like a man. He didn't. Anse felt the man's shadow on him, unmoving. He felt the others gathering around him, solemn. A ring of them, striped like green tigers, their rifles barbed against the world. There could be an enemy reaction force on the way, but no one said a word.

Huey was whining now, whole stories of hurt escaping through his clenched teeth.

A hand on Anse's shoulder.

"It's time," said Wilde.

Anse lifted his face. His cheeks were smeared with blood and fur.

"I'll do it."

"No, you won't. Detroit, you and Whoa-Boy take him behind those trees."

The shot, when it came, broke Anse's heart.

Master Sergeant Wilde emerged from the green razors of palm. He pushed his boonie hat far back on his head, a ragged halo over the bald dome of his skull. His face was painted black, white-streaked with sweat or tears. He knelt in front of Anse.

"He died game, kid, with the bull in his teeth."

He handed Anse the dog's chain collar, along with a scrap of black velvet, red along one edge. The inner folds, white-pink like a rose, were tattooed with a series of greenish dots: HU421.

Huey.

"Hate Charlie Cong, kid. Or me. Not yourself."

Anse lunged at the man, but the others were ready; they held him back. Anse thrashed and growled and spat until he sank between them, exhausted, slavering.

Detroit, silent, untied the leather thong from his neck, pocketing his own talisman—a medal of Saint George, patron saint of the cavalry—and Whoa-Boy handed Anse his knife. Anse looked up at them, his vision blurred with tears.

"Take him with you, kid," said Wilde. "He'll keep you alive."

Anse took the makings, looked at them in his hands. His eyes burned, as if he could feel the image being seared into his vision. He kissed the scrap of flesh, which smelled like Huey. Then he punched a hole and strung the shorn ear from his throat, like the trophy of a thing he'd killed. A creature too noble for the world of men.

CHAPTER 15

WHISPERS

"It's time," said Anse.

Malaya looked at him. It was just past dawn, the world still bruised with night. The old jockey's face was hard in the early light, creased with wear.

"Time for what?"

Anse lit a cigarette in the nest of his palms. His sunflower seeds were gone. He nodded toward the center of the sanctuary.

"To fill the empty enclosure."

Malaya watched the smoke curling from the man's nose. They were standing in front of Matilda's pen, ready to fork the elephant's daily ration of alfalfa through her feeding chute. Hers was the only electrified enclosure at Little Eden. The wires thrummed with eight thousand volts of charge, meant to keep the elephant from edging too close. In reality, she could swing the three-ton wrecking ball of her body through anything short of a brick wall—and maybe that.

She came hobbling toward them, her wide gray ears flapping gently, swimming through the dawn like a pair of manta rays. Malaya watched her come, then looked at Anse.

"You talking about the cage I think you are?"

"*Enclosure*," said Anse.

"Why now?"

"It's time. I can feel it."

Matilda was standing before the fence now, head turned, one great black eye watching them. In Africa, Malaya's team would find evidence of elephants meeting one another in the dead of night, in the deepest bush, as if by appointment, their tracks converging from miles and miles apart. The distances were too vast for the herds to hear one another. Rather, biologists said the elephants could sense seismic vibrations through hypersensitive nerves in their feet. The earth spoke to them, it seemed—underground messages passing through the land, rising through the roots of their flesh. In the dry season, matriarchs could detect thunderclouds rising on the far sides of nations and steer their herds for the lifeblood of rain. In the Sudan, the very day a peace treaty was signed after two decades of war, refugee herds had begun their long migration home, as if they could sense the cessation of the guns. As if their ears were satellite dishes, their trunks antennae. As if Reuters whispered headlines on the wind.

Anse shook his head again.

"I just know," he said.

Malaya nodded. She knew this day would come. Henrietta's memory haunted the sanctuary. The spirit of the lioness seemed ever-present, lying in the shards of sunlight scattered beneath the trees, in the breaths of wind that rustled the leaves. Malaya had seen the other animals casting long glances in the direction of her empty enclosure. The elephant, the ocelot, the monkeys. She'd seen the pantheress, Midnight, freeze midstride on the beam of her cat-tree and swivel her ears toward the heart of the sanctuary. Even the circus tigers sometimes stood staring in that direction, their jaws open, as if trying to taste her ghost on the breeze.

She looked at Anse.

"Where is he, this lion?"

Anse blew smoke from his nostrils. His eyes roamed the vast swell of the elephant's body, like the scarred terrain of a moon.

"What makes you think it's a he?"

Malaya grinned, cocked her head.

"I just know," she said. "I can *feel* it."

Anse blew a wisp of smoke from his mouth, almost smiling.

"I'll show you tonight."

They drove north on the interstate after work. The sun hung fat and orange over the dusky pines and a string of red taillights raced between the trees. Soon they were crossing dark rivers and broad prairies of marsh grass where old rail trestles flanked the interstate. Seaward lay the barrier islands, like giant freighters anchored just off the coast.

Anse lifted his hand from the wheel, pointing across the wetlands.

"I heard that's how Savannah got its name, all the marshes surrounding the city like savannah grass."

Malaya looked across the wide expanse of salt marsh. The cordgrass wavered in the dusk, high enough to hide lions or leopards. She cocked her head.

"Never thought of that, but I can see it. In school, we learned it was from a band of Shawnee that settled down here—their name sounded like Savannah, meant *southerners.*"

"That's more likely, I reckon."

"I like your version, though."

Malaya looked out across the marshes, squinting, as if she might spot a pair of eyes smoldering from the reeds or floating along a mudbank. She shivered. More than once lately, she'd caught a flash of light in the trees around the sanctuary, like the lens of a spotting scope might make, or glimpsed a flutter of shadow in the underbrush. She thought of the tattooed man at the grocery store, whose clear eyes cut her naked.

"You ever wonder if anybody suspects us? Sometimes I feel watched."

Anse growled, steering the big pickup around a minivan.

"We ain't doing anything wrong."

"Well, it's illegal to start."

"*Malum prohibitum,*" said Anse.

"*Malum* who?"

"Latin," said Anse. "Means 'wrong because prohibited.' Wrong because it's against the law. As opposed to being wrong in and of itself."

"Where'd you learn that?"

"My daddy used to say it growing up, when we were hungry and he'd kill a deer out of season or make a little whiskey in the woods."

"Sounds like a rationalization."

Anse flashed an eye at her, iron-hard beneath his hat brim.

"You ever had hungry mouths to feed?"

Malaya eyed him back.

"I was one."

They were back again into the pines. She looked at the billboards floating past, advertising fireworks stores or accident attorneys or Jesus Christ.

"I'm sure Robin Hood and Jesse James thought the same way. *Malum* whatever."

"Probably they did," said Anse.

"See how that turned out for them."

Anse cocked his chin her way, keeping his eyes on the road.

"You getting cold feet?"

Malaya had removed her work boots. Now she leaned back and set her socked feet on the dashboard.

"These feet are blazing, old man. Ready for hot coals."

Anse grunted. Malaya thought he'd tell her to get her damn feet off the dashboard but he didn't. He kept looking straight ahead, jaw muscles throbbing, as if working a bone.

"What is it?" she asked.

"What's what?"

"You're gonna be sipping your meals through a straw, you keep grinding your teeth like that. Now spit it out, whatever it is you're chewing on."

Anse's temples quit pulsing. He blinked a couple of times.

"I've been wanting to tell her," he said.

"Who, Tyler?"

"Yeah."

"Well, why haven't you yet?"

Anse stared down the highway. Far into the distance.

"I'm afraid," he said.

Malaya nodded. "She's a tough one. I might be scared, too."

Anse cast an eye her way.

"You ain't exactly helping right at this moment."

Malaya took her feet from the dashboard and folded them beneath her, perching cross-legged on the leather seat.

"You ever hear the story of the blind men and the elephant? My grandfather used to tell it in the day."

"I don't know. Might have."

"There's six blind men examining an elephant. Each touches a different part. Trunk, tusk, ear, tail, leg, et cetera. Just one part. Of course, each blind man thinks it's something else. One says it's a tree branch, one a spear, another a sail, a rope, a tree trunk, so on. They can't agree. Finally they come to blows, trying to pound what they believe into one another."

Anse squinted. "So the elephant's the world and what, we're each just hanging on to some little piece, never grasping the big picture?"

"Maybe," said Malaya. "Or maybe we're all just groping blind for body parts. Either way, I think you should give her the whole story, or else you're liable to catch an ass-whooping. Can't say I'd blame her, either."

A thin smile quivered across the old jockey's face. He cocked his head, talking from the side of his mouth.

"I like the story of the blind elephants better," he said.

"Yeah, what's that?"

"Six blind elephants. First one feels a man. Says, 'Man is flat.' Rest of the elephants feel the man, too." Anse looked at her. "They all agree."

They were nearing Savannah when sleep fell over Malaya, heavy as a spell, her head bobbing in the gentle hum of the cab. She'd been rising early to run along the dewy streets of town, pausing to squeeze out sets of pull-ups and dips on the monkey bars of the county playground. The sun would be unrisen, a cool glow in the piney air, and she would wring her flesh with knuckled ferocity, like a dishrag, squeezing out the black feelings of anxiety and fear that always seemed to build up overnight. They would turn cool on her skin. She had a mission now. A purpose. She could feel her body hardening, tightening, her body honed sharp as the point of a spear.

She drifted now, riding the edge of dream. She was seated high on the back of a mammoth, woolly and thunderous, convoying through a valley at night. The yellow eyes of wild things glowed from the hillsides. Hyenas or wolves or wild dogs. Waiting, watching the heavy sway of ivory and meat. The night grew darker, quieter. Malaya was sure a blast would come at any moment and the wolves would descend from the hills, but the rising sun broke across the land, overwhelming the ridges and avalanching down the slopes.

Then they were out of the valley and moving through the thornveld, a landscape she knew. They were passing through Zululand, she realized, heading toward Thula Thula, the game reserve of Lawrence Anthony, hero of the Baghdad Zoo, struck dead by a heart attack at sixty-one. The woolly mammoth she rode was no longer a mammoth but one of the elephants from the rogue herd that Anthony had saved, giving them refuge on his reserve.

The entire herd, twenty-some members strong, had walked twelve hours through the night and turned up at Anthony's home the very weekend he died, as if they'd sensed the stoppage of the man's heart. A man the Zulu called *umkhulu*—grandfather. Who could, they said, speak to the elephants. The herd had not visited the house in months and they spent two days roaming around the compound, their cheeks streaked black with stress secretions. While the people scattered Anthony's ashes in the dark water of the Mkhulu Dam, the solemn gut-rumbles of the elephants were heard in the surrounding bush, like the sound of distant thunder.

Malaya, who'd been on the riverbank that day, was among the elephants now. She was buoyant upon their backs, among the stone-gray boulders of flesh, until she saw what she hadn't seen the day of the memorial service. She saw men bunched at the boundaries of the reserve, watching, waiting to strike in the wake of the great man's death.

Poachers.

"Malaya." A whisper. "Malaya."

A touch on her arm. She exploded awake, opening her eyes to find Anse holding her wrists, keeping her fingernails just short of his face. His hat was knocked off.

"Whoa," he said. "Whoa, now."

Malaya dropped her hands. Tears were swarming her eyes.

"I'm sorry," she said. "I was dreaming."

Anse nodded. "I know."

Malaya leaned her head back on the seat and breathed, her chest thumping.

"I'm sorry."

Her window hummed down.

"Go on, get some air," said Anse.

Malaya leaned her head out the window, dizzied, her hair hanging over her face. Within weeks of Lawrence's death, poachers had descended on Thula Thula, breaching the fence and shooting one of the rhinos in broad daylight. Malaya had been on a contract elsewhere in the country, unable to help. Rage and guilt racked her at the time—she could do nothing as the reserve was picked apart, perforated. Thula Thula would survive thanks to the steely resolve of Anthony's widow and a team of loyal rangers, but Malaya still carried that wound, like so many others, bleeding into her dreams. Now she felt a warm light on her cheek, calling her to lift her head. She looked up, cracking one eye open.

There, high against the night, glowed a giant yellow paw. It was bigger than the moon, brighter, drowning the stars. An emblem, gas-filled and electric, that blazed day and night. Now her eyes came to rest on the giant cage at the foot of the sign. It was the size of a shipping container, double-fenced and strung with razor wire, the iron bars shining in the floodlights. She got out of the truck, slowly, and approached the outer fence, hooking her fingers in the wire, squinting into the darkness. She saw nothing until the lion lifted his head, his eyes gold-fired inside a ragged black wreath of mane.

Malaya's heart purred and she heard a distant whisper inside her head.

The only good cage . . .

CHAPTER 16

AMBA

Horn approached her enclosure from upwind, as he always did, moving in a crouch, his bare feet avoiding loose sticks and fallen leaves—any sound that might betray his presence. He was shirtless, the curved blade of his karambit sheathed at the base of his spine. Dusk was falling, smoking the world, while a crescent moon rose through the pines.

Amba would just be coming awake, prowling the twilight.

The air rose, shuffling the leaves overhead. Horn could hear the moan of the island's abandoned buildings, their broken windows sieving the wind, their chambers and porches clotted with the wrack of hurricanes and storm surges. Horn paused to look through a break in the trees, landward, where strings of headlights flickered in and out of the trees, following the coast road. Christ haunted that stretch of highway, the shoulders staked with hand-made crucifixes and plastic flowers, while chemical plants and pulp mills shone on the horizon. The singlewide he'd grown up in still lay along that road, vine-snarled, canted in the weeds like a derailed boxcar, subjected to storm after storm.

During his long nights in the dog box, Horn had transformed. He could hear the scream of tires in the night and the chug of shrimp boats through the marsh, some heavy-hulled with bales of marijuana or cocaine. *Square grouper.* He could feel the moon hanging high in the black sky, drawing the beast from his flesh, summoning the power from his throat. Black bristles sprouted from his adolescent cheeks and chin, as if drawn toward the moonlight that shafted down through the perforated box. If he was to be caged like a dog, he would become the most savage of the line.

A wolf.

He hardened his body against the world, punching the walls of juvenile detention cells and the fence posts of foster homes until his knuckles were calcified, cruel as sledges. He rolled fifty-pound dumbbells over his shins, month after month, hardening them like Louisville Sluggers—hard enough to shatter the bones of lesser men. He grew his chest beneath the iron bar of a weight bench. A juvie inmate performed his first tattoo, pricking the words across his back with guitar string and cigarette ash, swiping away the blood with a dishrag.

MAN IS TO MAN EITHER A GOD OR A WOLF

Horn would have no fear of cages, for he was made in one.

He circled upwind of Amba's enclosure and knelt in the trees, watching. There was the giant cat-tree he'd built her of treated pine, branching with platforms and catwalks and treehouses of every kind—big enough to rival those of the Lost Boys or the Swiss Family Robinson. It sprang from a heavy understory of saw palmetto and holly and creeper vines, even a few stands of bamboo he'd planted for her. The walls of the enclosure were more than thirty feet high, the sky fenced against the acrobatics of her kind, draped with camouflage netting in case of snooping drones or satellites.

Horn squinted, trying to find her amid the bush. He never could. She would sense his approach, always, and nestle in one of her hides to watch. He knew her eyes were already upon him, moving across his skin, as if she could read the words tattooed there. He approached the fence.

When he whistled, she shot like a streak of fire from a bamboo thicket, straight for him, turning at the last second to run her long body against the fence, chuffing at him. He pushed his belly against the fence wire.

"Amba," he said.

She was an Amur tiger, *Panthera tigris altaica*. The largest species in the world, evolved in the spruce forests of Siberia, the taiga. She was nearly six feet long and three hundred pounds. He'd raised her from cubhood, hand-feeding her, his hands slicked with the blood of her meals. He'd trained her for the flaming hoops of the circus. They performed for years together, rattling from town to town in the whirring caravan of animal cages and folded big tops and electric lights—a tent city that bloomed in fairgrounds across the nation, offering trapeze artists and tightrope walkers and other aerialists who seemed to float on the very gasps of the crowds.

There were the stunt acts, the performers who breathed fire or swallowed swords or hurled knives at daughters bound spread-eagle to spinning wheels. Strongmen who performed four-hundred-pound bench presses from beds of nails or tore phone books in half. Unicyclists who juggled chainsaws, contortionists who twisted themselves into human knots.

Then there were the exotic animal acts. Acrobatic elephants that moonwalked on wooden barrels, seals that bounced beach balls on their noses. Wolves trained to howl beneath the electric bulbs of the big top, as if summoning the bones of their ancestors from beneath the strip malls and parking lots of local townships. There was Horn, the sideshow wolfman and tiger tamer, who led his tigress through rings of fire with his thin wand, as if conducting a long banner of flame through the arena, and engaged her in the traditional mock battles of the act, fending off the big cat with only a chair. A final hug, burying his head in her mouth to show that their true relationship was love, which *was* true. He had never found in human companionship anything to match the warm white fur of her chest, the hug of her deadly paws.

Later, when the gates were closed and the children gone, Horn might be found in one of the smaller tents, bare-knuckled before the local champion, the pair of them circling inside a wire cage while the bettors roared on every side of them, shaking their crumpled bills. The local champion would soon be straining red-faced in an arm-bar or Kimura or triangle choke, tapping out his submission, or else slipping to sleep in the hard cradle of Horn's arms. His specialty was the rear naked choke, known in Brazil as *mata leão*—the "lion-killer."

They had traveled together—man and tiger and wolves—in a pair of tandem trailers, towed by an ancient snubnose semi with a sleeping cabinet behind the seats. A coffin sleeper, two feet wide, where Horn spent his nights after feeding and tending to the animals. They were free agents, taking their show from circus to circus, sometimes hiring out to train tigers for other acts. They performed until Horn had saved enough to move them all to this bankrupt island, which he defended from looters and treasure-hunters in return for this plot of land.

Their refuge from the world of men.

Amba slunk back and forth, rubbing her body against the fence. Her fur was fire-bright, like it hadn't been for so long. Her hips swayed with power. A little more than a year ago, at only eleven years old, she'd begun to cough and sag at her midline. Her coat seemed to fade, her eyes dimming. Then one morning Horn had won their game—the first time ever. He'd found her lying on one of her platforms, unaware of his approach. She hardly rose at his whistle.

Cancer, said the vet. A tumor in one of her mammary glands.

In the last year, Horn had spent everything he had for her treatment, bringing her to a veterinary oncologist on the mainland for care. He'd sold the semi-truck and the trailers and the buggy he used to haul food and supplies around the compound. He'd spent his savings and his emergency fund and maxed out what little credit he had. He'd sold wolf-dog pups to buyers he didn't like, who smelled wrong to him. Bearded men in dark parking lots, who'd scratched perfect answers on his questionnaire—too perfect, as if they'd taken this particular test before. After Mystic Tiger's death, he sold the skin and bones and claws to a shadowy dealer at the local port, who would smuggle them to Asia on a transoceanic freighter or container ship, where the tiger's parts could fetch a handsome sum on the black market.

Whatever it took.

Amba's coat blazed newly before him, like a stoked bed of coals, her spine weaving and cracking along the fence. The breeze rose, fluttering the leaves, lifting an ammoniac sting into his nostrils. Her scent-marks. She was entering estrus, radiant with heat. The first time in months. Likely the last. She had sprayed around the enclosure, signaling her readiness to mate. Now she turned her gaze upon him. The gold flashed newly in her eyes, bright as coins. They cut through the panels and ink of his flesh, as they always had. Burning into his heart. She was demanding a last wish, he knew.

Horn bowed his head.

BOOK IV

CHAPTER 17

THE KING OF SAVANNAH

The yellow paw of Lion Gas hangs high over the truck stop, smearing out the stars. Big rigs snooze far beneath the luminous emblem, huddled in long parking lanes, while motorists pump gas under the bright lights or peruse the store aisles, snatching gummy fish and pork rinds and beef jerky from pegboard hooks. The mascot's enclosure sits at the base of the sign, crowned in razor wire and spotlights.

Mosi stares out across the wire, watching the people come and go, as from a waterhole. He watches the wiggle of their toes on dashboards and the bumble of their rumps in sweatpants. How he longs to taste their meat, their blood dripping hot from his chin. He longs for prey besides the bald chickens that come tumbling through his feeding chute, so cold and bloodless they hurt his teeth.

He hasn't roared in so long—not since that day on the riverbank, beneath the bloodied hull of the impala. He is alone here. He doesn't have the company of other lions to swell his chest. A lion without a pride is nothing. He is empty and thin. He has no lionesses to hunt for him, to stalk so handsome through the bush grass and bring him antelope. His shoulders are bony and raw. His mane feels thin. A sign hangs across the top of this cage:

THE KING OF SAVANNAH

There's no night here, when he should prowl beneath the stars. Only the white barrage of floodlights, which blind and expose him. He thinks of the dark belly of the ship that brought him to this shore, groaning through the swells of the sea. He rode inside a pinewood box with holes for him to breathe. His thirst in the box had never been so great. His tongue was a desert. The metal bowls, when they came clanging and slopping into his box, were too shallow to slake him. He could hear the squawk and scream of other beasts. Their anxiety was a stench. They were sick with fear, each a font of bile and defecation. His eye would float in the holes of his box, witnessing their agony. He could do nothing for those beasts, who deserved, at the least, the mercy of his teeth.

Still, he sometimes longs for that pinewood box. For darkness.

The yellow torch of the lion's paw flickers against the sky—once, twice—then winks out. The whole bubble of light alongside the interstate shivers and bursts. Night floods over the place, as if leaping down from the hills, coursing over everything but the amber parking lights of semis and the odd pair of headlights swimming in the blackout.

Drivers stand amazed in the sudden darkness, night-blind, holding their pump guns like oversized pistols. Their mouths fall slack. Some wonder if this could be the end, the impact of a bomb or missile or meteorite. A returned Christ, beamed down from heaven at light speed, or the eruption of a supervolcano, ejecting the earth's crust into the stratosphere. They wait for the aftershock, the blast wave or megatsunami or four horsemen ripping open the sky.

No one thinks to look in the direction of the enclosure, where a black vehicle has come rumbling from the service road, lightless, and parked behind the cage, the driver wearing a pair of green-lensed goggles that amplify starlight. They don't see the figure that emerges to crouch at the edge of the fence and shoulder a rifle, nor the hiss of the dart through the iron bars.

Mosi leaps from his platform, wheeling to swat the offending hornet or scorpion or snake—whatever has just stung his rump. He's still turning circles, his tail whirling after him in the darkness, when his hindquarters give out. He sits down clumsily on his flanks, staring about. His jaw sags. His tongue falls out. A black sleep is washing over him, drowning him, thick as blood in his throat.

This is not the darkness he wanted. To drown in this iron box, stung by an evil hornet. He wishes to die with his chin bloodied, the taste of a rival in his mouth, or else amid a pride of his own, his muzzle gray with age. He swells his chest, as he did that day on the riverbank.

He is Mosi, the black-maned, who should die with a roar—
He drops splay-pawed in the dirt, tranquilized.

Motorists are still staring up at the black heavens, gape-mouthed, as if waiting for the stars to turn back on. Truckers turn over in their sleeper cabs, unaware. A shift manager, in the dark of a back office, dials the power company. When the bucket truck arrives, the linemen will find the cutout fuses of the nearest transformer pulled open, their brass rings hanging down like grenade pins—killing power to the truck stop. The black vehicle will be miles gone, racing south through the night.

CHAPTER 18

TROOPER

They were still on the interstate, several miles shy of their exit, when blue lights splashed into the cab, the *whoop-whoop* of a siren. Malaya clenched the wheel, the leopard screaming awake over her heart.

"What should I do?"

"Pull over," said Anse.

The rumble strip shuddered through the wheel. Malaya parked on the shoulder. She was thinking of cuffs and snares and cages.

"I can't go to jail, Anse."

The old jockey squinted in his door mirror, the flesh crinkling around his eyes.

"You won't," he said.

The trooper stepped out of his cruiser and stood a moment beside the door, tall and erect, smoothing his tie and leveling his campaign hat. Malaya could feel the pistol hard against her hip, concealed under her shirt. Her heart was thrashing against her ribs, wanting out. She could only catch shallow bits of breath. She stared straight ahead, wondering how far they would get if she punched the gas.

"I can't go, Anse. I'll die first."

Now a hand on her forearm, firm and sure. She smelled the old jockey's Marlboro breath, so much like her grandfather's.

"You won't go," he said.

He reached behind the seat for his hat.

Meanwhile, Malaya watched the trooper's approach, holding her breath. As trained, the man lifted his hand from his side, as if to palm the swell of the fender, and tapped the tailgate firmly with two fingers, marking the vehicle with his fingerprints. Malaya jerked at the touch. Then the man was standing at her window with his flashlight out, long and black as a billy club. He rapped the handle against his own shoulder, his right hand palming the butt of his sidearm.

"You folks coming from the truck stop?"

Malaya wondered if the man could see the pounding of her chest. She opened her mouth, but Anse spoke first from behind her, his voice crackly and drawled.

"Said we wasn't stopping but once this trip, and this'n here already needs her a pit stop. Bladder the size of a quail egg, I tell you."

Malaya, still looking at the officer, took up the lie. She squeezed her knees together.

"Power was out," she said.

The trooper didn't seem to notice. He stood like a man at attention. A Boy Scout.

"You know why I pulled you over, ma'am?"

"Was I speeding?"

"No, ma'am. I just received a report that the King of Savannah has been stolen from his enclosure."

"The truck stop lion?"

"That's right. There's a BOLO on suspicious vehicles in the vicinity."

"Are we suspicious?"

The trooper leaned back, taking in the heavy body of the truck, the chrome exhaust stacks, the smoked windows of the bed cap. Then he looked at the occupants: Asian female, mid-twenties, black hooded sweatshirt. Caucasian male, late fifties, green outdoors shirt.

"License and registration," he said.

They'd first discussed the operation in the butcher shed while Malaya disassembled a whitetail buck for tiger food. Anse was sitting on one of the battered deep freezers, clicking his boot-heels against the side, railing on lion farms and canned hunts.

"See now, the farms collect pay-to-play money from the tourists while they're cubs, then sell them to the hunting ranches."

Malaya held the cleaver high against the blade, driving it firmly, firmly through the shoulder joint. The foreleg broke free of the trunk. She bucketed the shorn limb and looked to Anse. He was staring far off, chewing his lip.

"Now a real hunt, that could take two, three weeks of hiking through the bush, maybe a fifty-fifty chance of shooting a wild lion. These canned hunts, some son of a bitch just wants a head for his wall. The guides release a farm-raised lion into a fenced enclosure. Bait them, maybe, or hit them with a low-dose tranq. Ninety-nine percent chance of success."

Malaya had the other leg cut free from the trunk. The empty sockets dribbled blood, spattering the green rubber boots she wore. She looked at Anse.

"'Least nobody shot this one. Sign says he was saved from a canned hunt."

Anse growled.

"Which would you rather? Be shot once by a five-hundred-grain bullet, or a thousand fucking cameras and spitballs every day of your life?"

"Still, isn't it just one cage to another?"

"*Enclosure.* What else can we do, turn him loose in the streets?"

Malaya thought of the truck stop lion loosed from the interstate, disappearing along the nearby Savannah River and turning up in the streets of downtown, trotting heavy-pawed beneath the gothic oaks of the squares, rumbling past statues of dead men with their swords or hats or Bibles raised, as if to address him, or along the cobbled streets of the waterfront. People would flee screaming before him, leaving a trail of spilled beers and leather sandals and shopping bags in their wake, their ice-cream cones and cocktails bleeding between the cobblestones. Helicopters would swarm overhead, stabbing their spotlights through the trees, while the wails of cruisers converged. The lion would pass the barking dogs of front porches and apartment windows, unconcerned, and float among the ghostly statuary of Bonaventure Cemetery, a creature rarer there than any ghost. His paws would stamp a trail of crowns across the city, pugmarks that residents would cast in plaster for their mantels and curiosity shops. Perhaps he would come to stand finally at land's edge and look east, dreaming of his home across the ocean, while a SWAT sniper loaded the round that would wreck his heart.

Malaya thought of her grandfather, who died with a bullet in his chest. Sometimes she wondered if he'd wanted it that way— better than some hospital room or nursing home.

"If we turn him loose," she said, "'least he wouldn't die behind a fence."

Anse shook his head, knocking his heels on the deep freezer.

"He'll have some measure of peace here. And room to roam. Some dignity."

Malaya nodded, sliding the severed foreleg into the bucket.

"What about Lope? You thought about bringing him into this one?"

Anse shook his head again.

"We don't need him," he said.

Malaya cocked her head, eyeing the cleaver held dripping from her hand.

"It's a high-profile heist, Anse."

Anse leaned and spat out the door, wiping his mouth with the back of his hand.

"*Rescue,*" he said.

They practiced with a four-hundred-pound body bag full of

Quikrete, sweating in the shadows of the old overgrown enclosure along the river, rolling the simulated lion into the bed of a custom-built lowboy litter outfitted with buggy tires. Malaya had gone with Anse to see the builder, an ancient biker named Spider with a shop off the highway. Out front, a row of raked-out choppers with chrome engines and leather tassels. The biker smiled at Anse when they walked in.

"Old man, have you come to let me build you a bike?"

"I'm not ready to die just yet," said Anse. "When I put a motorcycle between my legs, you'll know." He handed the man a sheet of grid paper, a penciled design rife with arrows and notes and measurements. "I come because we're needing something like this. Built low, so it'll fit beneath the height of a truck bed."

The biker studied the sheet, scratching the spiderweb inked over one elbow.

"You looking to transport bodies?"

"Just one," said Anse. "A lion."

Malaya jumped at the word. She cocked an eye at the old biker.

"You ain't a snitch, are you?"

The man only smiled, lifting his chin. A dashed line tattooed across the front of his neck, along with the inscription: CUT HERE.

Malaya tried to slow her breath, worrying the trooper would notice the swell of her chest. While she fumbled for her wallet, the man leaned back on his heels, eyeing the bed cap. The windows were tinted to the legal maximum.

"What y'all got in the bed?"

Malaya's heart bounced in her chest.

"Tree-trimming equipment," said Anse. This was not untrue—the litter lay hidden beneath the deck of a truck bed storage system, which was covered with chainsaws, climbing ropes, and gasoline cans. "Took down a couple widow-maker limbs up in Savannah this afternoon. Historical district. They call me in for the dicey stuff."

"No lions?"

"Not that dicey."

Malaya handed over her license and registration.

"I wish," she said, surprising herself. "We'd be doing the poor thing a favor."

The trooper grunted, eyeing her license.

"Buddy of mine from the DNR worked a tiger case not too long ago. Not the first big-cat theft of late."

He leaned back again, looking at the bed cap, thumping the license against his thumb. Deciding. He would ask to search the truck. Malaya knew he would. The trooper cleared his throat, about to speak, but Anse's voice came first, barked like a gunnery sergeant.

"You serve, son?"

The trooper straightened at the question—reflex. Malaya turned to Anse, shocked to realize he wasn't wearing his regular bush hat but a darker Stetson, perched high atop his head with a yellow braid around the base and a pair of crossed cavalry sabers on the crown. Beneath the brim, the old jockey's eyes were steely and bright, as if newly polished.

Malaya had been sitting at the wheel of the truck, alone, when the bubble of light over the truck stop shivered and burst. Blackout. Anse had come climbing down the utility pole, leaning back on his flipline, kicking his tree spikes in and out of the creosoted pine. He waddled to the big truck and hauled himself into the cab.

"Hit it."

Malaya nodded and pulled the truck into gear, driving down the service road without headlights, using a pair of night-vision goggles to see. Everything had been plotted, timed. The truck stop had no backup generators. Anse, still wearing his spurs and harness, pulled a balaclava over his head before replacing his eyeglasses. The truck rocked over the curb behind the enclosure and Malaya pulled in along the outer fence of razor wire, leaving the motor running. Anse unracked the tranquilizer gun from behind his head while she stepped down from the cab, leaving the goggles on the dashboard and reaching for a pair of heavy bolt-cutters stored behind the seat. She knelt before the outer gate, ready to cut the padlock. Anse crouched beside her, facing the opposite direction, scanning the truck lot.

He tapped her shoulder and she cut the shackle and eased open the gate. Now Anse crept past her, the dart gun cradled against his chest. A Cap-Chur tranquilizer gun from the 1970s, built like a high-powered rifle, with a long black barrel and walnut stock. It fired 20-cc aero syringes, effective at ranges up to thirty yards. Anse knelt before the inner cage, threading the barrel through the heavy iron bars. The lion was sitting erect on a plywood platform in the very middle of the enclosure, watching the pumps. They could see the sharp ridge of his spine, the black shock of his mane. The tufted tail swishing along the platform. Surely his eyes were boring through the rare darkness of this twenty-four-hour oasis, watching the interstate travelers paw blindly about the aisles and gas pumps. He looked like a giant housecat, monitoring the world beyond his window.

Anse's chest rose, fell, his breath loud as a deer hunter's. He was squinting through the starlight scope. Malaya watched the lion. His mane looked strangely human from the rear, like the wild locks of an eighties rock star. When she looked back at Anse, he was holding out the dart gun, long as a sword across his palms.

"You do it," he said.

"Me?"

His eyes looked slightly wet.

"Please."

Malaya shrugged and took the rifle, spiraling the leather sling around one arm and sighting through the bars. The lion looked an eerie green through the starlight scope, as if seen through swampy water. The barrel hissed, a chuff of gas.

Soon they were winching the King of Savannah into the bed of the truck. The sedated lion lay on his side. His paws, big as softballs, were curled against his chest, his eyes twitching beneath their lids. Malaya thought of Hemingway's old Cuban fisherman, who dreamed always of lions come slinking from the dusk to stand on the beach. She looked at the beast in the bed of the truck, wondering if lions ever dreamed of men.

"Eighty-second Airborne, sir."

Anse's eyes glittered beneath the wide brim of the cavalry hat.

"I ain't no *sir*," he said. "I worked for my living. First Cavalry Division, Airmobile. Vietnam, seventy-one, seventy-two." He growled. "Now there was a war run by a bunch of pasty-faced pencil-pushers out of Washington, D.C. Wonder Boys, they called them. The hell they were. Take a hill one day, give it up the next—"

"Oh, let's not start," said Malaya.

Anse squinted at her, his square jaws rumbling beneath the crossed sabers of the cavalry hat. "Listen, young lady, I spent all afternoon trimming that rich lady's oaks while you sat on your got-damn cellular phone smacking chewing gum."

"Those trees weren't all of hers you wanted to trim."

"The Christ," said Anse.

The trooper gestured toward Malaya with the license.

"You his daughter?"

"God, no," she said. "He won't touch Asians. So it's all his wife will let him hire."

Anse growled in confirmation.

The trooper shook his head, then handed Malaya her license back. Her body was trembling as she slid it back in her wallet.

Anse leaned forward in his seat and thumbed up the brim of his Stetson.

"Say, Trooper, you said this ain't the first big-cat theft of late? Buddy of yours worked a tiger case?"

The trooper hooked a thumb on his belt.

"Just across the state line," he said. "High school mascot. Could be related to tiger trafficking."

Anse leaned forward, cupping a hand over his ear.

"Tiger what?"

"Trafficking, sir. They busted a ring in the Midwest was rounding up old tigers and parting them out like stolen cars. Pelts, bones, paws for the black market. Like a chop shop. They say a hide can sell for twenty grand in Asia, case of tiger bone wine for twice that."

Anse growled—every inch the curmudgeon now, rarely loosed from the local VFW bar.

"Ought to be a special rung of hell for sons-of-bitches would do that," he said. "Same's dogfighters. Line 'em up for me, I'll send them down on a rail of fire, every one."

The trooper nodded, heavy and slow, as if to say *Amen* or *Hooah* or *Get some.*

He tapped the door sill with one finger, lightly.

"There's a rest stop 'bout five miles up the road, clean restrooms. Sorry to keep you waiting, ma'am."

He touched his hat brim and turned for his cruiser. On the way he lifted a hand to rap the bed cap window—once, hard, to see what might wake—but didn't. He kept walking, sliding the flashlight back into his belt.

Malaya pulled back onto the highway. Her body was trembling, her blood fired with adrenaline. She breathed in through her nose, out through her mouth, exhaling through the pinhole of her pursed lips. Counting her breaths. She imagined the heavy throb of the lion's heart in the bed, steady as an engine. She imagined her own heart that steady, that sure.

She looked at Anse. The cavalry Stetson had vanished into the backseat, quick as a magic trick, replaced with his battered bush hat. The old man was kicked back in his seat now, his hands laced across his chest, his eyes shut beneath his hat brim, as if he were asleep. A sly smile raked his face.

Malaya shook her head.

"You sneaky bastard."

CHAPTER 19

WAR EAGLE

Malaya stood cross-armed in front of the gift shop's television set, head cocked. The owner of Lion Gas—a large man in a khaki safari shirt—was on the news, speaking teary-eyed before a bank of microphones. Winter Melton was offering a reward for the return of his beloved mascot. He said thousands of children would be disappointed not to see their favorite lion along the interstate. He said the thought broke his heart.

"You seeing this?" asked Malaya.

Anse huffed, not looking up from the bills and paperwork spread across the cashier's counter. He was scribbling out checks, his handwriting tiny, jagged.

"I seen it," he said.

They had placed the lion in the old enclosure along the river, a ten-acre tract. The fence was so overwhelmed with vines and kudzu no one could see him roam. On television, the truck stop magnate railed away at the act.

A striking blow to conservation.

A crime against wildlife.

The work of evildoers.

Meanwhile, newscasters speculated on the perpetrators'

motives, citing any number of theories: kidnap-and-ransom, wildlife trafficking, even environmental vigilantism.

"What should we do?" asked Malaya.

Anse didn't look up.

"Pick up Lope," he said. "It's feeding time."

The golden eagle stood on Lope's heavy gauntlet, her black talons hooked over his fist. She spread her wings, her flight feathers spanning nearly seven feet.

His uncle Delk had been the one to name the bird.

Aurora, pretty as the dawn.

Uncle Delk had stepped in after the death of Lope's father. The man was a giant. Six foot six, the same as Lope, but twice as wide, built like a brick shithouse. An ox-yoke of muscle crossed his shoulders, oak-hard, and he wore a black dart of beard that never grayed, even into his fifties.

In the 1980s, Delk had played football alongside the great Herschel Walker, the patron saint of Georgia—a tailback who'd raced freight trains to build his speed and thumped out two thousand push-ups per day, transforming himself from a boy into a god. *Oh you Herschel Walker.* This human locomotive, built of an iron will, had roared through linebackers across the South until the radios crackled there was *sugar falling out of the sky, sugar falling out of the sky*—the Georgia Bulldogs were going to the Sugar Bowl. Delk had been there that championship season. The only man, said the papers, who could keep up with the rabid mania of Herschel's training regimen.

During an away game at Auburn University, Delk had toured the campus's Raptor Center, which cared for injured birds of prey from around the country. There he met the opposing team's mascot—War Eagle V, a golden eagle—and strode down the main aisle of the barn. There were eagles, owls, ospreys. Hawks and harriers, kestrels and kites. They stared one-eyed or wing-shot from their perches, stern as old gods. Here, he learned the golden eagle of Zeus had carried thunderbolts in his talons and fetched men to heaven before ascending among the stars—the constellation Aquila. He learned the Plains Indians had believed eagles carried their prayers to the heavens. They made whistles of their thigh bones and healed the sick with fans of their feathers. For the seal of their new nation, the forefathers of the republic had chosen a bald eagle with thirteen arrows in one talon, an olive branch in the other. War and peace, as if neatly twinned.

In that raptor barn, Delk fell in love.

Lope could still remember the first time his uncle took him to fly a bird. It was on the high school football field, a month after the stable fire. Uncle Delk, this childless giant who'd worn armor and wrecked other men for sport, emanated such calm on the field that day. He wore it like an aura. Valk, his peregrine falcon, stood hooded on his fist, still as a statue. Delk's voice was baritone, risen from the deep bellows of his chest, but strangely sweet, rounded with a lisp.

"A raptor is a live wire, baby. Electric. She can read your energy, she's *attuned*. The peregrine most of all. She's been clocked over two hundred miles per hour, diving. She's life shot through the glass of God's eye, magnified, beamed down on the earth. A laser, baby. A motherfucking thunderbolt. Her heart will beat nine hundred times a minute. She's triply alive compared to us. She can see the twitch of a rabbit tail from three miles, the slither of a moccasin from one thousand feet. So you got to be cool, baby. Collected. You got to be scaled, smooth as glass. Sometimes you got to sing."

His great lungs expanded. The song rose like a sweet bird from his throat:

"See that angel, in the middle of the field. That angel is working, on a chariot wheel."

The falcon stood listening. The words humming, perhaps, in the hollows of her bones.

"Not too particular, 'bout workin' on that wheel. I just want to know, how that chariot feel."

Valk shifted slightly on his fist. Her wings were slate, her nostrils baffled like jet intakes so she could breathe at high speed.

Her wings swelled slightly, as if the song were a wind beneath them.

"Now let me fly, O, now let me fly..."

Delk slipped off the raptor's hood, gently, and the bird rose from his fist. The raptor would orbit high against the sun, half a mile from the ground—watching, watching—then fold her wings and dive for the earth, striking shorebirds and songbirds and waterfowl in midflight, severing their spines with the clenched hammer of her foot, then wheeling back to catch their spinning, broken bodies from the sky.

Death from above.

Delk watched the falcon rise.

"Your daddy died doing a good thing. That's rare, boy."

Lope licked his lips. He felt the guilt-pain rising inside his chest, licking his ribs like roof beams. His hands squirmed one into the other, his knuckles crackling.

"I can't quit thinking about it. Him burning like he done. I don't want to go to sleep, because I know I'll dream it again."

Delk nodded. The falcon spiraled higher and higher, riding an invisible column of heat.

"We gonna put a raptor on your wrist," he said. "She'll make you aware of powers you never knew you had. Draw them up out of you, through your veins like tree sap. It's biofeedback, boy. Autonomic control. Get you tapped in, wired into your own brainwaves, heartbeat, skin conductance. Your own pain. Give you the power to let go, give that pain up to God above."

Lope was skeptical. Uncle Delk had always been strange— unexpectedly sensitive for a man who'd played two seasons in the pros, sending running backs home on stretchers before he blew out a knee in a preseason game. Lope's mother blamed it on his Geechee blood. After all, his father's side of the family had sprung from one of the Georgia sea islands where descendants of freed slaves had lived in near isolation since the end of the Civil War.

"Them Saltwater Geechee always been funny," she'd say,

wringing the suds from a dish towel. "They had their own world out there so long, they hardly at home in this one."

But Uncle Delk was right. It had worked. The falcon was like a mirror of his insides—Lope could read his own anxiety in her mood. She would step lightly on his arm, agitated, as if his flesh were too hot through the glove. Watching her, he could will himself to calm, to turn down the hissing flame in his blood. In time he learned to let go. Every summer, working the resorts with Delk, he would watch the raptors soar high over the beaches and cabanas and swimming pools, scattering the gulls. Lope would release the burdens of the previous year—grief, anxiety, heartbreak—letting them be carried off into the sky, burned up in the sun.

Now, twenty years later, he needed help again. He was writhing in bed at night, slimy with sweat. He was replaying the shooting of the lioness, looking for his fault in the matter, his guilt. The same as he'd done over his father's death, winding himself deeper and deeper. He worried he'd been too quick to shoot. That he should have trusted Anse's instincts. That he'd broken an old man's heart.

He found himself itching for the firehouse alarm to sound so he could slide down the greasy brass of the fireman's pole and race toward the burning torch of a trailer or bungalow or corner store, forgetting all, gone to a place where flames leapt from windows and rolled tumbling through doors—beasts tamed beneath his hose. He worried, sometimes, that there weren't enough such fires. That he could light one himself.

Aurora stood ready on his arm. She was flying well. A week ago, she had taken her first drone, descending high-winged on a cheap quadcopter and driving it into the ground. European police had started the trend, using eagles to take down unmanned flying vehicles. Suspicious drones had been reported over secure facilities, hovering over airports and radar installations. It took little to have the eagles target them; they seemed to attack the drones on mere principle.

Aurora seemed slightly troubled, edging back and forth on his arm. Lope took a deep breath, thinking of the things that gave him peace. He thought of his wife at home, their baby throbbing against her chest, suckling, and he thought of his uncle Delk, steady as oak. He thought of the eagle calming on his arm. Settling. Both of them, together. Then he sucked another breath into his lungs, gathering a wind between his ribs.

Lope opened his mouth and began to sing.

Malaya lay in the bed of the truck, staring up. The ribbed metal thudded over the roots and ruts between enclosures, rocking her insides. Five-gallon buckets rattled and slopped on along the bedrails—feeding time. A cast of turkey buzzards was already aloft, circling stiff-winged over the sanctuary, waiting for leftovers. They scrawled lazy-eights on the thermals, their wing feathers slightly translucent, like blackbirds in white dresses.

A *kettle* of vultures, circling. A *wake* of buzzards.

The bravest would descend into the tiger enclosures to pick clean the bones. The big cats would only watch, too sated to bother, their eyes full of a menacing tolerance. People hated the turkey vulture, a redheaded carrion bird that haunted the land, broadcasting the whereabouts of roadkilled dogs, calves strangled in barbwire, husbands fallen dead at the plow. A sort of black weather, come corkscrewing over any site of death. But they had their uses, Malaya knew. They'd found her father.

She was five when his helicopter disappeared in the rolling hills surrounding Fort Benning, Georgia. It was a night exercise and no one saw the crash. No Mayday call from the pilots, no fire or smoke. For three days, search-and-rescue choppers flew day and night, combing the hills for signs. Malaya was only in kindergarten, but she knew something was wrong. Her mother and grandfather had become silent, still as the painted saints that stood in the corners of the Catholic church in town. Waiting, waiting. She curled up in the warm chair of her grandfather's lap and he absently stroked her hair. He seemed so quiet he might be hearing something she could not. The distant thunder of searching helicopters, perhaps, or the slice of vulture wings.

"It was the turkey buzzards that led them in," said Malaya. She was leaning over the truck's toolbox now, arms crossed, talking to Anse and Lope through the rear window of the cab. "A cyclone of them. Fifty or more. The helo had struck a big sandhill crane. They said it crashed through the windshield, activating the fire suppression handles, and the engines lost power at low altitude. They said men were spilled in pieces for a hundred yards."

She set her chin down on her arms. She could hardly believe how much she was telling them, Lope especially. She'd only known him for a few months, but somehow she felt safe around him, calm. At feeding time that afternoon, they'd found him crooning to his bird in the field, singing her lullabies, his long throat vibrating like an instrument. Someone like that, you could tell them anything.

"It haunted me a long time," she said. "Thinking of those birds hunched over my father, pecking at his eyes. I can barely remember him, but I can remember that. Just like I was there. I couldn't shake them. It was like they were inside my head, peck, peck, pecking at my brain."

Lope nodded slowly. He seemed ill-made for the cabin of a truck, his long limbs knobbed and folded to fit into the shotgun seat. He turned his chin over his shoulder.

"You know what they do over in the Himalayas?"

Malaya shook her head.

"When a person dies, they lay out their body on a mountaintop for the vultures to eat. Eurasian griffons, lammergeyers. Old World vultures. The priests club the body first, breaking all the bones, to make it easier for the scavengers. They say it's good karma, the dead offering themselves for the living. They call it sky burial."

A tingle went up Malaya's spine.

"That's beautiful," she said.

Lope nodded, scratching the tops of his knees.

"You heard of Ebos Landing?" he asked. "The Flying Africans?"

"No."

"My grandmother used to tell the story. She grew up out on one of the barrier islands—one of the last Geechee communities, founded by slaves' descendants. She was full of tales, but this one was true. You can look it up. It happened on one of the other barrier islands. St. Simons, I think. The Igbo tribe, from West Africa, was known across the South for being rebellious. A shipload of them revolted at the landing, overthrew the crew. Then, instead of letting themselves get captured, they went marching into the river, chained together, chanting, drowning themselves. People say they transformed into vultures or buzzards, so they could fly back home to Africa. Myth of the Flying Africans. Then you got the Cherokee, they have a special name for the turkey vulture. They call it the 'peace eagle' because it doesn't kill. In Latin, its name means *cleanser* or *pacifier*."

Tears swam into Malaya's eyes. She blinked, trying to hold them back. *Peace eagle.* She lay back in the bed of the truck. *Sky burial.* She closed her eyes, imagining her father's flesh risen in fragments from the earth, carried inside the ribs of wheeling eagles. His blood greasing their wing-joints, fueling their flight. His name translated, heard in the whisper of air beneath their wings. A man returned to the sky out of which he'd fallen.

Her heart boomed. She opened her eyes, staring up. The cast of vultures was gone, scattered. A single raptor hung wing-blazed over the sanctuary, high as an archangel. Malaya squinted, trying to make out what species. She wondered whether it was a buzzard or bird of prey. An eagle of peace or war.

Lope rode shotgun as they rattled from enclosure to enclosure. They had fallen into a pattern these last weeks. About the time he finished with his eagle, Anse's truck would come grumbling up the drive for feeding time. The old jockey would throw his head out the driver's window and crow like a train conductor.

"All aboard!"

The words never ceased to scratch a spark of excitement in Lope's belly. They would go rumbling around the sanctuary in the waning light, feeding the residents of Little Eden. At each enclosure, he and Anse would jump down from the cab while Malaya stood in the bed, handing down the meat or feed earmarked for each animal. The big cats loved the dusk, when the shadows grew long and they could slink like shades through the tall grass, stalking the keepers who delivered their meals.

Last they came to the enclosure of the former circus tigers. Past here, the drive terminated at a padlocked gate overwhelmed with vines and kudzu. A breeze skated down the fence, bobbing the shield-shaped leaves. Thousands of them, endless as an army.

Lope scratched his chin.

"What'd you say is back there?" he asked.

Anse stopped short of the tiger enclosure, a pair of deer legs held dripping at his sides.

"I didn't," he said.

The old jockey had seemed distant the last few days. His jaws were pulsing constantly, his eyes hard and squinty under his hat brim.

Lope looked again at the fence. The leaves purred. He licked his lips.

"You hear about that truck stop lion off the interstate?"

"What about him?"

"Got stolen a few days ago."

"I seen it on television."

"That Winter Melton is making a big fuss, acting like it's some big tragedy. Put up a bounty. Fifty thousand dollars, no questions asked." Lope shook his head. "Mercy mission, you ask me. A lion like that—like Henrietta—made to live in a cage, breathing exhaust fumes all day. It's a crime."

Anse was staring at the tigers. They crisscrossed before him, ready to feed. The heavy shanks of meat hung dripping from his arms, like a pair of bloodied clubs. He cleared his throat.

"It ain't even the start," he said.

Lope waited.

"The start of what?"

The old man kept working his jaws, chewing on words, mincing or grinding them between his teeth.

He didn't say.

CHAPTER 20

PIT

They stood at the edge of an empty swimming pool. The blue bottom, pale as a robin's egg, had not been mopped or scrubbed. There were random streaks of blood across the floor, pocked with the muddy prints of boots and paws.

Malaya shook her head.

"Christ," she whispered.

"At the end of a whip," said Anse.

The house was a five-bedroom behemoth with a Spanish roof, embowered in a jungle of overgrown vines and palms and shrubs. A foreclosure, vacant for months, sitting on the edge of the St. Johns River outside Jacksonville, Florida. The subtropical flora had run rampant in the absence of weekly landscaping crews. No men in masks and neckerchiefs, wielding weed-whackers and shrub shears and motorized trimmers. The nearest house sat more than one hundred yards away, hidden behind a veil of ivy and honeysuckle—vacant, too.

Malaya stared into the stained belly of the pool. An iron mount had been bolted into the deep end, trailing a ten-foot length of heavy chain. At the end of the lead lay an empty leather collar, chewed ragged.

"Dogfight?" asked Malaya.

Anse shook his head.

"Looks more like a bait."

"What kind?"

Anse squatted at the edge of the pool.

"Don't know. All I see is canine prints."

Malaya balled her hands at her sides. Her fists felt small, brittle. She thought of being chained and collared in the pit, facing the red jaws of dogs. She thought of Camp Liberty. Her heart wailed. She wished for some way to channel the pain, to transform her hurt into a roar.

"We'll find them," said Anse.

"Who?"

"Whoever it was did this."

"Find them and what?"

Anse turned his head and spat.

"Whatever we have to."

They descended into the pool, using the steps built into one corner. The walls rose high as the bottom sloped toward the deep end. The ghosts of dogs whirled and roared, their fury echoing inside the sky-blue belly of the pit. Malaya's eyes burned, blurry with tears. She swiped them away, scanning for clues.

The tip had been anonymous, left on the answering machine of an 800 number they'd started posting on telephone poles and gas station corkboards up and down the coast—hoping for a lead on any exotics that needed new homes. The caller gave no specifics—just an address.

They policed the knee-high grass of the yard, cutting back and forth, back and forth, until they passed beneath the low-hanging moss of the oaks along the riverbank. Nothing. There they sat, staring across the noon glitter of the river.

Here the early European explorers had sailed beneath the billowed canvas of their three-masted ships, erecting stone pillars of dominion among the tattooed tribes of the New World, who welcomed them as sons of god. Log-rafts and steamboats followed, hauling out the last virgin timber of the land. Dark

veins of pollution slipped into the river, sprung from the pulp
mills and chemical plants that lined the banks. Strange formations of algae bloomed in the water; lesions grew on the scales
of fish. Manatees paddled just beneath the surface, their backs
grouted with scars, while powerboats blasted along the river,
heedless of caution signs.

Malaya sat hugging her knees.

"Sometimes I wonder if we don't deserve it," she said. "Some
plague to wipe us from history. Some flood."

Anse took a soft pack of Marlboros from his pocket, lit one.

"You been hanging around me too long."

"From the lion pits to the Coliseum to now. Nothing changes,
except there's more of us."

Anse blew smoke from his nostrils.

"All we can do is try and be the good guys, best we can."

Malaya envisioned the rivers rising, swollen by the ire of God,
and the works of man swamped, drowned under inland seas. People
swept beneath the surface, wheeling like spirits in the darker currents. Some clinging to life in high apartments, perched just above
the lapping flood, or throwing one another from listing cruise ships
or freighters. She pictured men lording homemade arks, wielding
bangsticks or assault rifles like the staffs of prophets. Men who'd
said again and again that the time was nigh for fire and flood.

Her fingers lay in the swales between her ribs, fingering her
new tattoo. A spiral of peace eagles, raised tender from her side.
She wanted to claw them from her skin.

"I thought we'd find something today. Some clue."

Anse swallowed hard.

"I'm sorry."

Malaya shook her head.

"Nobody gets what they deserve."

Anse broke the back of the cigarette under his thumb.

"Some do."

Late that afternoon, Anse drove to the back of the sanctuary,
alone, a bison shoulder riding in the bed of his truck. He parked

and stepped down from the cab and bent his head to squint through a keyhole-sized opening in the kudzu. There was plenty of room along the river for the lion to roam. Pools of sunlight where he could laze, letting the lesser creatures peck the mites from his fur, and bowers of shade for the heat of the day. Larger prey could even be living inside the enclosure, left from the days before they closed the gate.

Anse had rarely seen the lion since the night of the rescue, but he felt a drumming in his chest every time he looked through this fence. A heavy tattoo, low and proud, that seemed to call his heart back to itself, calling home the bloodied shreds, the blasted parts of himself. He felt a warmth in his chest, a healing. He thought of Henrietta, how she would like this maned lion prowling heavy-pawed along the river, crossing her burial bluff, telling her she was not alone.

But there was something else now. Anse knew he would spend the night lying in bed beside Tyler, his eyes watching the whirl of the ceiling fan, his jaws flickering, grinding his molars to nubs. He would want to tell her about the beast on the other side of the fence, the kidnapped king. But he couldn't—not yet.

He took a folded bandanna from the chest pocket of his safari shirt. A clue he'd found at the edge of the pool, which he hadn't told Malaya about.

Slowly, he began to unwrap it.

Malaya lay in a damp snarl of sheets, unable to sleep. She kept thinking of the blue belly of the pit, streaked with blood. She kept thinking of the rhinos and elephants in the reserve, their carcasses discovered hours or days or weeks too late. How little she'd helped. She kept thinking of the house on the edge of the Okefenokee Swamp—the animals caged on their barge-ark, awaiting some storm or flood.

She rose from bed.

In an hour, she was surrounded by the night sounds of the swamp. The surge of crickets, the croak of bullfrogs. The very air seemed to buzz and whine, clouding her—thousands of tiny motors with wings. She was dressed for night-walking, head to toe. Black compression shirt, Teflon-coated pants, soft-soled jungle boots. At the last moment, standing before the hollow-core door of her rented room, she'd set her pistol on the bedside table. Her baby Glock. She felt almost faint leaving the gun behind, but she didn't want to risk a replay of Africa. The riverbank.

Now she lay prone in a thicket of palmetto, glassing the property. She swept the stilt-house where the brothers lived, the brick pit where Mighty Mo had been chained. She focused on the barge floating on the creek behind the house, the wire crib full of mismatched crates and birdcages and aquariums. A hive of activity—creatures bobbed and twitched, slithered and paced. Meanwhile, weak yellow light spilled from the windows of the house.

No movement.

Malaya rose and began circling the property, moving through the trees. Slowly, slowly, testing the earth with every step, walking on the outer edges of her bootsoles. She willed all of her weight into her head, away from her feet, trying to touch the ground but barely. A soundless creature, floating through the trees, no more than a wrinkle in the night.

The dock planks hardly groaned, scarcely aware of her weight, and then she was crouching before the corncrib, removing a small can of WD-40 from her fanny pack. She greased the hinges and unhasped the door, swinging it wide without a creak. She stepped inside. A hundred beady eyes surrounded her on every side, shining in the night's dark— hungry little planets drawn into her orbit. She imagined their hearts, sized like seeds or cherries or grapes, beating newly at her presence. She could hear the hopeful scrape of their claws, could smell the taint of their urine and fear.

She began working catches and levers and slides, opening crates. Creatures scurried out, a river of fur and scales and skin that rumbled over her boots, flooding out under the moon. Raccoons and squirrels, marsh rabbits and gophers and a pair of otters. A red fox and a gray fox and a small bobcat that flashed through the door. Malaya thought she could feel the barge rising higher on the water, lightening, as if the creek were rising. She could feel her own spirit lifting, as from the blue belly of the pit, and her hands worked faster, faster, loosing opossums and cottontails into the night. She was nearly finished with the bottom row of crates, the heaviest creatures, when the door of the crib clanged closed behind her, the hard snap of a lock.

She wheeled, throwing her hand to her hip, but no weapon was there. On the far side of the iron-barred door stood the boyish swamper with the sky-blue eyes, holding his bangstick in one hand. A heavy brass padlock hung from the door hasp, still swinging.

"Didn't bring your weapon this time, did you?"

Malaya imagined raising the hard black shape of a pistol, two-handed, superimposing the glowing tritium dots of the night sights over the boy's head. Her hands wouldn't shake.

"If I had, you'd have a third eye already, staring at the moon."

The boy's face was serene.

"But you didn't," he said. "It could mean something."

"Means you're in luck, that's for sure."

"Maybe," he said. "Or maybe you're the one that's lucky."

"How's that?"

"You'd have to live with what you done."

Malaya opened her mouth, but no words came out. She cleared her throat.

"Tell me something," she said. She swept a hand around herself, at the cages and crates. "What the hell is this? What're y'all trying to do out here?"

"To keep the seed alive upon the face of the earth."

Malaya crossed her arms, cocked her head.

"Well, I'm afraid I just don't know what *in the flying fuck* that's supposed to mean."

A slight blush in the boy's cheeks.

"I'm talking about the Flood," he said. "Like with a capital *F*. They say the melting of the ice sheets is accelerating, sea levels rising. Miami and New Orleans under water in fifty years. The sea swimming inland, swallowing up the coast. The Flood."

Malaya sat down in place, cross-legged, and shook her head.

"Fuck," she said, then looked up at him. "Like with a capital *F*."

Anse stared at the fence of the old enclosure along the river, grinding his teeth. Something was wrong. Malaya hadn't shown up for work in three days. She hadn't called or put in her notice or left a note. He'd tried calling—her phone was dead or off. Earlier that day, he'd driven past the motor inn where she rented a room by the week. Her car wasn't there and the motel clerk said he hadn't seen her. For twenty dollars to think harder, the man's answer was still the same.

Anse pushed his hat back, staring at the fence. Creeper vines curled through the chain link and kudzu hung in heavy reefs along the top, hiding the rusty snarls of barbwire. Past that, the King of Savannah roamed under the trees, black-maned, the sunlight rippling across his golden hide. A thing unseen, hard to believe, and true. Anse lifted his thumb to his chest, tracing the triangular scrap in the breast pocket of his shirt, tucked flat over his heart. The clue he'd found at the pool—a trace of the animal pitted against the dogs.

A wolf.

A velvety scrap of flesh just like the one strung from his neck an age ago, in Vietnam, when it was his talisman against the black-sandaled men who haunted the jungle. The ghosts. The Cong. When the ear of the dog could hear the rumor of feet, the whisper of fronds. When the scrap of flesh would tingle at his throat, telling him what secrets it heard, and the men of the patrol would look to this boy, their youngest, who could outspook the Cong. He'd buried that last relic of the war, finally, in a maize field in Africa, alongside the body of a blind lion. He'd buried the ghosts. Buried the hiss of gun barrels through elephant grass, the patter of sandaled feet. But here was another scrap of flesh, singing against his heart. It told him something was wrong. Malaya had missed work. She hadn't called.

He could feel a storm rumbling in his blood. He could hear distant sounds.

Anse slipped the bison shoulder through the old feeding chute, then started back up the drive in his truck. He stopped at the gator pond and got out, looking through the fence. There was the Nile croc, Mighty Mo, cutting a black wake in the scum. Anse looked into the reptilian eyes of the creature—so swampy and ancient—and the wolf-flesh glowed against his heart. He could hear a black tongue of creek water, lapping at the shore, and the thrum of tiny hearts. He could hear a wind rising, moaning through halls of cypress, tugging at beards of moss. He could hear metal skirling through air.

Spinning, spinning, like a staff of power.

He knew where she was.

CHAPTER 21

SKUNK APE

Anse's truck skidded to a halt in front of the raptor barn, the chrome stacks trailing streamers of diesel smoke. The old jockey leapt down from the cab and came marching through the dust he'd raised. He was chewing his bottom lip, cracking his knuckles.

Lope had just removed the eagle's jesses and anklets, her bells and hood. She was free of him, untethered, but he could still sense the invisible wires of connection between them, like the plucked strings of a guitar. Still vibrating. Lope's ditties to the bird had been high and lonesome since Malaya had gone. He knew what the old man was going to ask.

"You still ain't seen her, have you?"

Lope shook his head.

"Not for two, three days."

The old jockey shook his head.

"Something's happened, Lope. And I got an idea what."

Now he cocked his head beneath his bush hat, flashing the hard iron of one eye.

"I need your help, Lope."

Lope nodded. He hung his gauntlet on a nearby hook and told the bird goodbye.

They crossed into the swamp at dusk, pushing eighty through the darkening pines. Fireflies rose like starry vision from the roadsides, bleeding past, and the sun squatted low behind the trees, scorching the cloud-bellies red. They might be rushing toward a giant, distant structure fire—a city burning just over the horizon.

The big truck hopped the joints of small bridges, pushing deeper into the wild. They were beyond the range of cell towers and emergency services now. Before them lay the Okefenokee Swamp, Land of the Trembling Earth. A place where the law grew weak, too short-armed to steer the actions of men.

A pair of heavy rifles rattled in the gun rack of the truck. Lope breathed in, out, willing his heart to settle, to perch calmly in the cage of his ribs. Night fell, the dark trees rumbling past them like so much smoke. They turned onto a perimeter road, then wheeled onto an unpaved track through the swamp.

"I thought nobody was allowed to live in here," said Lope.

Anse chewed his bottom lip like a wad of gum.

"We're right on the border of the park," he said. "Where all the old swampers came when the government pushed them out."

They crossed a dark slither of creek and Anse pulled off onto an old maintenance siding. Malaya's battered sedan flared in their headlights, covered in a three-day layer of tree droppings. The men elbowed open their doors and stepped from the cab. Anse kinked the barrels of his howdah pistol and loaded a pair of heavy cartridges from his shirt pocket. He looked across the seat at Lope, then at the double rifle still hanging in the cab— the same one used to stop a charging lioness those weeks ago. He looked back at Lope.

"You gonna leave that here or what?"

"I didn't know if you, if . . . after what happened."

Anse slung his holster over one shoulder, snugging the big howdah pistol butt-forward against his ribs.

"You can leave it if you want. But where we're going, I advise bringing more than them two gangly-ass arms of yours."

When Lope still hesitated, Anse nodded at the big double rifle.

"Think of it as a steel hose," he said. "That's all. Puts out a certain kind of fire."

Lope swallowed, looked at him. Anse set one hand on his shoulder, squeezed.

"I trust you," he said.

Lope nodded and reached into the cab, unracking the gun.

Malaya lay locked in the corncrib, surrounded by motley stacks of crates and cages and glass terrariums. The moon had risen silver and fat, like the bad nights in Africa when poachers scuttled through the bush. The Okefenokee Swamp croaked and chittered and hissed on every side of her, like life simmering in a pan. She could hear the rasp of claws, the hum of insects. The mosquitoes whined at her ear canals, as if trying to bore into her brain.

Deep in the nights, she'd seen strange lights floating in the trees, pulsing and weaving. *Swamp gas,* she told herself. Only that. She'd heard the crackle of unknown creatures in the woods, circling, and heard strange splashes of creek water, blood-thick, like knife-wounds being made. She'd tried not to think of the pig man or the skunk ape or how very alone she was in this place. How far from help.

Now she heard the clop of rubber boots and saw the angel-faced boy coming down the dock. The first night, she'd nearly gagged at the contents of the metal cafeteria tray he pushed under the door. Piles of worms and insects and dead baby mice, neatly scooped and arranged in various compartments. She'd pushed the tray back.

"You're kidding yourself, you think I'm eating this shit."

The boy sat cross-legged on the dock, his bangstick leaning in the crook of his arm.

"It ain't for you. It's for them." He nodded to the animals around her. "You feed them, I might could get you a plate of our leftover dinner. Fried gator tail."

"I *might* could starve instead."

The boy leaned his head on his staff.

"I believe you'd starve yourself. But the rest of these animals? I doubt it."

Malaya had sighed and looked again at the tray. Around her, the animals were rattling their cages, alive with anticipation. Their eyes beady, bright. *Suppertime.*

"One condition," she said. "I need a name."

"Name?"

Malaya nodded. "Name of whoever set up that big dogfight last week. I'm sure you heard about it on the news."

"We don't believe in television."

"I'm sure you heard about it, no matter what you believe in."

The boy smiled, nodded. He blew into his palm and stuck his hand between the bars.

"Deal."

They settled into a pattern. The boy would sit on the dock, Indian-style, while she fed the animals. She lowered mice by their tails to the snakes and spooned out beetles and worms. She watched the strangely nimble paws of the raccoons, glove-black, as they reached through the wire of their crate, and the scraping claws and nibbling teeth of the other animals. Sometimes she thought she could hear their breathing as one breath, the very swamp quickened with hunger.

The third night, she took the tray and cocked her head at the boy. There was a sweetness to him, how neatly he arranged the food for the animals.

"How come you keep them?" she asked. "Are they like pets?"

"They were my mother's," said the boy. "Before she passed on."

Malaya paused, the first mouse dangling from her fingers.

"I'm sorry for your loss."

"She fed the animals every night. They never went hungry. There was a river prophet up on the Altamaha River said flood times were coming. She said the scientists were saying the same thing, the sea levels was rising every year, inch on inch.

And if the prophets and scientists were in accord, you might ought to listen. Said all these, the snakes and rodents, the slimy things of the swamp, they was the last creatures the rest of the world would save. Said she'd die ere she saw them drowned. We'd make an ark of our own."

"What happened to her?"

The boy blinked again.

"Fire of oh-seven. Bugaboo Swamp Fire, they called it after. Powerline went down west of Waycross, igniting a fire on Sweat Farm Road. Five days later, bolt of lightning in the swamp started a second burn. They converged here in the Okefenokee, biggest wildfire in the history of the state. They say you could smell the smoke as far away as Atlanta, Fort Lauderdale, Mississippi. Astronauts could see it from space. Burned people's eyes, put them in the hospital for asthma."

"I remember it from the news," said Malaya. "They handed out masks for the smoke."

The boy nodded.

"Mama made us tow out the ark first. She wasn't ready to leave just yet. Brother tried to make her, but she wouldn't listen. Last I saw her, she was wearing a wet bandanna tied over her face, spraying down the house with a garden hose. We towed the barge down to the coast, tied it off on a buoy. By the time we came back, the creek was a tunnel of fire, water seemed near to boiling. Mile-high smoke blotting out the sun. The house was steaming like a hot pie—all that water she'd sprayed on the roof and walls—and Mama was gone."

"Gone?"

"We found her body a month later. Quarter mile from the house. Looked like a napalm strike had come down, or the finger of God himself had touched the earth, left a thumbprint there—everything stumped and charred. She was curled up in a ball next to a live animal trap she'd laid. She must of been making sure nothing was caught inside when the fire came."

Malaya realized she was sitting now, listening, the tray of food in her lap.

"Was something trapped in there?"

"Cage was empty. Door unlatched. There's times I'll see a flying squirrel gliding through the trees, stretched out white-bellied like a slice of bread, or I'll see a fox shoot through the scrub, and I'll wonder if that's the bloodline Mama saved. If it was that animal's great-great-gran she let free."

"Maybe she'd want you to let the rest of these go, too."

"I've yet to see a sign."

Malaya looked at the bulwark of cages and crates. The animals that surrounded her, they were emitting a low murmur or hum, a compounded whisper of scrambling paws, darting tongues, swelling ribs. They were breathing all at once. Malaya felt a whelming in her chest, a rising. She leaned toward the boy, her words rolling from her tongue like testament.

"I'm the sign," she said. "It's me." She leaned farther forward. "Don't you see? You caught something you never expected in this cage, something that can speak. *Me.* I've been locked in here three days with the rest of them. Breathing the same air, feeling the same fear. I'm the same as them. And I can tell you this: They'd rather die in a flood than live in a cage. They'd rather burn in a fire. They would rather anything than this."

The boy shifted on his sit bones.

"I don't know," he said. "Brother won't like it."

"Fuck what he likes. He listened when you put that bang-stick to his chest."

The boy shook his head against his staff.

"I lost my temper, is what happened. I shouldn't of done that."

Malaya felt her heart tilt toward this strange boy, nearly a man. His blue eyes, so bright. His white hair and white rubber boots.

"Listen," she said, "you got to stand on your own. You don't now, you never will."

With this, she tilted back her head and inhaled the wretched musk of the cage. It poured down her throat, into her lungs like

a flood, and she rose to her feet. Her hands went to the cage of
the mink. The most vicious of weasels, skinned for the stoles of
women in pearls.

Her hand found the latch.

Lope lay on the far side of the creek, one knee hugging the earth,
the double rifle tucked against his shoulder. The swamp cried
on every side of him, like the pop and scream of burning wood.
He aimed down the iron sights of the gun, watching the barge
across the creek. Inside the corncrib sat Malaya. He could see
her through the warped glass of aquariums, the metal wire of
crates. She sat cross-legged, leaning over a tray in her lap.

Below him, Anse was swimming across the creek, froglike,
a knife between his teeth.

Lope breathed in, out, trying to steady the barrel. He thought
of his raptor perched on his arm. He imagined her calming, her
wings sheathed against her sides. Her head swiveling slowly, her
eyes piercing long miles of woods and fields and sky. The barrel
steadied at the end of his arms. On the far side of the creek,
Malaya stood and turned to one of the head-high crates. To his
amazement, she slipped the latch.

The mink shot from the cage, unfurling like a black whip in the
night, striking Malaya's shoulder before leaping to the ground.
She hardly noticed, bending to unlatch another crate, then another and another. Raccoons leapt bandit-eyed from their cages,
swirling on the floor, followed by opossums and rabbits and
squirrels. An armadillo came rumbling from his pen. A black
racer sped across the floor. A weasel. At her feet, a roiling of bodies, tumbling and wheeling, unsure where to go. They hit the
limits of the place and turned back, crawling over themselves.
Some, by instinct, started to climb. They hugged the trunks of
her legs, her calves and thighs. She could feel them scrambling
up her body, their hearts tapping away.

The boy was standing now, his eyes wide and round and
blue, beholding the strange creation rising before him. A woman

crawling with living beasts, bejeweled with the hot beads of their eyes, flashing with their claws and teeth. She came toward the locked door of the cage, swaying in her armor of scales and fur, a creature risen godlike in the darkness. The boy stepped forward, slack-mouthed, as if caught in a spell. His silver staff, dragged, cut a line in the mildewed planks. He reached out with his free hand and unlocked the door.

Lope watched the girl step from the cage, whelmed with furs and skins. She fell to one knee and the animals burst free of her, skating and slithering from the barge, hurrying back into the creek or swamp. She knelt there, lean and dark, her body cut by claws, blistering with blood. Behind her, Anse rose slimy from the creek, his bare back spreading like a shield. Water streamed from his body. He drew the knife from his teeth.

The boy wheeled, his staff flashing in the night. The pair circled each other, the girl between them.

"Skunk ape," said the boy.

"Meaner," said Anse.

Malaya rose and held out her hands between them. She looked at Anse.

"No," she said. "The boy let me go."

The old jockey's jaw muscles flickered, his teeth grinding, but he slowly nodded, lowering the knife. Now Malaya turned to the boy. She leaned forward and lightly tapped his chest. The boy jolted at her touch, as if freed from a spell. He lowered the bang-stick. Malaya nodded, touching his chest again.

"Mama would be proud."

Now she turned and staggered past Anse, to the end of the dock. Her black shirt was ripped, her skin striped with blood. She eased into the black glass of the creek, as if into healing waters, and disappeared.

CHAPTER 22

KING BULL

They rode home three abreast in Anse's truck, the dark trees tumbling past their windows. Malaya kept nodding off, her head rolling onto one of their shoulders or the other. Leaves stuck to her wounds and wisps of gray-green moss hung in her hair. She might have sprung from the black muck of the swamp itself, rising through the deep roots of mangroves and cypress knees, seeking light. She smelled of the cage. An animal musk, sour and wild and old. Where she touched the men, their shoulders and collarbones glowed.

The big diesel rumbled under the hood, a lulling thunder, and the cabin was dim, lit only by the tiny lights of the dashboard, the steady needles. The old highway speared into the darkness, leading them out of the swamp. A jetliner blinked slowly across the sky. A whitetail doe floated at the roadside, pale as a specter in the headlights.

Malaya began to snore.

The two men looked at each other. Neither spoke.

They emerged onto the old coastal highway, turning for home. Traffic was scarce. The odd sedan or pulpwood truck flared twin-eyed from the darkness and bleared across the windshield, then vanished red-tailed into the night. They drove past the old

zombie neighborhoods, drowning in weeds, and passed Little
Eden itself, where the entrance yawned red-mouthed in the
night. Now came the bridge over the Satilla River and the highway descended through rows of storefronts, brick-built with
dusty windows and sagging awnings. The mural on the side of
one building flared in the headlights. A riverboat smoking at the
dock, surrounded by horse-drawn coaches and ladies in white.
Now they passed the barbecue joint and biker bar. Now the rows
of disused logwood trucks, hoodless with rusting engines.

Soon they were in Kingsland, adjacent to the Kings Bay
Naval Submarine Base, home of the Atlantic Fleet's nuclear
missile subs. As a girl, Malaya had come here with her grandfather, staying at the veterans lodge. She'd told them of long
days on the water with the old man, setting trotlines and casting bread for gulls. Tea-colored creeks and white riverbanks
and swallow-tailed kites—rare raptors, black and white, which
wheeled and darted over the water like acrobats.

No wonder she would come here after returning from overseas.

They turned in to the King's Suites, a faded motor inn offering weekly rates. The few cars that dotted the place looked
desperate, rife with balding tires and plastic bags taped over
broken windows. The hollow-core door to Malaya's room was
slightly warped, clad in a damp sheen. They found her keys in
the fanny pack she wore, wrapped in grip tape to prevent them
from jingling. Anse had to use his shoulder to open the swollen
door, which caved slightly before popping wide. They yoked
Malaya between them, each taking an arm, carrying her sideways
across the threshold into the musty room. She seemed heavy
beyond her weight.

The bedspreads were beige, a quilted synthetic that felt damp.
The whole room felt wet, as if coated in a cold sweat, sickly and
nervous. The wall unit was rattling away, set on sixty-five, the
windows clouded with condensation.

They laid her on the bed farthest from the stripes of amber-
orange light that blasted through the blinds—shot from the all-

night security lamp in the parking lot. They looked around, squinting in the dimness. The room was neatly squared, as if for inspection. No mark of dust, nothing out of place. Clothes hung in the doorless closet, neatly spaced, over a row of shoes set in ascending order of height, flats to wedges to boots. The beds had been planed flat by practiced hands, the bedside books stacked just so. No toothbrush or mouthwash or hair iron beside the sink—only a single canvas Dopp kit, OD green, the last name ANGON stenciled on the side. A roach crawled along the baseboard.

Malaya lay on her back on the bed, breathing heavily through her nose.

Lope rubbed his chin with two fingers and a thumb, looking at the room.

"Can we leave her here?"

Anse chewed his bottom lip.

"It ain't killed her yet."

"Those scratches she got, they could infect. Maybe we should call Tyler, have her look at them?"

Anse shook his head.

"She don't know anything about this."

Lope frowned.

"What is *this,* exactly? It about what you got hid in that old enclosure along the river?"

Anse's collarbones lifted, fell. A man readying himself, finding the air for his confession. But when he opened his mouth, Malaya's hand shot from the bed and clapped his wrist.

Both men froze, eyes wide.

"Please," she said. *"Find them."*

They sat in a pair of white plastic chairs outside her room, watching the erratic orbit of moths around the security light. The bugs were pale in the night, frantic, swirling about the amber bulb. The old jockey got out his pack of cigarettes and offered one up. Lope hadn't smoked since the day he entered the fire academy.

"Fuck it." He took one.

Anse lit his cigarette and passed the lighter. An old Zippo, nicked and scarred, like the kind Lope once kept in the box beneath his bed.

The old jockey's nostrils flared, puffing smoke.

"These drones you got, can you mount cameras on them?"

Lope lit the cigarette, feeling the tickling blue burn in his throat. There was the urge to cough, but he quelled his twitchy lungs—easy compared to the nervous wings of an eagle.

Autonomic control.

"Cameras," he said. "Sure."

"Live feed?"

"No problem."

"What about thermal?"

"Sure. Hog-hunters use them all the time. All it takes is money."

The older man leaned to one side, scrunching an eye, and extracted an ancient trifold wallet from his back pocket. It was thick as a textbook, the leather ravaged and chewed. He spread it across his lap and hunted through the credit cards, finally sliding one free and holding it out to Lope.

"Billing address is the same as the sanctuary," he said.

"Could get expensive, Anse."

"Whatever it takes."

Lope took the card, then looked seaward. Out there, not too distant, lay a fleet of American submarines, each more than five hundred feet long, skinned in black steel and carrying enough nuclear warheads to end the age of man. He looked back to Anse.

"What are we looking for?" he asked.

"Wolves."

A week later, they parked beneath a causeway bridge outside of Savannah. An ancient dock, storm-shredded, was toppling back into the water and a pair of aboveground gasoline tanks sat rusting in the trees, empty for decades. Upriver stood the vari-colored shipping containers of the Port of Savannah, stacked like

Lego ramparts along the shoreline, craned day and night from transoceanic ships.

They launched the drone from the bed of the pickup, watching the tiny rotorcraft disappear into the night. Lope hunched over the controller in his lap, thumbing the joysticks, squinting into the tablet mounted on top. The screen displayed a bird's-eye view of the world, delivered in the gray scale of thermal energy. Heat burned white, the hotter the brighter. Anse and Malaya leaned in from either side, watching the screen.

The place was a quarter mile away, located on a tiny speck of land called Tadpole Spit. Malaya had come out of the swamp with the name of the place. Her intention all along, she said. *Actionable intelligence.* According to the boy-swamper, the coast's king breeder of fighting dogs lived here.

They could see the dark creeks that squiggled and branched through the marsh, feeding the tide. A bird seared across the screen, wings spread. Now a spit of land slid into view, just big enough for a house and yard. It was built from the spoil of a dredging operation, a roundish plot of high ground connected to the mainland by the thinnest string of a road, forming a tadpole shape. They could see the dark rectangle of a doublewide house, elevated on concrete blocks, and a narrow dock that led to a nearby creek and twin-engine boat. A large pickup truck sat in the drive. Now they saw the dogs, a ragged pack of them chained behind the house, their bodies glowing white-hot beneath the eye of the drone. Each was staked just out of reach of his neighbor, with a 55-gallon oil drum for a doghouse.

"Can you bring us down to one?" asked Anse.

Lope nodded and the drone descended toward the dog at the center of the pack, a heavy brute with a beer-keg chest and lean hips. At his widest, he was nearly the size of the steel oil drum behind him. His name was torch-cut into the top of the barrel: KING BULL.

The quadcopter descended closer, closer. The dog's ears were battle-cropped, shorn to tiny spikes against his skull. They snapped erect, quivering like antennae, and the animal began turning in place, puffing his chest this way and that, expecting his enemy to come from the dirt. The drone was nearly on top of him before he looked straight up. His head was heavy and square, wide as a cinderblock, his shoulders rocky as a weightlifter's. He cocked his head, his face crisscrossed with dark scars. Perhaps he saw a strange dragonfly hovering over him. His monstrous mouth fell into a wide, sloppy grin. His tongue flopped out.

Anse leaned over Lope's shoulder, squinting at the dog. He thumbed the chest pocket of his shirt.

"Bingo, motherfucker."

Lope looked up from the screen.

"What should we do?"

Anse chewed his bottom lip.

"It's too damn many to take them all in. Reckon we'll have to call the police."

"Hold on," said Malaya. "Owner might could tell us something."

"Like what?"

"Like where he got that wolf he baited, for starters."

Anse nodded, pressing his thumb against his chest pocket. "True."

Lope ascended to two hundred feet, watching the pair of them scurry up the narrow causeway toward the house. They moved in echelon, white ghosts of heat in the night. They were wearing masks and gloves and carrying shotguns from the truck's toolbox. They'd cut through the marsh to slip the security cameras at the main road and stepped over the pneumatic tube detectors stretched across the drive, intended to alert the house of approaching vehicles.

Now they approached the gate at the front of the property. Lope's heart banged hard in his chest, as if keeping him airborne. He watched them cut the padlock and slip through the gate, one after the next, then scamper toward the truck in the front yard, crouching behind the rear fender. Here they were squatted, making hand signals to each other, when a red thunderbolt began to blink in the corner of Lope's display.

"Damn."

The drone had only twenty minutes of flight time. He hovered overhead as long as he could. They were creeping toward the house, crouched low, when he hit the HOME button, calling the drone back to the truck.

Lope waited, staring across the marsh and pines. He had the windows down and the marsh bellowed and barked around him. The night seemed louder than normal. Closer. Malaya and Anse had been gone nearly thirty minutes now. He was worried what might happen. He was not accustomed to sitting in the truck. He was used to breaching doors and hauling in hoses.

He leaned his head back on the seat, thinking of the hunters of the Kazakh steppes—*bird lords*—men who rode aback stout winter ponies with eagles on their fists. They climbed mountain cliffs to capture their eaglets and hand-raised them to adulthood, raptors so large they could blot the sun from a man's shoulders. They flew their eagles against hares and foxes, even wolves. Lope pictured himself clad in the fur of a Tibetan wolf, saddled on a horse whose breath smoked in the night, an eagle on his fist. Bird lord. He pictured his raptor beaming down from the darkness, laserlike, cutting loose the dogs. He could see King Bull trotting through the country midnight, slop-tongued and jaunty, following his scarred nose.

But that was only a dream, he knew. Such a dog would be a trespasser wherever he went. He would always be stopping at the edges of fields and roads and yards, raising his head, ears spiked, alert for barks, screams, shots. Listening, listening, as Lope was now.

They returned after forty-five minutes, jogging out of the darkness, their guns angled high across their chests. They were breathing hard as they climbed into the cab. When they pulled their masks to their foreheads, their faces were bright with sweat, like firefighters just emerged from a burning house. Lope looked from one to the other, waiting.

"Well, how'd it go?"

Anse tucked his mask into his pocket.

"Better for us than him."

"You find out anything?"

"There's some ex-cage-fighter, apparently, raises wolf dogs."

"Where at?"

Anse shook his head, showing his teeth.

"Some island. Couldn't get it straight."

"You called the police yet?"

"Waiting till we got back here."

When the old jockey reached for the ignition, Lope saw the cuff of his shirt.

"Is that blood?"

Anse cranked the truck.

"Better call from a pay phone."

They parked beneath the shot-out light of a gas station several miles down the road. The place had iron grilles over the windows and neon beer signs. Through the windshield, Lope watched the old jockey lean against the side of a battered pay phone, the receiver wedged between ear and shoulder, his face shadowed beneath the brim of his bush hat.

"What happened back there?" he asked.

Malaya leaned her head back on the seat.

"We didn't feed him to the dogs, if that's what you're thinking."

"Well, that's a relief."

"You sure you want to know?"

"Don't I?"

"It's . . . awkward."

"Awkward?"

Malaya crossed her arms.

"You asked for it," she said. "So, we come up on the house and check through the windows first, right? See what we can see.

Den is the only room with a light on. Dude is sitting there in his La-Z-Boy, kicked back, eyes mashed shut. And he's just going to town."

"Town?"

"Pants down," said Malaya. "Like he was gonna rub a genie out the damn thing."

"Oh, Jesus," said Lope.

Malaya shook her head.

"Right? I don't reckon he thought the genie would look like us."

"No," said Lope. "I reckon not."

"'Least we knew he didn't expect us. We come through the door and he jumps about five feet from the chair. I thought his head would go through the ceiling. He lands, trips in his own pants, goes flat-face on the floor. We cuff him. Anse goes to clear the rest of the house while I watch the guy, and that's when I recognize him. He's got this long-ass beard, like ZZ Top or somebody. Waist-length, nearly. I realize I saw him in the grocery parking lot a few weeks back, he was buying something in a dog crate."

Malaya cracked her knuckles.

"About that time Anse calls me into the back bedroom. There's one of those dog treadmills back there, has a live marsh rabbit in a cage like a lure. Canine tactical vests hanging from the walls. Chains and sleds and weights, like some kind of dungeon gym. Pill bottles, syringes, veterinary tools."

She shook her head.

"We go back to our man on the floor and start asking questions. Asking about the bait and where he got the wolf from and what he knows about anybody on the coast breeding big cats or selling them for their parts. Instead he just keeps telling us he's got the right to do whatever he wants with his dogs. Breed 'em, pit 'em, bury 'em. Says he's got dominion over the beasts of the field. *DOUGH-min-YAWN.* That's what he says. You can tell this ain't the first time he's been pushing this particular piece of rope. He isn't even hearing our questions, let alone answering them."

Lope's mind flashed to the bloody cuff of Anse's shirt.

"What did you do?"

Anse's door swung open and he climbed back into the cab, settling himself behind the wheel. He looked at them, one hand smoothing the chest pocket of his shirt.

"I asked him whether he paid a couple hundred bucks for King Bull and the rest of those poor sons-of-bitches to have their ears battle-cropped by a licensed veterinary professional, or if he used that ear brace and set of shears I found in the back bedroom."

The old jockey put the truck in reverse and slung his arm along the back of the seat, revealing the blood on his sleeve.

"Wrong answer," he said.

They drove south along the coast, heading home. They were ten minutes out from the gas station when a string of police cruisers came curling around a bend, wailing and flashing between the trees. They blasted past, headed to Tadpole Spit, where they would find the owner of the kennel bound and gagged in a twelve-by-twelve dogfight pit, missing the tip of an earlobe. They hadn't been able to get a warrant to search the place. Now they wouldn't need one.

Anse shrugged.

"Just a nip," he said. "Had him a little gold earring he got to keep."

Lope looked at Malaya, but she was staring out her window, watching the night roll past. Lost in thought. They jolted over the short bridges of the coastal highway, crossing tidal creeks and salt marshes and the dark mouths of rivers. Now and again, Lope sighted the chain of barrier islands strung along the coast like a blockade. Rumor was, the cage-fighter kept more than wolves on his island. The dogman had heard tell of tigers.

Lope shook his head and leaned back against the bench seat. He felt wearied, emptied out. Sleep fell over him, slowing his blood. His body grew heavy, his thoughts roved. Soon he was drifting, rising through the roof of the cab and spreading his arms, lifting into the night. He was high over the coast, kiting against the stars, reading the white language of heat across the earth. The pulp and paper mills smoldered from the pines. The barrier islands lay like giant ships anchored just offshore— some dark, some aglow with souls.

Lope woke as the truck rocked down from the highway, crackling across the gravel lot of the sanctuary. He wiped the corner of his mouth and sat up, blinking at the dashboard clock. Past midnight.

"Was I snoring?"

"You slept like a babe," said Anse. He threw a thumb toward Malaya. "That one there was the freight train."

She was just coming awake, stretching and yawning in her seat. She grinned.

"Choo, choo, motherfucker."

Anse drove toward the main entrance. The headlights illuminated the roaring mouth of the lion, the long fangs. The visage grew before them, as if they would drive right down the red throat, swallowed whole into the belly of the place. They were nearly to the curb when Anse stabbed the brakes, throwing them hard against their seatbelts. Dust rose before them, whirling from the skidded tires.

"What?"

Anse pointed over the wheel.

There, on the lion's tongue, lay the glittering wreckage of the entrance doors, the shards of glass gleaming like shattered teeth.

BOOK V

CHAPTER 23

EDEN

Mosi looks out across the river. Birds stand slender and white from the golden savannah of marsh grass. Seahawks slash from the sky, tearing fish from the water, while alligators bask on the riverbank, heavy with pride. Now and again they bellow across the river, defiant, or slide into the black water to hunt.

Mosi has sensed other beasts here, too—creatures that remind him of home. Yesterday he heard the hoots of the silver monkey, and the wind has brought him traces of lesser cats, too—lone hunters who rely on speed and stealth. He's caught the scent of a leopardess—she who snipes her prey from the tall grass and drags her kills into the trees, protecting them from the hyena and wild dog. Mosi has even heard the gut-rumbles of an elephant—the only beast of Eden he would rather avoid.

Most often he hears the two-footed gait of a man, along with the heavy tread of the machine that carries him. Mosi studied these machines during his time in the iron cage, watching them race along the hard tar of their migratory route, season after season, colliding every so often in a screaming tangle of fire that brought wails and whirling red lights. Mosi relished these clashes, for sometimes they delivered the scent of fresh kill on the wind, fresher than any tasted inside the bars of his cage. He would stand open-jawed, tasting the dream-flesh of deer and men.

That cage had been the least of his homes. He felt naked beneath the ever-present eyes of men. The gold of his coat felt tarnished, his hide too thin. His mane so heavy he could hardly rise. There was no night in that place, no stars—only the endless glare of white light, which bleached his vision, and he could no longer see the black cloak come curling around the shoulders of the doomed.

When darkness came, Mosi never expected to be reborn along such a river, in a realm so vast. There are no flashbulbs or iron bars or chattering children here—only the long wall of tangled vines and the woven wire of the fence along the river. The man on the other side of the wall, he's different from the others Mosi has known. He remains unseen, delivering shanks of bison or cattle at dusk, when Mosi grows hungriest, longing for hoof-flesh. He's unlike the man they called Winter, who would stand just outside Mosi's cage—just beyond reach of his claws—and spread his arms to accept the flashes and smiles of his pride. How Mosi longed to slice his round belly and gorge on his entrails, rising red-chinned to roar.

But this man on the other side of the vine-wall—he's only a sound, a scent, like the unseen force that springs green shoots of grass from the earth or splinters the sky with light, spearing the parched lands with rain. Like the wind, which asks nothing for delivering the scent of prey to his nose, or the trees, whose leaves feed the antelope he loves.

Mosi lies at the woven wire of the fence, listening to the whisper and chirp of his new world, the flutter and hum. He hears squirrels scraping along pine bark, doves whistling to flight. The *knock-a-knock* of a woodpecker. The river lazes beneath him, bright beneath the sun, and now a new scent touches the pink of his nose. His senses come awake, his ears swiveling. His heart floods the coat of muscle that powers his bones.

There is a deer in these woods, a meal fit for a king.

Horn drove south along the old coastal highway, crossing creeks that jagged darkly through the marshes. The outriggers of shrimp boats swung past, their nets like rotten sails. He passed the hulks of one-story motor inns, gaped windowless and tangled in kudzu, and rotten roadside stands that once sold paper sacks of boiled peanuts and fresh shrimp from Styrofoam coolers. PEENUTS. SRIMP. He passed once-famed fish diners where rats now scurried along the counters, braiding the dust, and warped trailers with cars beached hoodless in their yards. The interstate lay farther inland, where fast-food restaurants and truck stops shone stadium-bright in the dusk, each emblem thrust higher than the next.

This wild coast seemed to him a glimpse of the world to come. Horn believed—even hoped—that the First World of Man would collapse. The icecaps were melting, the seas rising, the hurricanes coming harder and faster every year. As if the very earth were spinning faster, hotter, raked with solar flares and radiation. A man on the coast could feel it. He'd ridden out storm after storm, the highways directing eight lanes of traffic inland while hurricanes the size of small nations came wheeling ashore, toppling trees and powerlines, throwing boats into high branches and sucking whole islands into the sea. The storms would not stop, nor the pipelines or pumpjacks or births of sucking mouths. The cities of men would be flooded and choked, their fuel burned up. Their water grown toxic. They would be forced to hide again in caves, afraid of the darkness they'd worked for ages to dispel. They would have to kill to eat. Their fears would no longer be vague illnesses and anxieties—they would have claws and teeth.

Thousands of lions and tigers and leopards, loosed from their cages, would race like wildfire across the Americas, rewilding the concrete jungles of cityscapes and the long migration paths of superhighways, hunting the children of men. They would interbreed in the wild, spawning whole new bloodlines of apex cats. Thousand-pound hybrids, mighty as the saber-tooth cats of prehistory. Already the grizzly bear was moving north with the melting ice, breeding with the polar bear, springing white-coated giants with brown paws. *Grolars.* Meanwhile the eastern wolf, decimated by overhunting, was mating with the western coyote. *Coywolves* and *woyotes* were spreading fast across North America, migrating along railroad tracks and greenways, filtering their way into suburbs and city parks. Living among man. The narwhal and beluga were coupling, too. Various species of seals. The continents were shrinking, the seas lapping higher and warmer at their shores.

Horn shook his head. He would be in the high mountains of the West, far from flooded coasts and urban tragedies. Alone against the cataclysms of an ending age. He would be with his pack, his wolves safe beneath the strength of their alpha. His ties to men finally cut. His transformation complete.

Mosi feels the moonlight slinking over the vast country of his body, the craggy mountains of his shoulders and the sharp ridge of his spine, the golden steppes of his sides. He is but a whisper through the pines now, despite his size. He has circled the deer, trapping her against the river. The night silences itself before his presence. The opossums and raccoons stand motionless, watching the beast cruise past them, and the barred owl no longer hoots. Even the frogs fall silent, sensing his presence through the thin tympana of their skin.

Mosi aligns himself behind the trunk of an old pine, arrowing his body toward his prey. The deer, if she looked, would only see one of his eyes edging from behind the tree, floating in the black shadow of his mane. The moonlight falls broken through the overhanging branches, the silver shards of light magnified beneath his gaze. Burning. A vast twilight. The leaves float purple before him, trembling, and Mosi stalks closer, closer, his spine snaking soundless through the brush.

He watches from across a palmetto thicket. She is a white-tail doe, alone, tawny and delicate. She dips her head, eating some leafy thing. He sees her nose so black and small, the pink dart of her tongue. The squirm of her chewing mouth. He studies her high haunches and tapered legs and the fine black hooves that bounce her weightless across the earth. Her high ears, big as little wings, and her pale underbelly, as if she's lain in snow. Her eyes, so round and unknowing.

Mosi's mouth hangs open. His breath burns across his tongue. His blood is alive, risen hard and angular beneath his hide. He has never wanted something so much in his life. He will snap her neck between his jaws, snuffing the light from her eyes, then tear her limb from limb, burying his face in the hot gore of her belly. He will consume her, heart and bone, leaving nothing for the worms and crows. Now she lifts her head, alert, and Mosi sees a pair of shadow-antlers rise gnarled and spiked from the smooth cast of her skull. A black crown of death.

He pounces.

Horn drove through a dark canyon of pines. His van was from the 1980s, outfitted with four-wheel drive and heavy tires and a three-hundred-channel police scanner mounted under the dashboard. The rear seats were gone, replaced with a wildlife litter that could be winched into the cargo hold. A built-in locker held heavy leather gauntlets and telescoping capture nooses, dart guns and ampules of sedative stolen from rural veterinary clinics.

The moon had risen skull-bright from the trees, waxing, and Horn could feel the swell of power, the rising of blood. Beasts would soon be waking across the land, chewing through leashes or ripping off neckties. Emergency room nurses would dread their shifts. Children, unable to sleep, would notice strange silver gleams in the eyes of their stuffed animals, and wives would find their husbands in the garage, sharpening lawn shears or cleaning their grandfather's guns.

Lunacy. The mad blood stirring beneath the moon.

Horn's wolves would be as ravening demons, howling in their cages, and he would long to howl beside them. Surely his ancestors had squatted in the high branches of giant trees, clad in animal skins, and jabbed their spears at the moon, howling with the dire wolves.

The silver light crept up his arms, revealing the bandage taped over one forearm. The work of Onyx, his beta wolf, who'd struck for dominance that morning. It was just past dawn and Horn was feeding his pack fresh strips of venison from a road-killed deer. For days, the beta wolf had been watching him side-wise, reading his master for any sign of weakness. Any limp or favored joint. Any show of fear. Horn didn't blame him. He loved Onyx for the black dart of his spirit, ever testing the world, seeing what might bleed. Still, Horn's love was hard.

The wolves had whirled about him that morning, waiting to be fed. A dark whirlwind of desire. Onyx was among them, smile-mouthed as any, and this was his mistake. So often the beta wolf stood apart, waiting, as if fighting for food were beneath him. Horn held out a red rag of backstrap, the tenderest of cuts. He knew what was coming. The wolf lunged not for the meat but his master's throat.

Horn reacted without thought, his instincts honed for years in dojos and cages. He thrust his forearm into the flying jaws of the wolf and fell neatly onto his back, pulling the animal into the trap of his open knees. He wrapped his legs around the wolf's torso, cross-hooking his feet. They lay this way a long moment, chest to chest, like mates or lovers. Then Horn torqued the wolf squealing to the ground and rolled on top of him, reversing po-sition, pinning the beast belly up, his free arm driven hard against its throat. There they lay, man over wolf, the beast's breath coming wet and ragged. Horn stared into the fierce gold of the creature's eyes, unblinking, crushing the wind from his throat. His veins stood quivering over the hard burls and ridges of his body. The words on his skin shone with sweat.

Arch type of ravin.
Six hundred pounds of sin.
Beast of waste and desolation.

He would stare down the beast until it yielded, or else. Slowly, the fierce sparks in the creature's eyes began to dull, even soften, the life dying out in those dark worlds, death rolling in like a fog. The other wolves stood in a ring, watching, their tongues hanging red. Some whined with anxiety or growled, as if urging one champion or the other. Onyx's eyes were white-rimmed with fear now, but he did not let up. His jaws were locked, his lungs choked with death-fire. His hind legs scrabbled uselessly at the man's rump, his paws unable to gain purchase or leverage. Horn gave no words of encouragement. He simply stared, spearing his dominance into the yellow eyes. If the animal could not live as beta of the pack, it would die.

Horn saw the shift in the wolf's eyes, the precise instant of release. They broke from their spell of power, the pupils widening, like tunnels accepting light. They diffused into a haze of submission, even love. The animal's body went slack, as if releasing its spirit, and Horn watched the teeth unsheathe from his flesh, his arm bubbling with blood.

If the wolf were a man, it would live under the shame of defeat. Not the wolf. Onyx began licking the wounds of his god, which his own teeth had made.

Horn cut the headlights five hundred yards short of the sanctuary and killed the engine, letting the van coast between the trees. He'd been watching the place for weeks—glassing the property from the high branches of neighboring trees, noting the workings of the place, recording the habits of the animals and their keepers. He'd even installed cellular trail cams at various points, which tracked the comings and goings of the staff.

The van slowed to a crawl and the tires crackled into the gravel and Horn wheeled the machine into a lightless corner of the lot. The owner's truck was gone, as he knew it would be. The jaws of the place yawned wide in the night, the lion's fangs waiting. Horn slung his pack over one shoulder and headed for the throat.

Mosi lies at the fence along the river, feasting. The doe is spread flimsy-necked before him, one black eye reflecting the stars. Her long legs are crisscrossed to one side.

She went rigid when he pounced, too startled to flee. Mosi sank his teeth into her neck and slung her to the ground, crushing her throat. He's torn away swathes of her silver-brown hide, revealing the red luster of her meat. Now he buries his face between her ribs. Her blood, still hot, covers his cheeks and chin and tongue. Her bones crack between his teeth. He looks across the river, where the alligators and seahawks must watch him eat.

He is king.

Mosi bends again to his meal, scraping a thigh bone with the pink rasp of his tongue. It gleams beneath him, slick and white. The wind moves through the trees, purring through the needles and fronds. A new scent comes skulking beneath his nose. A creature sharp-shouldered, ravenous.

Mosi's nostrils flare.

Wolf.

His ire rises. This kill is his. No rout of wolves will steal his meat.

Mosi lifts his bloodied face to the moon.

He roars.

CHAPTER 24

TIGER LADY

Tyler came fast awake, sitting upright in the snarled sheets of Anse's bed. A roar was echoing in the chambers of her heart. She swiveled and set her bare feet on the floor, hanging her head over her knees. Her chest was heaving.

She'd been dreaming of Anse. They were standing on a beach at dawn, their sleeping bags crumpled behind them in the dunes. The rising sun shone on the ravaged flesh of Anse's torso. A land of fissure and striation, carved as if by storm and hoof. She saw the hard little cobbles of his stomach, which spread and converged with his breath, and the bluish rivers that branched down his arms. The scars from bullets or claws or teeth. He turned slightly, letting the dawn-light lick farther across his flesh, and Tyler gasped. An angry scar lay in the hollow of his sternum. Like a surgical wound but rougher, meaner, risen from a dark storm of bruise.

Anse was turning toward the sea, the crashing waves. Toward the east, where so much of his history lay, that ghostly country of jungles and velds.

Just going for a swim, he said.

Tyler wanted to tell him to wait, but no words would come. He turned fully toward the ocean, revealing the ragged chevron of scars in his back, as if someone had ripped out the roots of wings or plastered over a set of gills. She worried he would not come back from the swim. That he would drown in a riptide or undertow. The sound that rose from her throat was not a word but a roar, and she woke upright in bed, heaving.

She stood now, naked in the dark room. Alone. Anse was gone—one of his midnight drives that could last until dawn. Tyler swung open the door of the trailer and stepped onto the stoop. Fall was coming. The cool edge of the night pressed against her skin. She stood there wondering whether the roar was hers. Whether it came from inside her or out. Finally she stepped down from the stoop and walked into the night.

Malaya jumped down from the truck, shotgun in hand, and approached the lion's mouth of the entrance. Anse was close behind. They posted themselves on either side of the shattered doors, their chests heaving. The old jockey jammed his bush hat harder on his head and eased open the breech of his shotgun, checking for a chambered round. Then he ducked through the door. Malaya followed him down the darkened hallway, her weapon held high over the squeak of her boots. They spread out in the gift shop, scanning the T-shirt racks and display cases for intruders. The skulls stared back at them from their shelves and pedestals, hollow-eyed.

Nothing.

Lope appeared from the hallway with one of the elephant rifles. The three of them looked at one another, eyes wide in the dark. The cash register was untouched, the merchandise.

If the intruder didn't come for that . . .

Together, they turned to face the big windows that looked onto the sanctuary grounds.

The door was ajar.

"You want me to launch the drone?" asked Lope.

Then they saw it: a flicker of stripes in the darkness.

"Tyler," croaked Anse. He was through the door before they could stop him.

Tyler walked down the drive between enclosures. The woods were growing paler as the season turned, thinner, and sound traveled farther through the trees. Spanish moss seeped silver from the oaks. The firefly larvae were out, wingless and earthbound. The bulbs of luciferin in their tails emitted a cool, bluish-white glow, like stars scattered through the grass.

Other lights hovered in the night, bodiless, blooming from deep tangles of brush or the high limbs of trees. The eyes of servals, ocelots, tigers. Their iridescent interiors reflected even the dimmest scraps of light onto their retinas, maximizing their night vision. Tyler wondered how she might glow for them, her skin near phosphorescent under the moon.

She found herself standing before the enclosure of the black leopard. Midnight. A sign hung from the hurricane fence, which explained that the black panther was not a distinct species but the melanistic variant of the leopard or jaguar. Midnight was the former: *Panthera pardus.* Tyler had typed up the language herself. Now she squinted, searching for the green eyeshine of the felid. Anse said the state wildlife commission had found her in the backyard menagerie of a suspected wildlife smuggler. He said they'd called him, needing a home for the animal. The story felt suspicious to her, though she couldn't say why.

Tyler stepped closer to the fence, hooking her fingers in the links. Closer than visitors or staff were allowed. She squinted. It had always been this way with Anse. There were whole secret worlds inside him. Memories hidden in the flicker of his jaws, the bite of his lip, the grind of his teeth. She trusted him—always had—but it hurt to be outside his skin, unable to know the dark country of his interior. The tongue was too small a bridge, too hardly used. Perhaps she was being paranoid, even jealous. But she *knew.*

She'd never believed in supernatural phenomena—didn't need to. She knew the powers of nature were uncanny, underestimated, scarcely understood. There were the thousand-mile songs of the humpback whale, heard from sea to sea on naval anti-submarine systems, and dogs that could detect, hours in advance, the onset of seizures and strokes. Acacia trees whose leaves, when chewed, released a warning gas that drifted from tree to tree, triggering the production of leaf tannins lethal to antelope and other browsers. *Hormonal sentience.* African elephants that could detect rainstorms from one hundred miles away, sensing the thunder's vibration in the earth, and Amur tigers capable of premeditated vengeance, tracking down and assassinating poachers. Tyler could even give cautious credence to various premonitions of her own species—intimations of doom or bliss too subtle for clipboards or electrodes.

When no leopard came slinking from the darkness, Tyler turned and started walking again, striking deeper into the sanctuary, toward the unseen glow of the river.

The loose tigers cut back and forth before Anse, their faces bobbing in the darkness. It was the former circus tigers, Snow and Fire, released or escaped from their enclosure, prowling the sanctuary grounds. Their eyes never deviated from the man before them, despite their switchbacking bodies, the restless whip of their tails.

"Anse!" hissed Malaya.

She was crouched on the back deck of the sanctuary, Lope beside her. Their guns were leveled on the rail, their barrels tracking the crisscrossing tigers.

"Anse!"

The old jockey was standing in the middle of the sanctuary grounds, arms wide, speaking to the animals. Comforting them. He paid no attention to the scream of the monkeys or the foot-thunder of the elephant or the pleas of his own species. He seemed entranced, caught in the tigers' spell.

Lope thumbed the sweat from one eye, looking down the sights of his rifle.

"Don't make me do it again," he whispered. "Please, old man."

Anse didn't seem to hear. His voice was low and kind, floating like a lullaby on the night air, but his big howdah pistol was out, the twin hammers cocked. Malaya saw Lope inhale beside her, deep and slow, his chest rising toward his chin. He exhaled slowly, a faint whistle through his lips. Then closed his eyes, opened them. The man seemed changed, calmed. He rose and leaned his rifle against the rail and stepped down from the deck.

"Lope," said Malaya. "Lope!"

The tall man walked straight toward the old jockey. The tigers were turning tighter circles now, agitated, their stripes flickering in the night, Anse standing spread-armed before them. Lope came to stand beside him, touching the smaller man on the shoulder. Anse jumped at the touch, turning to look.

"There's blood on their chins," he said.

"We left out meat to thaw," said Lope.

"You sure?"

"I'm sure," said Lope. "Come on now, we'll corral them with the buggy."

He tugged Anse's shoulder and the old man relented. Malaya covered them as they backed their way toward the deck— slowly, so as not to trigger the tigers' reflexes. They reached the steps and Anse looked up beneath the round brim of his hat. His eyes were wide, boylike, and the big howdah pistol hung forgotten at his side.

"Where is she?" he asked.

Then they heard the scream.

Tyler walked toward the river, stepping carefully among the tiny blue bulbs of firefly larvae, dim constellations under her feet. Next summer, the survivors would rise on newly sprouted wings, blinking in the dusk. She passed the enclosure of Snow and Fire—her favorites. They rose to approach the fence, chuffing at her presence, but she couldn't stop. She was being pulled toward the river, as if the current bore its own gravity, an invisible thrall. She walked past the fenced pond of the crocodile, Mighty Mo, then passed beneath the last amber security light of the sanctuary, where moths fluttered and pulsed. She strode on, the path lit only by the moon.

Before her loomed the old enclosure along the river. The chain-link fence was swarmed with vines and kudzu, solid as the wall of a hedge maze, the topmost leaves shining like shattered glass. She knew Anse came sometimes in the evenings to visit Henrietta's grave. Once or twice she'd seen bloody chunks of meat in his truck, offerings perhaps to her ghost. She imagined the door of the old enclosure would groan wide beneath her hands, the rust-seized hinges giving way.

She stopped short.

A brass padlock hung from a length of heavy chain, securing the gate. That was strange. She knew of no reason to keep the enclosure locked. No chains could hold back the memories buried along the river. The wind moved through the trees, and the dream-roar echoed again in her chest. The larvae glowed and the river still called. The night felt newly alive, sentient. The throb of blood in darkness.

Tyler walked along the fence until she found the old feeding chute. She touched the lower edge of the pipe, then held her hand to her face.

Blood.

Fear jolted her, sure as a shot. She was not alone. There was something back here, kept from her. She stalked along the fence, looking for an opening in the mass of vines. Here was one. A single diamond of chain link. She bent to the spyhole, squinting through the wall of vines, searching for a shadow of movement, a secret in the night.

She leaned closer, head cocked, her breath rattling the vines. Leaves tickled her chin. She was about to look away when a bronze eye, enormous, rose to meet her own. Tyler leapt backward from the fence, reeling and stumbling, crushing the blue worlds of glow bugs under her feet. A cry rose in her chest. She opened her mouth, screaming as an arm came curling around her neck, choking off the sound in her throat. The hard ball of a bicep jumped against her carotid artery, cutting the blood from her brain. She staggered, her vision tunneling, her nostrils filled with the scent of a man. Sweaty, feral. She dropped to her knees, clawing streaks in the fleshy noose of the arm. Her eyes caught a scroll of words rounding the pale cap of shoulder.

BEAST—

Now darkness.

"There!" cried Anse, leaping from the buggy.

Tyler was locked in one of the safety cages, her hands bound behind her back. A bandanna had been tied through her jaw, baring her teeth. They retrieved a pair of bolt-cutters from the gear-bag and cut the padlock. Anse jumped into the cage, cutting away her binds and gag with a pocketknife.

"Baby," he said. "I thought you were tiger food."

Tyler ripped the bandanna from her mouth.

"You're hiding the King of Savannah in the back enclosure."

It was not a question.

Anse opened his mouth to reply, but she stabbed a finger upright between them. His mouth clamped shut. Tyler swiped the jags of hair from her face, turned on her feet, and walked away, out of the safety cage and past the buggy, heading for the front of the sanctuary. Her shoulders were wide and squared, her wild blond hair bouncing in the night. Snow and Fire were still loose. She walked right past them. The tigers dipped their heads before her, expecting to be fed or addressed. Tyler kept walking.

Malaya's mouth hung open.

"Damn," she said. "Tiger lady."

They sat on the back deck of the gift shop, drinking instant coffee from chipped mugs. The eastern sky was paling, edging the pines from darkness. The tigers were back in their enclosure, persuaded with raw buffalo shanks, and the King of Savannah was gone. Taken. The heavy padlocks of the river enclosure had been cut with an acetylene torch, the scorched brass remnants set atop the coil of anchor chain. The animal had been darted either from the trees or through a break in the vine-wall.

His pugmarks turned three curlicues of widening circumference before his heavy chest had beached in the underbrush, flattening a bed of chickweed. There were marks where he'd been dragged or winched onto a litter, terminating at the fresh tracks of a heavy vehicle reversed to the gate for loading. The perpetrator's footprints had been raked away and the sanctuary's security cameras deactivated, the hard drive removed from the computer tower—the only thing taken from the office or gift shop.

Malaya held her mug with both hands. Her knees were tucked against her chest.

"Slick job," she said. "Professional."

Lope nodded. "You think it was that guy owns Lion Gas? The one from the news? Winter-something?"

Anse stood chewing his lip, squinting across the palms and cages of the sanctuary.

"Melton," he said. "Winter Melton."

He shook his head.

"It ain't him. If he knew we had the lion, he'd call in everybody he could. Police, news. Make it a public relations bonanza. Televised rescue or something. Whereas this looks like a small crew, possibly a one-man job. Looks like only one set of tracks raked clean back there."

"*Beast of waste and desolation.*"

They turned quickly to find Tyler standing on the deck. No one had heard her approach. She was fresh from the shower, twisting the blond rope of her hair, wringing water from the braid. Drops pattered against the planks at her feet. Anse, openmouthed, stared at her.

"Say that again?"

"A tattoo," she said. "He was shirtless, covered in tattoos. There's only one I saw up close, when he put me in the sleeper hold." Here she straightened and Malaya saw the bruised cords of her throat, which tightened.

"'Beast of waste and desolation' is what it said."

"Sounds like scripture," said Malaya.

Lope shook his head. "It ain't, not from the Bible."

"No," said Anse. "It's from Teddy Roosevelt." The old man's jaw muscles twitched. "Writing about the wolf."

Malaya felt a cold breath at the back of her neck, prickling the hairs.

"Then it's him," she said. "The one we've been hunting."

Tyler looked at the three of them, then back at Anse. She crossed her arms.

"*Hunting?*"

Anse ground his teeth.

"We've been calling him the wolfman. Breeds wolf hybrids, possibly big cats, too. Could be a tiger farm or chop shop, shipping parts straight out of the port."

Tyler lifted her chin, her arms still crossed.

"Where?"

"Some island," said Anse. "Our informant kept saying *Lion Claw.* Could be a nickname for a place, or else our man misheard it." The old jockey tugged absently on one earlobe. "It was kindly hard to tell at the time."

Lope set down his coffee.

"*Yamacraw,*" he said. "Yamacraw Island. Just off Savannah. My daddy and uncle grew up out there in the sixties and seventies. Investors bought it all up about a decade back, aiming to build a resort. All the old families sold and moved off, the few that were left. They built a beachfront hotel out there, golf course, tennis courts, cottages, the whole nine yards—just a couple years before the recession hit. It all went bankrupt soon after, is what I heard. Everything left to rot. It's isolated out there, no bridge." Lope shook his head. "It's perfect."

Anse growled, his brow gathered stormy over his eyes. He looked at Tyler.

"You want to be part of this?"

Tyler looked out across the sanctuary. She brushed one hand up the sleeve of her T-shirt, over the long swell of her upper arm. Then higher, lightly touching the bruise at her neck.

"In Chinese mythology, they say a tiger, at five hundred years old, will turn white and transform into a god, a guardian of the western sky and autumn lands—but only if virtue rules the land. But white tigers are no longer rare, are they? The world's full of them, bred father-to-daughter for circuses, sideshows, pets. For generations."

Now she swiveled back toward the others and uncrossed her arms, setting her hands on the back of a deck chair.

"Has Anse ever told you about our first rescue here, Polara? She was a white tiger bred for a Las Vegas magic show. When the show folded, they couldn't afford to keep her, so we took her in. She was slightly cross-eyed, with a clubbed rear foot. She sort of bounced around her enclosure, goofy-pawed, chuffing all the time, slapping at Boomer Balls." Tyler leaned closer to the rest of them, shaking her head. "I don't know what it was, but I loved that fucking cat. I really did. When she died, we dug her a grave along the river. Our first."

Tyler squeezed the back of the chair, the muscles standing from her arms.

"I've had enough sad stories crusted under my nails. I want claws."

CHAPTER 25

THE ISLAND

The full moon floated high in the dusk, a silver bullet in the purple glow of sky. Beneath it, the sea was dark, sharp, lapping at the hull of the boat. *The Catbird Seat.* Three days ago, they'd found the old shrimp trawler abandoned at her moorings, the owners fled. They'd swabbed the feathers from the decks and cleared the bilge and scrubbed the scum from the wheelhouse windows. Anse had fussed over the Detroit 8-71 diesel for hours, clad in rubber boots and headlamp, wielding wrenches and screwdrivers and aerosol cans until the old motor woke from greasy slumber, throbbing rhythmically in the hold.

That morning, they'd unwound the mooring lines and shoved off from the dock, chugging seaward through the lower delta of the Altamaha River, passing mossy hummocks and miles of salt marsh. Here or there, a scummy sailboat or cabin cruiser lay heeled on the bank, holed or scuttled alongside the alligators and cypress knees. Once or twice, while standing at the rail, Malaya thought she heard strange birds cawing along the river, as if to bless or curse their passage.

They broke from the river and cruised north along the Intracoastal Waterway, passing the string of sea islands that buffered the coast. Over the years, these islands had been home to tribal chiefdoms and Spanish missions and colonial forts, to antebellum plantations and reclusive millionaires and communities of freed slaves. Some still harbored small, isolated populations of exotic animals marooned long ago. Wild horses, feral cattle, white deer imported from Europe for hunters. Malaya glassed the shorelines, searching the dunes and oaks beneath the falling dusk, as if strange beasts might reveal themselves.

Now they floated a mile off Yamacraw Island. It was five miles long, two miles wide. The beach was littered with the skeletal remains of fallen trees, gnarled and sun-bleached, like some prehistoric boneyard—the work of erosion, shifting sands. A row of beach houses lurched from the trees, warped strangely over shattered seawalls, their windows broken. To the north, a lighthouse peeked over the trees, the glass of the lantern room dusted over, the once-white catwalk greened with neglect. Somewhere in the trees sat the deserted hulk of a fifty-room hotel, set back several hundred yards from the beach, hosting who knew what forms of life.

The southern end of the island speared into a mile-long point of tidal sands, where great rafts of pelicans and other shorebirds congregated, picking over the remains of dead fish and horseshoe crabs. Gulls wheeled over the boat, expecting mounds of shrimp and other catch to come pouring from the nets. Behind them, a container ship floated against the seaward horizon, its running lights burning in the dusk. The foghorn bellowed across the water.

Anse lowered his binoculars.

"It's time."

They lowered a black rubber boat over the side of the trawler, followed by a rope ladder. Anse climbed down first, then Malaya, who handed him the oars. Tyler came last, dressed in heavy overalls and boots, her hair knotted beneath a black skullcap. They wore shortwave radios clipped to their vests, the rubber antennas sticking over their shoulders, and their bodies were strapped and webbed with flashlights and wire cutters, maps and glow sticks and flexi-cuffs. Malaya wore a double long-gun

case slung over her shoulder. Tyler seated herself on the center
thwart and slid the oars through the locks. Lope waved from the
bridge of the trawler as Tyler dug the oars into the swells, heaving them away from the hull.

They were a thousand yards from shore when the drone
passed overhead. A winged model, newly purchased, capable of
staying aloft for hours. The breakers crashed over the outer sand-
bars and Malaya, riding in the bow, glanced back at Tyler. The
veterinarian, facing backward as she rowed, had removed her
pullover. Her muscles shone wide from the racerback of her overalls, almost winglike, her arms braided with power. Now Malaya
turned back to shore, watching the shadow of the drone scamper
over the dunes and into the trees.

She felt the leopard spots throbbing on her calf, the talons on
her foot. She thought of her father and her grandfather. These
men who lived inside her, roaming the tangled jungle of memory. She closed her eyes, imagining them swinging peacefully
overhead, watching over her.

They came ashore before the row of abandoned beach houses,
each hovering on a thin set of stilts. The concrete seawall
had shattered and the high ground bled away, exposing the
cement anchors of their pilings. French doors creaked on
hinges. Porch stairs ended in midair. An in-ground swimming pool sat like a giant bowl in the sand. The house before
them sagged hard at one corner, just short of toppling, while
strange ribs and points of furniture jutted from the sands beneath the porch, half buried, like fragments from a shipwreck.

They splashed through the knee-deep surf and dragged the
boat up the beach, the drier sands squeaking beneath the wet
soles of their boots. Beneath the beach house, it was damp and
cool, almost like a cave. They left the boat here, tied to a piling,
and started down the beach, hiking through the pale skeletons
of trees, the dull roar of wind and surf. The sun was nearly
gone, a reddish flush. A disheveled boardwalk loomed before
them. An old beach access. As planned, they stomped up the

sand-ledged steps and took the boardwalk inland. Ghost crabs scuttled beneath the planks, and the dunes were stitched with the tracks of various animals. Birds, rabbits, feral pigs. Dry grasses and shrubs stood wind-raked, as if pointing them on.

At the tree line, Malaya paused, looking back over the dunes, sighting *The Catbird Seat* off the coast. The trawler glowed under the risen moon, a small white fortress on the swells. She felt a throb of recognition at the sight, like a remembered dream. Now the wind rose, skirling over the sand, and Malaya felt the weight of the case on her back. She knelt and unslung the burden and unzipped the long flap.

They set off into the forest, armed now, the trees murmuring overhead.

Lope stood in the wheelhouse, bent over his screen, watching the live feed from the drone. Three bodies, white with heat, winked in and out of the trees. Ahead of them, a narrow strip of pavement burned pale, still holding the day's heat. A pair of deer seared across the path, ghostly, fleeing the humans crunching inland through the bush.

In shape, the island recalled a feather. The mainland lay across several miles of rivers and salt marsh, the cordgrass veined with blackwater creeks. No bridges or boats. Ancient tribes had inhabited the place, leaving rings of shucked oyster shells in their wake. Then came conquistadors and cotton planters and shipwrights who felled the hardwood timber of the island for the hulls of sailing ships, making room for ever more fields. When the plantations folded during the Civil War, the slaves stayed or fled from the mainland in stolen barques. For generations, they lived in near isolation from the rest of the country, speaking the creole language of the sea islands—Gullah—a fusion of English and African tongues.

Lope's grandmother had been born, lived, and died on this island. Her bones were buried here. The only time he ever saw her on the mainland was the day of his father's funeral. She came with a chorus of women who spoke only Gullah to one another, swilling scuppernong wine from a plastic jug. She was the grandmother who told stories of slaves striding into black rivers, enchained, flying free of their bonds. Lope hadn't been out here since her death more than two decades ago. He hadn't seen what had become of the place.

The remnants of a golf course slipped into view. Dogleg savannahs pocked with fairway bunkers and sand traps, the links weedy and overgrown. He saw oceanfront cottages with storm-felled limbs stabbing from their roofs, swimming pools covered in pond scum. Tennis courts like the cracked terrain of the moon. The hotel itself lay double-winged beneath the trees, massive, like the temple of some forgotten civilization. The developers had hoped to build a resort to rival Hilton Head or Sea Island or Kiawah—a haven for the well-heeled, who came ashore armed with racquets and golf clubs.

Deeper in the trees lay the manufactured housing of the resort staff. Singlewides arranged in once-orderly rows. They were canted and swollen now, their walls webbed with creeper vines and kudzu. Furry carpets of turf sprouted from their roofs. Lope shivered. A whole world without people, swallowed in a rising tide of jungle. It was as if the Rapture had come, sucking the souls from the place, and nature had run amok in their absence, multiplying with strangling vines and prowling things.

Lope watched for the marsh tackies his father had ridden as a boy—horses descended from the hoofstock of old Spanish garrisons. Small and sure-footed, with no fear of swamps and marshes. They'd been the preferred mounts of the Swamp Fox, Francis Marion, whose fighters struck like lightning from the swamplands, as well as the mounted beach patrols of World War II, who hunted remote shorelines for Nazi U-boats. Gullah riders had raced them on the beach, levitating over their thundering haunches. Those horses were mostly gone now, preserved only in high-dollar paddocks and old photographs.

For a time Lope saw only trees, acre on acre. For all he knew, fantastical beasts glowed beneath their canopy, wild horses or feral hogs or big cats, but he saw no sign. He began to lose hope.

There was nothing here but shell and bone. Even the ghosts had fled. Then, in the very middle of the island, far from the eyes of looters or campers or fishermen, the trees broke onto a small plot cut squarely from the forest.

A compound, arranged tidy and exact as a microchip.

There was a row of shipping containers and a greenhouse and a pair of generators that pulsed with heat. A flatboat on a trailer, a fat-tired ATV. A row of kennels with tin roofs, their long runs covered in camouflage netting. Now came a rectangular enclosure, vast and roofless, with a razor-wire fence. Lope could see dogs or wolves inside. He descended for a better look. Some of the canines lay curled in the grass, swaddled in their bushy tails, their shoulders bubbling and twitching in their sleep. One paced along the fence, pausing now and again to stare into the night, knife-eared, while another followed a scent-trail, nose prowling through the weeds.

The largest of the pack sat high atop a square shelter, watching the others. His tail swished slowly, softly, and his neck wore a jagged ruff. His body burned a snowy white beneath the thermal lens of the drone, though his fur could be jet black. Now the wolf lifted his nose toward the drone and swelled his chest. His mouth formed a small black *O*.

The first howl rose in the night, high and ghostly. Malaya froze mid-step, as if yanked at the end of a leash. So much pain in that sound, like the first wail of the damned. Now more of the cries, racing like banshees through the trees.

Wolves.

Malaya dropped to one knee, weapon up. The howls blew across her bones, goosing her skin. For all she knew, a pack had been loosed.

The radio crackled on Anse's shoulder.

Lope's voice: "You hear that?"

Anse didn't answer at first. He stood upright, ear cocked, his double rifle cradled in one arm. With his free hand, he thumbed the chest pocket of his shirt.

The radio crackled again.

"Anse, you copy?"

The old jockey shivered awake. He cocked his chin to the mike.

"Roger, we heard them, all right. You got eyes on?"

"Yes, sir. Pack of six in an open-top enclosure. It's eerie. Every last one of them's got his nose in the air, like they know I'm up here watching."

A shiver ran through Malaya.

Anse shook his head. His face looked hard in the night, battered. He thumbed the mike.

"Moon's full. They're howling it down, not you. You got a location for us?"

They moved single file through the woods, following the thin sinews of game trails. Slim corridors, hoof-worn paths. Woody vines snarled through the understory, threatening to trip them, while Spanish moss hung in curtains from the oaks. Barbed thickets of saw palmetto were everywhere, chafing and rattling.

Malaya carried her black carbine high against her chest. Her boots seemed too loud as they cracked twigs beneath her, crunched leaves and oyster shells. The ground felt dangerous, eager to give away their presence. The very night seemed to be listening, watching. Malaya felt exposed, more prey than predator. Now and again, she swung the carbine toward a crackle or crash in the outer dark. Tusked hogs, big as whiskey kegs, were known to roam here, and the dogfighter had heard tell of big cats kept on this island. Who knew if one was loose, or a wolf. Anse and Tyler seemed to feel it, too. When they knelt to take their bearings, Malaya could see it in their heaving chests and wide eyes.

They were not the apex predators here.

Soon the forest broke onto an unexpected meadow, a narrow savannah that wound and rolled through the trees. The grass was chest-high, thick enough to hide lions or leopards. Anse led them down a golf-cart path that ran along the fairway. Here or there, the heavy knees of oak roots had erupted through the pavement, and bright ferns stood from the gapes and fractures. They snaked around a pond carpeted with algae. A golf cart sat in the shallows, the front bumper bearing a tarnished name-plate: E-Z-GO. They passed sand traps sprouted with weeds and climbed the flat crown of the green. Anse pulled the stick from the hole and rubbed the flag between his fingers, slowly, like the shred of a fugitive's shirt.

They clopped across the short arch of a cart bridge, the planks soggy and loose, and the path ran alongside a chain-link fence clumped with vines. Inside the enclosure, a drooping succession of tennis nets. A serving machine stood on a tripod, the hopper loaded with mildewed balls. Others lay about the courts, soggy and dark.

A thick reef of kudzu and ivy whelmed the clubhouse. Only the roof was visible. The hedges lining the porch had exploded with growth, wreathing the rails and balusters. Through gaps in the foliage, they could see filmy windows, broken panes. Shattered glass twinkled on the front steps, the entrance doors barely visible through the snarled morass of leaves and vines.

Anse rounded the corner of the building and jerked to a halt. There stood a lone pony, feeding from a bed of delicate ferns on the putting green. Malaya watched the animal over Anse's shoulder. The horse's legs were thin and tapered, black-stockinged beneath the dun barrel of her chest. Her tail, black as a feather duster, flicked her rump. Now she raised her head, ears perked, and Malaya saw the rubbery flare of her nostrils, catching a scent—them or something else.

The pony wheeled and fled into the night, as if chased.

Lope felt weightless, as if he floated high over the island him-self, his heart making a delicate electric hum. His wingspan would be some seven feet, wide as a peace eagle's, his long fingers riding the invisible currents of wind and pressure. He would steer with the long rudders of his feet.

He watched his companions moving across the island, their

body heat winking now and again through the trees. Fear prodded him when, for long intervals, he couldn't see them beneath the canopy. There was a burden in being the eye in the sky, he realized. A pressure. If he failed to alert them of a threat or gave the wrong directions, their fates would be on him. He thought of God looking down on the whole swarm of his creation and how he must not feel guilty when he didn't slip them the right signs and they walked right into passing buses or abusive husbands, again and again, all over the place and every minute.

Beneath him, the pony swam into view.

A marsh tacky, her mane hanging dark over one shoulder. Her whole body was cocked rigid, her ears pricked, as if awaiting some signal. When she bolted for the woods, Lope scanned in the exact opposite direction. The vector led him back to the compound. The wolves were standing in a row along the fence now, pointed like arrows, as if directing him. He followed their pointed snouts, finding a circular arena shaped like a circus tent, domed with the thin silk of a giant cargo parachute. He'd noted the arena on his previous pass but not the heat blooms just visible through the canopy. There were two of them, shaped like giant scimitars, circling slowly inside the enclosure. Lope descended closer, trying to make out what they were. What order or species. His heart quickened as he neared, as if he could sense their heat on his cheeks. The wind was thumping the big top of silk. He was squinting, willing the animals to reveal themselves, when a gust peeled back the canopy.

His eyes went wide. A sharp stab of breath.

Lope keyed the radio mike. He sent his words, like a prayer, across the waves.

CHAPTER 26

TIGRESS

She circles Mosi. A long tongue of flame, ember-bright, her breath smoking in the night. She is longer than any lioness, her hips sharp and lean. Her huge paws dab the earth. Silent, almost. She's a fire flickering behind a black forest of stripes. Her eyes are gold. Her lips pulled back, showing her teeth. She's tasting him on the air.

She is something Mosi knows and doesn't know. A member, perhaps, of some distant pride. The wolves howl again and her ears swivel rearward, revealing their eyespots—a second pair of eyes, guarding her flank. So Mosi knows her pride must have been scattered long ago, cast across the earth. They must burn alone in jungle darks or mountain snows. A lone hunter, with no pride to watch her flank.

No mate.

Mosi's heart drums loud, swelling his flesh. He circles, circles. A cloud crosses the moon, darkening the night. The fangs drip from her mouth, curved and sharp, and Mosi can see the golden length of his body reflected in her eyes. He can see the black mane about his neck, heavy as a wreath of wolves.

Horn sat high on his perch, a small platform built in the crown of the compound's single oak tree. The big cats were circling inside the high fence of the arena, their tails long as whips, their muscles flexed jagged beneath their hides. Closer they circled.

Closer.

When, a week ago, he heard the lion roar across the grounds of Little Eden, he knew it was the one from the news. The King of Savannah. The mascot taken from the truck stop on the interstate. Fifty thousand dollars had been offered for the animal's safe return, no questions asked. A king's ransom. Such an amount moved his blood. He could take his pack west with such money, high into the mountains they deserved. Far from the hurricanes that worsened year after year, threatening to drive the ocean inland—a shallow sea, as in the days before men. When the lion roared a second time, his breath fled his chest, sucked out into the night. His whole body tightened. He could feel his calcified knuckles, the sharp blades of his shins. He was ready. He'd only come to Little Eden for a tiger. A sire, for Amba, so that he could carry a cub of hers into the West. So that her blood would still move across the earth.

Here was a king.

Horn watched the big cats circling beneath him. Here were the greatest hunters that had ever lived, predators whose bloodlines had survived some three million years in the killing fields of evolution. Their ancestors had been the strongest and smartest of their generations, each successive line born harder than the last, sharper, more capable of bringing down the mastodon, the cave bear, the antelope. Kings of the forest and savannah, who battled the most formidable prey of the earth to live. They circled beneath him, smoke-breathed, like beasts of fire and light.

Like far worlds, converging.

His wolves raised their voices again, as if keening some loss. He could hear Onyx the loudest, as if the black wolf's heart had been ripped silver from his chest and hung among the stars. Their howls carried long miles across the water, so that shrimpers and crabbers spoke of ghosts keening on the wind.

The great lion seemed unfazed. He strode proud-chested before the tigress, as if indifferent to the fiery slink of her body, the long whisper of her tail. But Horn knew better. He knew the lion's heart was thundering bright—the same as his own.

Her fur burns in the night, firelike. Her eyes so gold. She bellies the earth before him, her ears laid flat. The white mitts of her paws nearly touch. Her tail swishes. Her muscles have marshaled beneath her shoulders, hard as stones. Her eyes track his every move. She might be readying herself to pounce, to tear the throat from a deer. The wolves howl in the distance, in worship or dread.

Mosi approaches, high-chinned and sidewise, wary as a housecat. Closer, closer. If she springs, he will turn his shoulder to the slash of her claws and drive his teeth into her neck, snapping the hot vine of blood that tethers her to the earth. She will run red through his jaws. His own throat is safe, hidden beneath the black of his mane.

He stands unmoved before her, waiting. His body so vast, a golden country of desire. A hot wind pours from his mouth. His blood burns like magma beneath his skin. The wolves howl yet louder, as if longing for flight, to run high among the stars.

She springs for his throat, so fast he can hardly react. At the last moment she lowers her chin and drives her broad forehead through his mane, her pink nose grazing his neck. His throat sings at her touch, as if sliced, and she bolts away, high-shanked and jaunty. Mosi trots after her, open-jawed, following the red zag of her body.

She tumbles onto her back before him, revealing the soft white fur of her belly. She rubs her shoulders against his forelegs and swats at his nose, her teeth clicking in the night. His breath smokes over her. They snarl like battlers through their fangs. Now the tigress rolls upright and hovers on her belly beneath him, haunches raised. One eye slides over her shoulder.

Mosi lifts his great maned head, whose semblance has ridden on the shields and banners of nations. He inhales, swelling his chest, and blasts his roar through the night. Trees bend and shiver. Birds explode to flight. Eggs quiver in their nests, as if they might hatch, and the very stars seem to pulse.

The wolves fall silent.

CHAPTER 27

LEOPARD GIRL

Malaya dropped to one knee, hard and fast, as if anchoring herself against a gale. The roar crashed through the trees, careening seaward. She imagined the surf breaking white-foamed against the sound, as if against a seawall. Shorebirds bursting to flight. Entire shoals of baitfish silvering with terror, darting for darker fathoms.

I am Mosi.

They'd come more than a mile since the clubhouse, directed now and again by crackles from the radio—Lope's voice, directing them from above. They'd crossed the main east-west road of the island, an oak-lined lane that once led visitors between the ferry dock and the oceanside hotel, then taken a dirt drive past the trailers of the resort staff. The singlewides sat moldering beneath the trees, with busted windows and open doors. Old belongings scattered before them, bicycles and beach chairs and mini-fridges. Cable satellite dishes, green with lichen, still listening for messages from space. The whole place lay beneath a heavy, organic film, growing back into the earth.

They'd passed a giant maintenance warehouse of corrugated metal and a fleet of diesel tanks shaped like submarines, rust-patched with red hazard placards. On the outside wall of the warehouse, a large button haloed with red paint: EMERGENCY PUMP SHUTOFF. An old bucket truck sat in the lot, hood raised, the tires puddled flat beneath their wheels.

Then the buildings had vanished, the road narrowing through the trees, only wide enough for a single vehicle. Anse had bent to the ground, running his hand along the ruts and treads.

"Been a truck through here since the last rain."

Finally they'd come to a narrow drive, double-rutted with a stripe of grass down the center. A single sign had been nailed to a nearby tree: BEWARE OF DOG.

The roar died away. The trees unbent and the stars reappeared and Malaya's ears thrummed, as in the wake of a blast. She looked to Anse, raising an eyebrow.

She was younger than they were, faster. For all they knew, the lion they'd taken as their charge was about to fight a tiger for the roar of ten thousand bettors scattered across the world, bent to tablets or computer screens.

Can I?

Anse curled his bottom lip into his teeth, biting hard. Then he unslung the howdah pistol and held out the walnut club of the grip.

"God forbid," he said.

Then Malaya was moving fast through the trees, darting over roots and fallen limbs, dodging briars and thickets, her eyes cutting a path for her feet. She could not take the drive itself for threat of traps and alarms. She skirted deadfalls and ducked branches and leapt a creekbed that crossed her path. She clutched the carbine close against her chest, ripping through sweeps of moss and spiderwebs with her free hand, breaking branches at eye level, leaving a trail for Anse and Tyler to follow. She was strong and tireless, as in a dream. Her thighs were sprung with power, buoyant, her breath storming through her teeth. She had trained for this. The predawn runs on dewy streets, the evening wind sprints. The thousands of push-ups and dips and squats.

The moon grew closer, stronger. Thorns raked her face. Slivers of blood burned on her cheeks. She felt freed, loosed into the night. Now a bubble of light rose through the trees and she broke into the clearing of the compound before the giant canopy of a cargo parachute, a secret carnival pitched beneath the moon. The big top of silk billowed in the night, skirling and popping, while the lion and tiger wrestled inside the arena, flashing in and out of shadow, their breath whirling from them in paling blades of smoke. The lion curling on top, biting the tiger's neck. The tiger rolling beneath him, swatting his face. Their teeth bared white. Bloodless. Their growls whipping strangely through the night, in and out of earshot.

Malaya approached the fence, slowly, stepping beneath the gnarled crown of an ancient oak. She held her carbine against her chest, her eyes wide. These crazed beasts, snarling and smoking, flashing out of the darkness in bright flames of power, as if twisting themselves into a single beast.

Snap—

Malaya jerked her head straight up. A creature dropping from the tree overhead—a man, his arms spread high and wide as a crucifixion. She jumped back and he hit the ground feet-first, straight as a spear, then balled and sprang upright before her, his fists raised on either side of his face. One hand gripped an evil, curled knife. He was shirtless, his torso cut pale and hard as living marble. She saw words scrolled over the heaving planes of his navel:

SOMETIME THE WOLF

Then she looked up, seeing his face.

"You."

Her heart jabbed in her chest. She drove the heel of her boot into his belly, forcing him back, then raised the barrel of the carbine between them. Too slow. The long-haired man rebounded, leaping upon her like a giant claw. He spiraled around her trunk, torqueing her hard to the ground, cutting the sling of her carbine and kicking it away. She found herself facing the sky, snared in limbs, her head locked in a hard triangle of arms. The man's biceps bulged against her neck. A blood-choke. Her artery pinched, the blood slackening to her brain. She clawed at the arm to no avail. Her vision began to dim, tunneling. The stars to bleed. The moon oozing out of round. She had only seconds before she passed out.

Malaya looked down her body, past the pair of legs that ensnared her. The lion and the tiger stood on the far side of the fence, their great ribs flaring with breath. Their jaws hung open, strings of saliva dripping from their chins. The night flooded in on them, lapping over their edges, drowning their bodies. Soon there was only the glow of their eyes, soon to vanish.

Malaya's hand found the grip of the howdah pistol.

Here was the vision that haunted her.

To uncage fire and light.

Her fingers tightened.

She would not miss.

CHAPTER 28

DAWN

Horn woke. He was lying flat on his back, high from the ground, his bare chest coated in sweat. Dawn light, pale and cool, rifled through the high fence of the wolf pen, seeking his stricken form. The pain throbbed along his femur, hammering at the socket of his hip. He lifted his head to look down his body, seeing the ragged slash of claws in his thigh, bone gleaming through the meat.

Sickness rose in his throat. He leaned his head back on the roof of the shelter, thinking of all the wolves caught in the jaws of iron traps. Century after century. Feeling the same pain he felt now. Knowing they would have to gnaw through their own flesh and bone to escape. To chew themselves free of a limb.

He'd tried so hard to break from the world of men. The world of mothers who died in the night, their eyes clouded with blood, and fathers whose keys rattled from brass rings on their belts, promising cages and locks. He'd found an island apart from their rule, cloaking himself in the fur of a new family.

Now he must go back.

Last night, when the girl raised the double-barreled pistol from her chest, both hammers cocked, Horn had seen what would happen. The long tongues of flame leaping forth, the bright shatter of the gate latch. The door blown inward on its hinges and the lion and tiger wheeling in panic, their eyes burning for escape. They'd come charging for the blasted door, big as battering rams, and Horn was already letting the girl slide unconscious from his arms. He was rising over her, spreading his arms wide, trying to divert their path, when the lion broke first from the arena.

Blazing eyes, a black halo of mane. A roar that filled the night.

Without thought, Horn sprang over the girl, howling into the roar.

In a single stroke, the lion swatted him far across the night, sent him tumbling through the air and along the ground, the flesh raked from his thigh. When he opened his eyes, Amba was standing over him, scenting him, her pink nose just shy of his wound.

Horn had reached up, stroked her chin.

"I'm sorry," he said.

Amba chuffled, a cloud of breath.

"Go," he said. "While you can."

The tigress hovered, reluctant to heed.

Horn slashed his arm toward the tree line.

"Go!"

She seemed to dip her head once, revealing the black mark of power on her forehead. Then she wheeled and vanished, quick as a flame winking out. Gone. Horn had turned and begun crawling through the night, making for the wolf enclosure, the shelter of his pack. They would protect him, he thought . . .

Now he looked over the edge of the roof. The wolves were swimming about the wooden sides of the shelter, circling black and gray, their tongues flopping from their jaws. A dark sea of them, whirling faster. A rising hunger. They could smell the power of their alpha slipping, seeping from his veins.

He who'd been a wolf—he was becoming a man.

Only Onyx stood beside him now, high atop the shelter, his hackles risen black and serrated from his spine. He snarled long-toothed at the others, keeping them at bay. Several had already tried to spring atop the shelter. Onyx sent them squealing and tumbling back to earth, scrambling to right themselves amid the snarls of the pack.

Horn reached out, ruffing the neck of the black wolf.

He knew what he had to do. His only chance. He had to climb down and walk through them, staring straight into their eyes. Never blinking. Showing them that he was still the strongest among them. The fittest, most worthy of their faith. That he was still their alpha. He must walk straight to the gate of the enclosure, showing no fear, no pain or weakness.

The shelter shook beneath him. The wolves were rubbing their ribs against its sides.

Horn closed his eyes a long moment, then opened them.

He descended.

Mosi strides through wide fans of saw palmetto, high-shouldered, heedless of the thorns and briars of the understory. He loves the scrape and sting of the bush. He was never meant to wear a faultless coat, he knows. The old savannah kings are in his blood. Rulers of the black mane, who wore their scars with pride. Their shredded ears and eyeless sockets. Their coats storied with old battles, never meant to shine in cages or trophy rooms.

The sun is rising, lancing gold through the trees, when Mosi emerges from the woods and crosses a long glade of grass, plowing chest-high through the blades. He feels strangely at home here, as if he might hear the hoof-thunder of the great herds along their migration paths. He pauses, watching a robin perch atop a swaying weed stalk, her breast balled red with song.

Soon he's trotting down a long hall of oaks. Moss hangs silver-gold from the trees and thrushes drape themselves branch to branch above him. Squirrels freeze spread-limbed, their tails curled bushy, their black-bright eyes watching his passage. Mosi strides through the hush, the watching eyes and tapping hearts. He pauses again, his eyes searching for a flash in the trees.

The tigress burns in his mind. She is prideless, he knows, meant to flicker through dark jungles or snowy forests. Silent, no shiver of brush in her wake. How he would like to feast on the entrails of a fresh-killed deer beside her, their faces blazed warm with blood. Their sandy tongues lapping flesh from bone. How he would like to drowse in a pool of afternoon sunlight beside her, pushing his nose through the white fur of her belly. Their cubs tumbling in the grass. But he's caught no sign of her, no scent. She's vanished.

Mosi continues down the hall of oaks, searching.

Soon a structure rises before him, vine-strung and giant, moaning in the wind. He sniffs at the stone pool at the foot of the place, filled only with dead leaves and stagnant rainwater and scattered flecks of copper. He approaches the black maw of the entrance, swiveling his ears. He can hear the scrabble of rats, the scuttle of roaches. The drip of water on stone. Now the wind rises, whistling through the shattered wreck of the place, the empty halls and chambers. Mosi lifts his nose, trying to catch the scent of the tigress.

Nothing.

She's gone. Retreated to wherever fire goes, leaving no trace.

Mosi hears only the distant crash of surf, calling him on.

Horn was walking among his wolves, through them, their bodies parting before the bloody stride of his legs. They watched slack-jawed, their tongues flopped out, stood awed by the bloody footprints he left in his wake. They dipped their snouts again and again, scenting the tracks, only to look up at him in disbelief, their heads cocked like dogs.

Horn reached the first of the double gates, yanked up the latch, and slipped sideways through the door. The wolves bunched at his heels, eager to follow, but Horn pulled shut the gate, slamming home the latch. His knee gave out at the clang of the lock, buckling beneath the shredded flesh of his thigh. He collapsed hard in the dirt. The pain, pent so long in his chest, came howling from his throat, raising the rooty veins of his neck. He writhed on the ground, clawing the dirt, his vision gone starry and wild.

When his eyes cleared, his wolves were strung along the fence, their dark bodies quaking like storm clouds. Anxiety pulsed through them, electric. They knew. They lowered their snouts, revealing the high razors of their shoulder blades, and stared through the steel waffling of the fence. Their yellow eyes searched him like spotlamps. They were whining now, pleading through the white flash of their teeth. He must not leave them. He was their alpha. Their king.

They curled their lips, showing their fangs.

They would kill him if he left.

Only Onyx stood apart, with his black fur and yellow eyes. He was certain his master would return. His faith unbroken. In the distance, Horn could hear the rumbling of storm, or perhaps the thunder of a helicopter heading their way. The machine-rule of man would converge on this island, he knew. Government boats would arrive at the dock, dispersing state rangers with catchpoles and dog boxes, and aircraft would circle high overhead, carrying men with binoculars. A white cutter would anchor offshore, as if to provide artillery support. His wolves would be wrangled and crated, transported to shelters and sanctuaries around the country. His pack broken, dispersed.

Only Amba might escape. After all, her kind had been known to slip the nooses of hunters and poachers time and again throughout the centuries, leaving no sign of passage. No prints. Horn felt his blood ebb, blackness throbbing in the corners of his vision. He closed his eyes. In the dark of his mind, he could see Amba flickering through heavy drapes of myrtle and moss, her body so unbelievably long, her tail weaving through the maze of fronds. Silent. She was pursuing a whitetail buck who stood beneath a mossy oak, his body propped on the thinnest legs, his flanks raked high from the earth. His antlers knobby and short. The buck stood as if hypnotized by her presence, jacklighted. The tigress bolted from the trees, aiming her jaws for his throat.

In this dream, her belly was heavy and round, pregnant with power.

Horn woke to the howling of his wolves. They stood together in the enclosure, their snouts pointed to the sky. Their cries so high and sharp, as if to wake the dead. Horn turned and crawled, dragging himself away from them, leaving a red trail of himself through the grass. His body shivered beneath their cries. The wrecked meat of his leg was nothing compared to his heart. He must cut himself free of them—the only way to live.

In an hour, he would lie heaving on the planks of the dock, his ferry barge gone. Taken, surely, by those who came for the lion. He would look west, seeing the green edge of the continent across the marsh. The same land that conquistadors and pirates must have seen, so lush and green, arrayed beneath the heavy guns of their ships. The same coast that rose before the eyes of the enchained, let topside to glimpse the nation that would be built upon the heavy burls of their backs. Horn would squint hard at this horizon, as if he might make out the distant mountains of the West. The snowy ranges of dream, risen high and ghostly against the sky, sharp as fangs. Then he would slip into the water, gnashing his teeth, and begin the long swim toward land, alone.

Mosi trots down a long path between palm trees, the pavement fractured with roots and furry clumps of weeds. The sharp fronds of the palms whisper overhead. Soon he's walking through a white valley of dunes, the shrubs and grasses wind-bent on the sandy slopes. A marsh rabbit flees before him, a pale thumping of sand. He can taste the sea with every breath, salty and thick in his jaws.

Now he stands amid a dead forest of bleached and toppled trees, their skeletal forms flung along the shore like the bones of his ancestors or the prey they felled. The great ribs and tusks, salt-rimmed, rise snarling on every side of him, lacing the sands in shadow. Mosi looks over his shoulder a moment, back the way he came. A single raptor hangs high over the dunes, circling in the dawn.

Hunting.

Mosi turns to descend the beach. He passes piles of sea wrack and driftwood, threading his way between translucent blisters of jellyfish and crabs the size of giant hooves. Shells crunch beneath his paws. He crosses the tide line, the darker sand cool beneath his toes. Soon he's standing at water's edge, letting the surf run foaming against his paws. He watches the white roll and spray of the outer breakers. A flight of brown pelicans skims low over the water, strung one after the next, their wing tips cutting across the swells.

Beyond them, a thunderstorm hangs over the ocean. A vast, dark range of power, throbbing in the dawn. Rain slants from the heavy bellies of cloud, forking with light. The air hums over the waves, electric. Mosi lifts his face to the wind, open-jawed, tasting the storm in his mouth.

He closes his eyes, opens them.

The raptor is there again, circling high overhead, and Mosi knows he's been found. He hears the hiss of gas, feels the dart of pain in his haunches. He knows what will happen. His muscles will turn to jelly, his head heavy as stone. Sleep will wash over him, thick and dark, and his spirit will grow dim, hibernating deep inside him. Already his hindquarters are sinking, his forelegs swaying beneath his ribs. Then the storm pulses and quakes, sending a roar of thunder over the waves and against the shore. A challenge. Mosi lifts his maned head to the sky. His chest whelms with thunder.

He roars.

I am Mosi. This land is mine.

CHAPTER 29

ASWANG

Malaya stood on the bow of the old trawler, the deck rocking beneath her feet. The sun was high now, the day cool and bright. Lope was at the helm, his large hands resting on the wheel, making small corrections back and forth. He nodded to her through the windows of the bridge. Malaya looked out at the small ferry barge cruising alongside them. Anse stood at the controls, shirtless now, the scars glistening on his back. He was watching Tyler, who knelt before the transport cage on the front of the barge, monitoring the darted lion.

When Malaya regained consciousness at the foot of the arena, she'd found the pugmarks of the cats haloing her body and head. The lion and tiger had forked into the night, missing her by inches. The wolfman was gone, only the swirling of his wolves behind their fence, their breath winging in silver shreds through the night. The howdah pistol lay on her chest, the barrels still smoking.

Anse and Tyler soon emerged from the woods, breathing hard, lifting her to her feet. They tracked the lion through the night, through heavy palmetto thickets and man-high weeds, down narrow trails cut by deer and wild hogs. Lope's voice crackled in their radios, directing them. His drone orbiting high overhead, unseen, tracking the white-hot form of the escaped lion through the trees. Lope aimed them along broken golf-cart paths and maintenance roads, across fairways and down the long hall of oaks.

Near dawn, they reached the ruined hotel. The once-grand edifice sat double-winged beneath the mossy oaks, the wind groaning through the shattered windows. They crept up the drive, where ferns and weeds sprang from fissures in the concrete. The white porch columns showed dark cankers of rot, the paint peeling and flaking. One had fully disintegrated, revealing a steel support core. They passed a stone fountain at the foot of the place, littered with greening pennies and dead leaves, and walked into the heavy shadow of the portico. The entry doors hung wide, the innards dim. They looked at one another. The drone was high above, orbiting. Lope had lost track of the lion—he could not say if the animal was inside the building.

Together, they passed through the shattered entrance doors.

The air was damp and cool here, like the inside of a cave. The ceilings dripped *tink-tink* on the tile floors, making black puddles here or there. Their boots crunched across the broken glass of the lobby, beneath chandeliers swathed with cobwebs. Wind-piled leaves lay along the baseboards, and the walls had been axed open in ragged swathes, mined for their copper wire. Smashed furniture in one corner, piled like kindling. The front desk was scattered with papers and a single Gideon Bible, swollen, the pages freckled with mildew. A soft layer of dust, moon-gray, covered the floor, crisscrossed with the spoor of scavengers. Raccoons, opossums, mice. Their own bootsoles left distinct imprints, recording their every step. A history stamped in dust.

Soon they cut the trail of the lion in the murky light, his pugmarks wending crown-shaped through the vaulted chambers of the place. They followed, their eyes stabbing into every dark corner, passing down hallways scattered with curling papers and past a long wooden bar with bottles of spirits still lining the shelves.

They emerged into a vast ballroom devoid of furniture. On

the far wall, a large stone fireplace where the lion must have
paused to sniff the stale ashes clumped in the grate—so said his
tracks. Then came the oceanfront dining room. On the hostess
stand, a laminated menu from Easter Sunday brunch, ten years
ago. A vast field of white-clothed tables, still set. The glassware
filmy and overturned, the linen napkins spotted with mildew.
As if the guests had simply vanished from their seats, vapor-
ized. The windows were shattered here or there, sieving the wind,
while storm-thrown branches lay on tables or serving carts, in
clouds of broken glass.

They emerged onto the back porch, where brown fronds and
wind-wrack had been blown inland by hurricane-force winds,
piling against walls. Vines snaked around the rails and balusters and slithered across the floor, as if wresting the hotel back
into the earth. The ceiling fans drooped like wilted flowers.
They followed a tabby path across the wide, knee-high lawn,
between rows of ragged palm trees. Soon they came upon the
old swimming pool, set like a wild oasis amid the overgrown
lawn. The shrubbery had overrun the place, exploding from
pots and planters, while vines snarled through the legs of deck
chairs and tables. The pool itself, once-blue, had grown into
a primordial lagoon, bloomed green with algae and floating
scum. Tiny fish darted through the roots of floating plants. An
overturned rubber boot held an empty tallboy beer—some last
worker's goodbye.

Finally they walked a trail through the dunes and emerged
among the skeletons of salt-killed trees, where they sighted their
quarry. The lion stood open-jawed on the beach, as if feeding on
wind or light, watching the dark pulse of a passing storm. Anse
slowly knelt, threading the barrel of the tranquilizer gun through
the crook of his thumb. Malaya could hear the man's breath, ragged through his nose. He blinked and blinked again, taking a
long time to shoot. His finger lay on the trigger, motionless. Tyler
knelt beside him. She reached out and touched his back, lightly,
where his scars were.

"Only a dart," she said.

Anse nodded, tears in his eyes.

He pulled the trigger.

They stood over the lion at dawn, his sleeping body curled in a swirling halo of surf. The red feather of the dart fluttered from his rump. Tyler knelt at the animal's neck, threading the disc of her stethoscope through his mane. In the distance, the storm rumbled and hissed, passing offshore, as if cowed. Just before he collapsed, the black-maned lion had lifted his head and blasted his roar across the waves. He had, like a true lion of the savannah, answered the thunder.

Malaya looked at Anse.

"What about the tiger?"

Anse squinted out across the water, at the storm offshore. Then he looked down the beach, his eyes tracing the great boneyard of trees, the deep forest beyond. He set his fists on his hips and spat.

"What tiger?"

Malaya watched the shoreline of the island slip past the bow of the trawler. They had already passed the abandoned beach houses, stilted high over the receding sands, and the broken seawalls. The weedy links of the golf course. Now came the deep ranks of trees, acre on acre, heavy with moss, standing behind the dunes. Malaya leaned on the rail, squinting, as if she might glimpse a flash of fire through the trees.

Nothing.

Now came the point of the island. A long spear of sand, covered in a vast raft of shorebirds. Pelicans and gulls and skimmers. Some stood spread-winged, drying their feathers in the sun, while others strode back and forth, pecking the beach for food. A few sat like roosting hens, their legs tucked beneath them, the wind riffling their feathers.

Malaya thought of another shore, a world away. Africa. The skulk of poachers. The dead. Her hands tightened on the rail. The thoughts were descending on her, heavy and dark, ready to pick the black carrion of her mind.

Then—as by a shot—the great raft of shorebirds erupted to flight. A vast cloud of them, arch-winged, rising like a single nation from the beach, thumping into the sky. They hung in fluttering suspension, like the feathers of an exploded pillow, their shadows crisscrossing the sand. Malaya's heart lunged. There, beneath their wings, sat an old man in green sunglasses.

He sat cross-legged, smoking, his hands full of bread.

Malaya blinked.

Gone.

The gray bones of a lone tree, grown wild from the beach.

CHAPTER 30
GHOST LION

The shrimpers and oystermen of the coast tell stories of the creatures that haunt their waters, the black jags of river and long beaches of sea wrack. These men stand in their white rubber boots, the toes flecked with bycatch, and speak through curling wraiths of cigarette smoke. Their fingers are square, bullet-hard, and they have voices of gravel. The amber lights of the docks hover above them, haloed with sea-mist, while ancient tires squeak against the iron sides of trawler hulls.

They will tell you of the Altamaha-ha, the sea monster that prowls the black water of the Little Amazon, sweeping like a living fossil among the knuckled roots of the cypress trees. They will tell you of century-old sturgeon the size of ship cannon, which lift from the water, smashing boats and killing men. They will speak of the skunk ape, which stomps through the mossy fens of the Okefenokee Swamp, glimpsed from the boats of paddlers and fishermen, and the feral cattle of Sapelo, long-horned and wild as the prehistoric aurochs. They may even whisper of the tribe who drowned in the waters of a nearby river, their chains heard rattling across the marshes on moonless nights, their spirits wheeling under the stars.

They will hitch their pants and speak of yard-built arks, inspired by the sermons of old-time prophets, who say that flood time is near. That the shape of the continent will be redrawn, this world vanishing beneath the melted ice of the poles. They will tell you these waters are prowled by the greatest killer whales of all—Ohio-class nuclear submarines, each bellied with sufficient firepower to wipe whole nations from the earth—while the wreckages of German U-boats and World War II freighters sleep in the muddy night of the seabed, filled with the bones of their dead. Some will speak of square grouper—the bales of Colombian crop that once fell from the heavens on moonless nights, keeping them fed.

These latter days, they will tell you of the wind that rose howling across the sands of the barrier islands, like a cry of wolves, and the beast that rose in their wake. Beneath the fat spotlamp of the moon, they say, you might see a giant cat striding the beach, ghostly in the night, flanked by the bones of toppled trees. Some say it is a lion, maneless, or a white tiger without stripes. Some say the ghost of a saber-tooth cat.

The crewmen of the transoceanic freighters line the rails on moony nights, lifting binoculars to their eyes, hoping to catch sight of the beast striding high-chinned and enormous among the glowing boneyard of trees. Some say exotic beasts were once caged on the island and one of them escaped, birthing this giant. Some say a prehistoric spirit stalks the coast, searching for a mate long extinct.

Many have sought the prints of the creature, but tide and moon are in conspiracy with the beast. Twice per day, they wash clean the slate of the beach. The island is under private ownership. No one is allowed above the tide line. There are signs that warn strongly of trespassing, though some have strode past them, into the trees, vanishing into the deep heart of the island. They return with faces paled, like ghosts themselves.

The shrimpers say, on the loneliest of nights, a roar of thunder can be heard along the shore, loud enough to rattle bones, even though the horizon is clear of cloud. They say that roar will stand your hairs on end, like a promise of the storm yet to come.

AUTHOR'S NOTE

This is a work of imagination. While I have endeavored to stay in proximity to the historical, geographical, and scientific record when possible, I have left the door open to mystery, instinct, dream—the essentials of fiction. I am greatly indebted to Stephanie Rutan of White Oak Conservation and to the people of Carolina Tiger Rescue, Catty Shack Ranch Wildlife Sanctuary, and Thula Thula Game Reserve, who answered my many questions during my visits. For further reading, I would like to recommend the following authors and their work: Lawrence Anthony, *The Elephant Whisperer, The Last Rhinos,* and *Babylon's Ark* (St. Martin's Griffin, 2007–2012); Francoise Malby-Anthony, *An Elephant in My Kitchen* (Pan Macmillan, 2018); Elizabeth Marshall Thomas, *The Tribe of Tiger: Cats and Their Culture* (Simon & Schuster, 1994); John Valliant, *The Tiger: A True Story of Vengeance and Survival* (Vintage, 2011); Dane Huckelbridge, *No Beast So Fierce* (William Morrow, 2019); Alan Green, *Animal Underworld: Inside America's Black Market for Rare and Exotic Species* (PublicAffairs, 1999); Jessica Adams and Andrew Miller, *Between Dog and Wolf* (Direct Book Service, 2011); Carson Vaughn, *Zoo Nebraska* (Little A, 2019).

ACKNOWLEDGMENTS

To my father, Rick Brown, whose well of faith in me never ran dry, no matter the odds. Rest in power, old man.

To my mother, Janet Brown, who has nerves of steel and a mother-bear's heart. I am so lucky you are my mom.

To my agent, Christopher Rhodes, who brings immeasurable love and taste to his work. Thank you for believing in me, early and always.

To my first reader and editor, Jason Frye, whose mentorship continues to steer me true. I am so damn thankful for you.

To AJ, who makes my heart go boom. I am so damn lucky for you. May the wolf pack keep us laughing and the paint fall true.

To my friend Francoise Malby-Anthony, who runs Thula Thula Game Reserve in the heart of Zululand. You and Nana are heroes.

To my friend Stephanie Rutan of White Oak Conservation, who has been so generous with her time. May your nights be full of chess and good bourbon.

To my friend Allen Taylor, firefighter and hunter, whose story laid the seed for this entire book. You have my highest respect. Thank you for what you do.

To my friend Brian Darrith, who was gracious and crazy enough to let me road-trip across South Africa with him. Thank God for that mallet and bicycle pump.

To my friends Ben Galland, Robert Darrith, and Harley Krinsky, who led me to mysterious islands off the coast. Thank You.

To the people of Carolina Tiger Rescue, Tiger World, Catty Shack Ranch Wildlife Sanctuary, and exotic wildlife sanctuaries across the world. Thank you for what you do. You inspired this book.

To my team at St. Martin's Press, who have transformed my wildest dreams into a reality. You are a dream team for a writer, truly, and I am so wildly thankful for your work, your brilliance, and your faith.

To booksellers across the country and world, who read and recommend my work. Your friendship, near and far, has been the unexpected boon of this whole endeavor. Much love to all of you.